Praise for *Low April Sun*

"*Low April Sun* is among the best novels that I've read in quite a few years. Looming over the lives of almost everyone in this taut, riveting, vividly rendered and deeply humane narrative are Timothy McVeigh and the terrorist bombing of the Alfred P. Murrah Federal Building in Oklahoma City on April 19, 1995. While immersed in these pages, I felt the earth move. Squires is an extraordinary novelist."

Steve Yarbrough
author of *Stay Gone Days* and *The Unmade World*

"*Low April Sun* is an eminently respectful, irresistibly readable exploration of an American tragedy. Part historical fiction, part ecofiction, part contemporary meditation, Squires's storytelling captures the lonely spaces within collective grief."

Sarah Beth Childers
author of *Prodigals: A Sister's Memoir*

"*Low April Sun* possesses the rarest and most important qualities a novel can hold: it has what Joan Didion called 'moral nerve.' Its bravery is constant and revelatory, and its relationship with notoriety and tragedy is never mawkish or sensational. Constance Squires is that singular artist who can engage forces and aftershocks as powerful as these with writing that is authentic, thrilling, subtle, and transformative."

James Reich
author of *The Moth for the Star*

"*Low April Sun* is a moving and elegant exploration of grief and forgiveness, of regret and redemption. Constance Squires also tells a helluva story, riveting from first page to last."

Lou Berney
Edgar-winning author of *Dark Ride*

"*Low April Sun* holds a mystery, a history, an acute sense of place. Balancing dual timelines in a propulsive narrative, this beautiful novel tells the untold story of *then* and *now*: how the pain of trauma radiates in waves long after the act of terrorist violence that ripped open the state and the nation has passed. Constance Squires writes with respect for the wounded, compassion for the lost. She's an extraordinary stylist, and here she's writing with the full measure of her powers. A richly compelling and important novel."

Rilla Askew
author of *Harpsong* and *Fire in Beulah*

"This evocative, deeply drawn narrative keeps the reader hooked and watching as its characters, in turn, watch us. A vibrantly insightful novel."

Anne Lauppe-Dunbar

author of *Dark Mermaids* and *The Shape of Her*

"Remarkable! Whatever load you're carrying, lay it down to pick up this terrific, important novel. In *Low April Sun*, three oh-so-human characters are rocked by the 1995 Oklahoma City bombing, oil company fracking, and the earthquakes each triggered in their lives. There's more than enough guilt to go around, but also a great deal of grace. A regional hero, Squires should be a national treasure, her books alongside those by Denis Johnson and Annie Proulx."

Mary Kay Zuravleff

author of *American Ending* and *Man Alive!*

Praise for *Hit Your Brights*

"So many characters in these stories are AWOL—from an aspiring future, from family, from jobs, and from each other. With great suspense, Constance Squires hunts them down, suspends them above the voids in their lives, and makes them choose to return or to go up in flame."

Thomas Fox Averill

author of *rode* and *Ordinary Genius*

"*Hit Your Brights* is a well-crafted collection focusing on Oklahoma and southern characters in a universe full of questions. Here are stories of husbands and wives, musicians, addicts, people whose lives are filled with tragedies that make us feel as if they are our own. Constance Squires writes prose with startling precision and beauty. At times humorous, at times sad, her stories are always profoundly moving."

Brandon Hobson

author of *Where the Dead Sit Talking*

"In *Hit Your Brights*, Constance Squires tells of 'another Oklahoma,' one that is not often fictionalized, and rarely written so truthfully. Some of these stories offer hope—others ask, can you forgive us for doing the best we can under the circumstances? It is a collection of deep and complicated humanity, and truly one of the best collections of stories I've read in a long time."

Jeanetta Calhoun Mish

author of *Oklahomeland: Essays*

"*Hit Your Brights* is an exercise in 'double vision'—grief always paired with the utmost grace. The nucleus of these stories, sometimes rock 'n' roll or sometimes Oklahoma, provides a touchstone for the wandering, a tether between suffering and joy."

Iliana Rocha

author of *Karankawa*

Praise for *Live from Medicine Park*

"Few people write about the seductive energy of rock music and the bewitching power of place with the grace and acuity of Constance Squires. With a quirky Oklahoma spa town as backdrop, *Live from Medicine Park* is a rollicking tale of bad love, good music, and unwavering ambition gone wrong—all set to lyrics so evocative, they're bound to haunt you long after you close the book."

Rilla Askew

author of *Prize for the Fire* and *Harpsong*

"Constance Squires's potent and lyrical anthem about love, music, and memory also has a lot to say about the complex transience of fame and fandom—and the price that musicians and listeners alike must pay for them. *Live from Medicine Park* is an aching, honest, unforgettable story of a fading legend, as well as a vivid portrait of one of the most mystical places in this country."

Adam Davies

author of *The Frog King*

"Neither roots rock nor the American Southwest has enjoyed such savvy and inventive celebration as in this novel. While the material touches on those clichés of rock 'n' roll, sex 'n' drugs, et cetera, at every turn its narrative pushes past the cartoon to the bruise, past the headline to the whimper, and way past air guitar to the spellbinding noise of families in crisis and fallen people struggling to rise. Bristling with stubborn hopes and wild detours, *Live from Medicine Park* restores us finally to the redemptive power of howling at the moon."

John Domini

author of *Movieola!*

"A rocky encounter with a rock icon changes a filmmaker's life in [Constance] Squires' heartfelt novel. . . . Squires gets it right on both sides, making Lena a convincingly grizzled rock [and] roll survivor while giving resonance to Ray's journey to personal redemption. You don't need to be a rock fan to appreciate this rite-of-passage story, but Squires' fellow rockers will also appreciate her attention to details."
Kirkus Reviews

LOW APRIL SUN

LOW APRIL SUN

A NOVEL

CONSTANCE E. SQUIRES

University of Oklahoma Press : Norman

Publication of this book is made possible in part through the generosity of Edith Kinney Gaylord.

Excerpt from "The Incognito Lounge" by Denis Johnson used with the permission of Harper Collins publishing.

Library of Congress Cataloging-in-Publication Data

Names: Squires, Constance, author.
Title: Low April sun : a novel / Constance E. Squires.
Description: Norman : University of Oklahoma Press, [2025] | Summary: "A moving work of literary fiction that charts the events and long, traumatic aftermath of the Oklahoma City bombing"—Provided by publisher.
Identifiers: LCCN 2024016838 | ISBN 978-0-8061-9474-5 (hardcover ; alk. paper)
Subjects: LCSH: Oklahoma City Federal Building Bombing, Oklahoma City, Okla., 1995— Fiction. | LCGFT: Novels. | Historical fiction.
Classification: LCC PS3619.Q57 L69 2025 | DDC 813/.6—dc23/eng/20240419
LC record available at https://lccn.loc.gov/2024016838

This book is a work of fiction. Names, characters, places, and incidents are either the product of the author's imagination or are used fictitiously, and any resemblance to actual events, locales, or persons, living or dead, is entirely coincidental.

The paper in this book meets the guidelines for permanence and durability of the Committee on Production Guidelines for Book Longevity of the Council on Library Resources, Inc. ∞

Copyright © 2025 by Constance Squires. Published by the University of Oklahoma Press, Norman, Publishing Division of the University. Manufactured in the U.S.A.

All rights reserved. No part of this publication may be reproduced, stored in a retrieval system, or transmitted, in any form or by any means, electronic, mechanical, photocopying, recording, or otherwise—except as permitted under Section 107 or 108 of the United States Copyright Act—without the prior written permission of the University of Oklahoma Press. To request permission to reproduce selections from this book, write to Permissions, University of Oklahoma Press, 2800 Venture Drive, Norman, OK 73069, or email rights.oupress@ou.edu.

1 2 3 4 5 6 7 8 9 10

for my family

CONTENTS

Part One.	BLAST	1
1.	August P.	3
2.	Edie	7
3.	Edie	14
4.	Edie	25
5.	Keith	28
6.	Edie	36
7.	August P.	41
8.	Robert	46
9.	Edie	50
10.	Keith	56
11.	Keith	61
12.	Edie	68
13.	Edie	75
14.	Keith	78
Part Two.	SEARCH	85
15.	Edie	87
16.	Keith	94
17.	August P.	101
18.	Edie	109
19.	Delaney	117
20.	Edie	119
21.	August P.	124
22.	Keith	130
23.	Edie	136
24.	Keith	140
25.	Keith	142

26.	Edie	154
27.	Edie	162
28.	Robert	166
29.	Keith	171
30.	August P.	173
31.	Edie	177
32.	Keith	186
33.	Edie	189
34.	Keith	195
35.	Delaney	198
36.	Edie	201
37.	Keith	204

Part Three.	RECOVER	209
38.	Brad	211
39.	August P.	214
40.	Edie	221
41.	Keith	224
42.	August P.	231
43.	Edie	233
44.	Edie	241

PART ONE

BLAST

*It was as if the great country were asleep,
and they wished to carry on their lives without awakening it;
or as if the spirits of earth and air and water
were things not to antagonize and arouse.*

Willa Cather, *Death Comes for the Archbishop*

1

AUGUST P.

What if I'd never met the bomber? On April 19, 1995, I'd have seen the shattered face of the Alfred P. Murrah Federal Building in Oklahoma City on the TV like everybody else in the world, and a couple days later when they caught him, I'd have said *look at that evil sonofabitch* like everybody else and that would've been that. Some other life would've been mine. But I did meet ol' Tim back in August of '94, and that meeting was enough for him to stretch his long shadow down the years of my life and make them dark as a highway without headlights. I been trying to make it right ever since.

    The day before I met him, the elders made me join the ranks of the other teen boys at Elohim City in guarding the perimeter of the compound. Ever since Ruby Ridge and Waco, they figured we were next and were always on the lookout for feds in the forest. Kurt gave me an old SKS rifle he'd made fully automatic and ordered me and these other two fellas my age to stand on the packed red clay in the heat and load and unload the weapons like we would on the day the whole US government came to kill us all, which they figured was any day. Boxes covered in Chinese writing held the cartridges laid in there like pencils on the first day of school and stacked on plywood ammo cases that were a basic building material around there—new residents lived in houses made of them, with orange tarps thrown over for waterproofing and cinderblocks for anchors against the wind. Kurt gave us lessons on the guns and sent us out to guard the place. I spent the night up where the dirt two-lane heading into the property meets a paved county road, sure a cougar was going to spring on me from the trees and eat my guts any minute, fuming at my momma for her bad taste in men, which is what got us out there instead of back home in Springdale.

    She'd met Gary shoulder-to-shoulder on the assembly line at the Tyson chicken plant, and they fell in love above the flow of cold dead bird corpses they were cutting up for packaging. My mom, she said once Gary could sever the thighs from the bodies with his eyes closed. He lost that job, though, despite his ninja skills killing what was already dead. Those talents got him the girl, though, didn't they? That's my mom for you. Why couldn't she have married someone normal for her third go-round? Some guy who likes to bike or barbecue or whatever, even the kind of guy who never got off the couch and was always asking me to grab a beer from the fridge, anything but what I got, which was Gary, who sat at his computer after he lost the job at Tyson muttering about Ruby Ridge and Waco and griping about America Online and America in general.

Elohim City was a dusty place in spite of being in a forest, part of the Ozark Highlands, a hilly place thick with blackjack and post oak that twisted like thousands of gnarled hands choked with briar and grapevine. The county's got hardly anybody in it, it seeming that not many folks try to live inside that rough Ozark fringe, but I guess to a fringe group like my mother's community, it was perfect. At Elohim City there was an elder—slicked-back hair, square-jawed like a cartoon superhero—whose granddad was one of the founders of the Nazi party back in Germany, or at least that's what he said. They were all in the Christian Identity Movement, them people, so they were real impressed by his story and he had some old swastika stuff that seemed to bear it out. That old boy never liked me, actually kicked me out of the way one time, like I was a dog. He'd been coming through the door of the meeting room where everybody was sitting cross-legged on the floor waiting for him, a silhouette against the light, and I think I blew his entrance. My mom hunched in the group with her hands gripping her knees and smiled up at him as if to say sorry that she had in fact given birth to a dog.

I kind of pity myself when I think about that stuff, but the fact is, I did meet the bomber, late in the summer of '94, and although it weren't my fault I was living there at Elohim City, it was my actions, my desire to get away from that compound and to set myself apart that made me think, when I saw Timothy McVeigh, with his stiff gait and military buzz cut and the stories that he'd been a decorated war hero in Desert Storm, that he had something to offer me in the first place. I sought him out, so this fate is my own.

White polyurethane domes were the style of buildings on the compound instead of the usual four walls and a ceiling because the leader didn't like straight lines. The result had a strong effect on my young imagination. I had cast my eyes around Elohim at the weird little igloos and told myself I was living on Tatooine, like Luke Skywalker. I was waiting for the video message hidden in the droid, for the old Jedi master to tell me I'm special, for a princess in a wavering projection to tell me I was her only hope. Maybe even for the scene where the humpback houses were burnt to the ground with everybody in them. Not that I wanted anyone dead, not even those folks there at Elohim City, goodness, but you know, when you're a sixteen-year-old kid, you can't get very far with your fantasies of freedom until you can figure out some way to move the grown-ups out of the way.

That's all I wanted. I just wanted them gone. Or, no, that's not right. They could stay right there in their outlaw waystation, their hidden fortress in eastern Oklahoma, if only they'd let me out. I wanted to go back to my friends in Springdale, my bike and Walker and his Nintendo and the 7-Eleven near our house where we did donuts in the parking lot and bought Big Gulps. I'd been thinking on it, how to skedaddle, the first time I saw Timothy McVeigh walking yonder in front of the church, sidewinding along the wall of knotty oaks that always made me feel that forest was like to reach over Elohim City and close around it like a giant hand. He didn't care about the forest, the red ground, the white sun, nothing. He walked head down with that inward gaze I've since learned means you leave that fucker alone.

No, wait—I'd seen him before that a time or two—I remember him in winter. Thinking at first that he smoked because of his breath on the air. He wore a coat, plaid lining showing when he walked—I'd seen him, just never sort of lit on him, focused like. But that hot lonely day after my first night on guard duty, I did, because I'd heard he'd been in the military. Not the military as we knew it there at Elohim, the perimeter guarding giving way soon to training for robbing banks, something the community's men ran around and did from time to time, since by their lights US currency weren't legitimate so it weren't wrong to steal it, but the United States military.

That's right, their enemy. This fellow had been in the army of their enemy, and yet here he was on this hotter-than-hell afternoon in the star chamber of the white nationalist movement, not just accepted, but I'd say kind of revered, like the way a normal town would treat the boy who's going to be a college football star and maybe have a chance at the NFL. Like they knew he was going to make them proud. And I guess he went and did, but I didn't know a thing about what was coming on April 19th, 1995, or who he'd turn out to be. Me, I just wanted to hear about joining the army so I could get out of there. Like I said, I figured he was my Han Solo, my older dude who could tell me about the world. But he weren't no Han Solo.

2

EDIE

1995

April in Oklahoma City forced metaphors of destruction into Edie's vocabulary. There was no getting away from words like "apocalyptic," "biblical," and "malevolent" during the unavoidable weather chat while making a customer's drink, sliding it across the bar under a coaster with a benedictory comment about preferring tornados to earthquakes any day. This morning, though, the weather was mild and sunny and it was she who was the fiend, the wrecking ball, the unrighteous-as-a-noun. She had been awake for a few minutes and was sitting on the front porch in a ratty wicker chair with a case of the shakes, possibly still drunk. The sun leveled its judgment, flooding her brainpan front to back like the aggressive end of a broom forcing filth from dark corners. She had come outside armored with coffee and stacks of overseas graduate school brochures, stamps and light-blue airmail envelopes, program-specific application letters detailing her academic achievements copied at Kinko's yesterday with today's date—April 19, 1995—ready for imminent mailing. She felt less out of control tending to her future this way. Each morning she quit drinking for good, she got a lot done.

Behind her, the door opened. Edie looked up at her half sister, who let the screen door slam and came to stand before her, blocking the morning sun. Delaney pulled her dark hair off her shoulders and shrugged on a paint-splattered army surplus jacket festooned with rock pins. Edie felt her energy like a blast of heat. "Going somewhere?"

"Downtown," Delaney said. "The federal building."

"I didn't know there was a social security office around here." Edie remembered now Delaney's good cheer about a new job at the Petroleum Club turning to panic when she couldn't find all the ID she'd need to fill out the hiring forms. "They'll hand you a new card on the spot?"

"Just a receipt, but that'll work until the real one comes in the mail." Delaney spun the ring of her boyfriend's car keys on her left pointer finger and seemed to take her sister in for the first time that morning. She stopped spinning the keys and reached down to rub the crease between Edie's brows. "It's going to be okay, Sis."

"I hope so." Edie peered up at her sister, who didn't look so carefree herself.

"Did you go out last night?" Delaney asked.

"I don't know."

"You don't know?" She laughed. "Like, literally?"

Explaining blackout drinking to Delaney was like trying to explain the nighttime to the sun. She could never believe in its totality, took Edie's explanations for hyperbole. There was a different kind of beer bottle on the coffee table than the ones she had started the evening drinking, though, so either someone had dropped by and hung out for a while or she had driven to the convenience store down the street and restocked, or both. Did that count as going out?

"Keith and I got stuck at Subterranean. He has to talk to everybody." Delaney planted a foot on the brick ledge that enclosed the front porch and tightened the laces of her Doc Martens. "I hate it."

"It or him?"

"Not him, but I'm getting close. Do you know what that lunatic just did, like," she looked at her watch, "ten minutes ago?"

"Loaned you his car?" Edie said. She gestured at the back half of the kelly green Bronco visible on the driveway at the side of the duplex

Delaney looked down over crossed arms at her sister. "Promise not to tell him I told you."

"Oh no." She said it like a joke, but the dread Edie felt was real. The inconvenient crush she had on her sister's boyfriend made it hard to hear Delaney's confidences about him.

"He asked me to marry him!" Delaney flung both hands in front of her like a magician flashing an empty hat. "Holy matrimony, for fuckssake."

Edie let out a weird bark of a laugh and dropped her gaze to the pages on her lap. Good god, she had to hold on to something. She gripped the chair's splintering wicker arms. Her hangover shakes got worse.

"Can you imagine?" Delaney's voice was pained. She seemed constitutionally incapable of facing heavy shit and was already, Edie could tell, turning her sunny disposition to smoothing over Keith's faux pas and chilling the vibe.

"Yeah. No. I mean, that's unexpected."

"I got out of there as fast as I could."

"Is he okay?"

"I never even said I loved him. What was he thinking?"

"You don't have to be mean to him, Delaney." They both looked at the front door like tall, skinny Keith might appear, scratching his hairy chest and looking sad. Some thin, warbling note of hope sounded in Edie's mind as she realized that Keith was almost certainly about to be available. But so what? He wasn't interested in her, barely registered her.

Delaney trotted down the porch steps, legs loose and graceful. From the sidewalk she looked up at Edie. "Right, I'll just say yes so he doesn't get his feelings hurt. Fuck me, anyway. Who cares about my life?"

"You know I don't mean that. Just—let him down easy."

Delaney waved it off. "He was kidding. That's my line. It was a joke, okay?"

"Yeah—that's the kindest way." Edie set aside the envelopes and stood up, shading her eyes to see her sister.

Delaney spun on the grass and walked backward toward the Bronco in the driveway. "Back in a while. Remember, I didn't tell you. Try to use your powers for good on the poor—Oh, hey, Keith."

Edie turned to see Keith standing in the doorway holding open the screen, his eyes on Delaney. His dark hair was a disheveled mop that half obscured his long face. He was barefoot, in jeans and a red and black striped T-shirt. Frustration came off him like cologne.

"Morning." Edie gave him an encouraging smile. She pulled the ends of her hair under her chin like strings to a bonnet and wished she'd brushed it.

He acknowledged her with a long blink. "Don't forget," he said to Delaney. "I have class this morning." He glanced down at his watch. "It's eight forty. I need to leave by ten."

"Have a cup of coffee. Tell your troubles to Edie. I'll be right back."

"Ten o'clock, Delaney!"

Keith and Edie watched from the porch as Delaney slid into Keith's Bronco, a 1974 soft top with a white stripe down the side and rivets dotting the wheel wells like sequins on jeans. It was just an old truck, but Keith was proud of it like it was special. When she turned the key in the ignition, they heard loud music start up behind the glass. She gave them a wave and backed out.

Edie bent down and collected her letters and supplies. "Come on, I'm supposed to offer you a beverage."

Keith followed her in. Awkward together, they talked about the O. J. Simpson trial, Keith making the case for O.J.'s innocence.

"You really don't think he did it?"

Keith shrugged. "I can't stand the thought. It's hard for me to tell what I think when I feel something strongly. You know? Feeling overdrive." He stepped to the built-in bookshelves next to the fireplace and leaned close to read the spines of her books. They heard a TV begin its muttering on the other side of the wall that divided the house into a duplex, a slab of sheetrock thin as paper right down the middle so that they heard their neighbors' coughs and clattering cutlery, felt their weight on the wood planked floors, like living with ghosts.

What could she do for him? She was under orders not to let him know she knew about his failed proposal, so her expressions of sympathy were limited to the general sort. He grumbled about graduate school, about the reading load and the bad prose of most of the historical texts about the Old West. He loved it, though. A natural scholar, that was how he described himself. Somehow, he moved on to the economic role of saloons in the Old West, then to poker, talking so much she realized he was in fact distressed. He gave her the history of Texas Hold'em in under a minute. Did she play? Did they have any cards around the house?

"I don't think so," she said over the sound of the coffee percolating. Her hands were still shaking, and dehydration hit her like a panic. She turned on the tap and downed two tall glasses of water, hoping he didn't notice.

He sat down at the round glass kitchen table, part of an outdoor patio set they were using inside, and picked up one of the blue airmail envelopes already sealed. "You're applying for grad programs, right? What's your top pick?"

"London School of Economics?"

He whistled. "Nice. That would be nice. You're dreaming big."

"Just willing to take on debt." She set a cup of coffee in front of him.

He folded his hands around it as if he were cold. "Do you think Delaney will finish her degree one of these days?"

"Not sure she needs to."

"She's got everything she needs, she's an artist, she don't look back," he sang. "Besides, she's already selling her paintings."

"To you."

He shrugged. "Yes."

"But I know what you mean. She's already—" she looked for the word.

"Manifest," Keith said. "I think of her that way. I'm always reading about Manifest Destiny—which was such shit. But those words when applied to her—they mean something else."

She stood at the kitchen counter and turned away from him. Delaney would surely break up with him now. A wall that had been between her and Keith was coming down, but Edie didn't feel good. Instead, she kept thinking about what her sister had said—*fuck me anyway, who cares about my life?* Delaney was the mellowest person Edie knew, an easygoing type with a natural balance she seemed to find like a landing cat in every moment, no matter the upheaval. But her voice had been constricted, her body bristling. Delaney had been thrashing like she was caught in a trap. Ashamed not to have seen her sister more clearly before, so lost had she been in her own unrequited spin, Edie wanted to call her sister back and say more strongly than she had, *I understand.*

"Hey," she said. "I'm going to shower. There's a whole pot, so drink up."

Edie had just finished rinsing the conditioner from her hair when she felt the blast.

She was standing on a nubby plastic shower mat letting hot water run over her. Her eyes were half open, and she was looking at the caddy that hung from the neck of the shower head, wondering if there was some way to clean the hard water deposits from its metallic shelves, crowded with her and Delaney's bath products.

Then two matching green plastic bottles, shampoo and conditioner, smeared vertically, as if they were melting down the front of some screen she hadn't known was there. The shower tiles ran like candle wax. Everything melted and went out of focus and for a second, as the sound waves continued vibrating her eyes in their sockets, she couldn't see. Registering the roar of the sound took a second, the noise so big her mind couldn't immediately take it in. Airwaves roiled and snapped like a bullwhip jerked hard, responding to a push from some distant source and surging back toward it like an undertow.

Every cell in her body shook. Her body trembled like a blender turned on high. She stumbled from the shower while beauty products flew from the shelves on the wall. Baby powder, toothbrushes, and two pink birth control cases clattered around her. The medicine cabinet sprung open, and aspirin and vitamin bottles dropped into the sink. Jagged edges of reverb ripped the air like tissue, like the sonic booms she would later hear in London when the Concorde broke the sound barrier as it flew overhead.

Then it was quiet. The airwaves settled flat. Her insides stilled. She wrapped herself in a towel and stepped over all the fallen toiletries to turn off the shower. Then she parted the café curtains covering the small window next to the sink and looked outside, fully expecting to see a passenger plane sticking out of the ground in her backyard. Whatever it was had to have been very close and very big.

"Edie?" Keith was banging on the bathroom door.

"Hey! Are you okay? Have you looked out?"

"Everything looks normal," he said.

"How could it? What was that?"

"Something massive."

She opened the door, peering up at him with one hand over the towel wrapped across her torso. They gave each other wary looks. "Maybe a transformer blew up," she said.

"Good thing all your dishes were in the sink. Your books are on the floor, though. All Delaney's paintings fell."

"My eyes went blurry."

She combed her hair, pulled on a T-shirt and jeans, and they walked around the neighborhood, looking for some clue as to the source of the noise. Edie and Delaney lived a block south of Northwest Twenty-third Street, one of the city's major east-west arteries. Keith and Edie walked to the corner at Twenty-third and looked up and down. Traffic was heavy. The Payless Shoe store on the corner was just opening, as was the pawnshop on the southeast corner. Across the street, the parking lot of a half-empty shopping mall, now mostly used for office space, was filling up by the main entrances. Morning light began drying Edie's hair.

She walked up and down, hands on her hips. "No sign of anything? How is that—"

"Look." Keith pointed at a rising column of thick dark smoke to the southeast of them.

"That? But it sounded like it was right here." She stopped pacing and stood beside him. They watched the smoke encroach upon the sky's blue, obliterating the space above the city's modest skyline like a hole burning through a painting. "That's—how far away?"

Keith stared, shaking his head. "Look at it. Look at all that."

"What the hell?" she said. "I bet it makes the local news tonight."

He dropped a hand to her shoulder. "If she's not here by ten can you give me a ride?"

"She'll be back," Edie said.

3

EDIE

2015

A tremor rippled across the wood floors and up the walls. It was a mild one, a rumble like a semitruck had driven too fast down the shaded neighborhood street outside her house. Edie Ash's bare toes clenched against the cool floor as she pushed her son's art supplies out of the way and set his backpack on the kitchen table. He was working on a school project, a dream catcher made out of blue string and a plastic hoop, being meticulous about the spider's web in the center and tying tiny Star Wars figures to the bottoms of the fringe.

"I give it a two on the Richter scale." Ian held up his small fingers, a peace sign.

"I'm going to say one point six." Edie zipped his lunchbox into his backpack and held the padded green shoulder straps out while he slid it across his small shoulders. "Here you go, Buddy."

He pushed a Teenage Mutant Ninja Turtle thermos into the mesh carrier on the side of his pack and raised his freckled face to her, questions in his green eyes, and she knew he needed reassurance again, for her to tell him that there would be no big earthquake, that the earthquakes in Oklahoma might be frequent but that they would be small. He was going to say that he missed London, his school, and his friends, the stillness of the ground, but he didn't get a chance because, from the next room, they heard Keith gasp.

Ian turned in the direction of Keith's voice. "What is it, Daddy?"

Keith's high-drama interactions with the computer were funny if she was in the right mood, damned annoying if she wasn't. He would shout, "No! What the fuck? Are you serious?" and Edie would think there had been another suicide bombing or school shooting somewhere. Her pores would fill with needles, and she'd come running into his study, bracing for horror, yelling, "What happened?"

only to find that he had sent an email without attaching a document or was on a website with a pop-up ad that he couldn't get to go away. Ian would bang into her legs, wide-eyed, and giggle when he realized it was nothing. But this morning there was something about Keith's quiet gasp that had real shock in it, a trembling quality she had not heard in a long time.

She leaned into his doorway. "What's up?"

Like a gangster in a restaurant, he had positioned his desk to face the door, his back against the wall. The rest of the room was full of still-unpacked book boxes stacked with a small path cut across the wood-planked floor from the door to his desk chair. He wore an old Bikini Kill concert T-shirt and gray sweatpants, his longish dark hair uncombed and pushed behind his ears in a way that made him look medieval, a knight with his helmet off. He was going gray in exactly the places about his temples where his hair had been Manic Panic Purple when she first knew him, as if the gods of punk had struck a bargain that was now coming due. He glanced up at her. "What?"

"You gasped."

"Another one of your earthquakes. Don't tell me you didn't feel it."

Her nails tapped an impatient tattoo against the doorframe. He liked to use the possessive pronoun with Oklahoma's many new and frequent earthquakes. They were hers, according to him, because she worked for Landon Energy, one of the oil companies that owned the wastewater injection sites people said were causing the quakes. The oil company that paid for their life, unlike his own small academic paychecks, and kept them from sinking under the debt of Keith's epic gambling binges—all of which were in the past, he swore. The night before, they had argued about what he called her "complicity in the whole fracking boondoggle." She had no intention of opening that debate up again. "Not that," she said. "Just now. You gasped."

"Oh." He waved a hand at the screen. "Nothing. Bullshit headlines." Keith whisked his phone and keys across the desk and rose. It was his turn to drive Ian to school. "Away we go," he said. He planted a kiss on the top of her head as he swept by.

Her fingertips brushed across his chest and she followed him into the kitchen. "He needs lunch money."

She pulled Ian into a quick hug. Would it ever get easier to let him go into his day, to let him out of her sight and away from where she could ensure his safety at all times? It hadn't yet and he was seven. Ian squirmed away from her.

"Sorry!" She watched the top of his head cross the kitchen and resisted the urge to kiss him again. "Love you!"

"I have a job interview on Tuesday," Keith said. "The hiring committee loved my book."

"Really?"

He picked up and scrutinized the apples in a bowl on the counter before selecting one. Rubbing it against his shirt, he said. "You don't have to sound so surprised."

"Babe, I'm not." She felt a surge of blood to her head—why was he so sullen? But meditation was teaching her about the pause between moments where, according to the experts on the app, our choices reside. She played a different meditation every day, usually gave them five stars and a big thumbs up, returning often to a few favorites. They spoke, one and all, in the slow, reasonable tones of someone trying to talk a jumper from a ledge. Nonreactive, that was the goal. She held that space between the shuttling seconds and looked around, feeling a flush of pride at her small victory of mindfulness. Had she begun to need approval from the voices on her meditation app? Christ. She took a deep breath and said, "I think everyone should read your book. It's great."

"Yeah, yeah." He ducked his head like the praise was a projectile to be dodged. The man could not take a compliment.

She was more surprised that a job in his area of specialization had opened right here in town. Those jobs were few and far between. "Where's the interview?"

That fall semester he was adjunct teaching in history at four of the universities in the metro area, trying to cobble together a cumulatively decent salary from bits and scraps, a class here, a class there, three online, four in person, all introductory courses he was overqualified to teach, a crushing load of grading for paltry money and no benefits at all. At the polytechnic where he taught in London, he had also been an adjunct, but it was different there—he had felt sort of respected and his course load had been stable, even if he had little chance to teach in his area of specialization, the American West. His one book,

The Great Excuse: Manifest Destiny and American Westward Migration, had been published just three years earlier by a small but respectable British press, a man and a woman in gray cardigans with two computers in a one-room flat in Islington, who had received Keith at their offices with the grim furtiveness of a couple of Le Carré's spies debriefing a defector. Still, they knew their business, got the book to all the right reviewers, stocked it in university libraries, and had even taken him out for a pint on the day it was published.

He told her about the job at one of the big state schools, its benefits and its pay, his large hand palming the top of his son's head as he steered Ian toward the back door. His tone was dismissive. Like it was no big deal. Which meant he was scared.

"Wow," she said. "It sounds perfect, right? This is your job. You've got this."

Their eyes met for a moment as Ian trotted through the open door and down the back steps. The look on her husband's face scared her. She had seen it before, the toxic cocktail of confusion and self-loathing. Someone tumbling end-over-end through space after jumping ship in a fit of pique might wear such an expression. Yet the job interview was a huge win, and he had seemed victorious after their fight about her job the night before. He loved the moral high ground, and he had it these days so long as he wasn't gambling, and while she was getting paid to blow smoke about fracking while her boss ran for cover. Much as she hated her own situation, and God how she hated it, part of her was happy to see Keith feeling strong. So why the chaos eyes? Maybe it was nothing. His voice was solid when he said, "Straight to the car, Ian. Don't disturb your grandfather!"

She looked after them through the back windows. The door of the detached garage rose, and Keith backed out of the driveway with one hand, while with the other he slid the car line ticket onto the dash, bright yellow with IAN FRAYNE-ASH in black magic marker under the school's logo, a roaring cougar. The drawn shades of her father's apartment above the garage opened. Now she had to go to work. Now she had to prepare for the shit tornado that would finally drop when the Oklahoma Geological Survey announced the findings of its report on fracking. The report was due any day now, and there was no question that Landon Energy wouldn't fare well. She would have to respond, to craft answers, to face cameras.

She started to cry. First a tightness in her jaw, then waterworks. Shallow breathing ramped up her tears like a lawnmower starting, and soon she was doubled over at the waist, sobbing with abandon. It kept happening these days. Afterward she felt humiliated and vaguely worried about herself but also more relaxed, the way nausea abates for a while after you vomit. She wiped her cheeks with the back of her hand and poured a cup of coffee. "Get it together, Edie," she said aloud into the empty house. In the living room, she felt around in the cool leather couch cushions for her iPad. No luck.

Her first meeting at work was in ninety minutes, and the drive from her house to the office took ten minutes. She'd begun some sort of low-level disassociating to get through the stress. Each day, she didn't think about work at all until she was at her desk. Even when she was walking into Landon Energy's glass-lined foyer, while her heels rat-a-tat-tatted across the marble floors, the very sound of purposeful presence, she wouldn't be thinking. Lately she reminded herself of her old, drunk self, walking, talking, smiling, remembering absolutely nothing later but whatever physical clues she could put together from her surroundings and her body. So, too, now. She would take the elevator to the eleventh floor, feigning absorption in her phone to avoid conversation during the ride, then exit the lift and glide to her office.

Then, action. Like surfacing from a drunken blackout, the way a corpse bobs to the surface of a river, she would come to in the middle of a sentence, finding herself reacting to some stream of bad news. Ugly meetings. People assuming the worst of each other. And of her! She felt close to no one at work, and only venting to her colleagues still in the London office kept her sane. Fight, flight, or freeze shouldn't be one's menu of choices multiple times per day, should they? Until recently, she had loved her job. Landon Energy had always felt like a fortuitous gig, the kind of match that seemed to prove that things happened for a reason.

Do things happen for a reason?

It was a nice daydream, but then she thought about school shootings, cancer, war, terrorism in general, and her own experience with terrorism, the Oklahoma City bombing. Did the bombing of the Alfred P. Murrah Federal Building on April 19, 1995, happen for a reason? Had her best friend and half sister, Delaney, vanished in the rubble of that catastrophe for some overarching logic? Such a notion was hard for Edie to buy. In fact, the idea revolted and offended her. Yet when things went her way, it was difficult not to feel that they were meant to be, that some benevolent presence was patting her on the back and rewarding her for being a good person, and her job used to be one of those things.

She had landed it, a plum PR job with a company based in her home state, while she was at the London School of Economics determined never to set foot in Oklahoma again. The hiring committee had been charmed by her Okie twang—normally a liability—and had said she would be perfect for the company, a woman with all the right training who could speak "normally," as they put it, but also with the same flat-voweled drawl as the company's owner, Theron Landon. For seventeen years, she had been key personnel to the PR side of the company in London, even becoming a familiar face in commercials aired on BBC1 in which she strolled along a twilit English coastline, looking fondly out to the North Sea at the twinkling lights of a drilling platform before turning her symmetrical features to the camera and saying, "Landon Energy. Progress in harmony with nature."

She had avoided promotion to VP for as long as she could, but eventually it had come and that meant moving to headquarters in Oklahoma City. Back home. And now? Now people were paying attention to oil and gas as never before, and a drilling technique she had only recently learned enough about to explain was a source of understandable fury, locally and worldwide. Fracking, ye gods. She was as disturbed about it as anyone. Now PR wasn't such a great part of the business to be in. Now she was the one who had to stand in front of cameras, stand up at town hall meetings, and show up at industry summits spouting the company line as scripted for her by Theron Landon. *We are not responsible. Why has Oklahoma's rate of annual earthquakes gone from two to over five hundred since we began injecting wastewater into the ground? Very good question, citizen. We say nature. We say natural causes. Nature's amazing, y'all, it's just crazy! But we're as concerned as anyone else. We're in close communication with the Oklahoma Geological Survey to help get to the bottom of this. We are eagerly awaiting their report.* It was killing her.

She told herself she'd quit if it weren't for her intolerance of financial instability, which she attributed to the years after her father left them, to moving again and again around the Oklahoma City metro to no-credit-check-first-month-free apartment complexes, dirty and dangerous, where she learned to listen for her mother's alarm clock in the morning and to pull her skinny body out of bed, to make her breakfast before getting herself to the bus stop for school, standing around the lobby of the plasma center dodging perverts while her mother opened a vein.

Because of Keith they were never more than a gambling binge away from chaos, and he didn't make enough money to save them from his own depredations. A year had gone by since his last nosedive into the betting life, and he swore it was behind him, yet his talk about gambling recovery invariably fell into gambling metaphors—what are the *odds* of relapse, and did she *want to bet* he was really through. Troubling. Whether she would ever feel safe enough to fall backward into his arms and trust him to catch her was doubtful. It just wasn't in her. If life had taught her anything, it was one simple truth: nobody's coming. No one will save you.

She walked barefoot through the house looking for her iPad, which was in none of the other likely spots around the house she checked—kitchen counter, bookshelves, coffee table. Until she bought her dad his own tablet, it always would be. She slid her feet into slippers and crossed the backyard, past the beds of daffodils and hyacinths she had put in when they bought the house last October, the inside of the house unboxed and unkempt while she had gone outside with her spade and her bulbs to be sure she'd have in the spring what now broke through the hard clay like fists through a wall. She reached the garage, an old carriage house, putty-colored stucco with black shutters that matched the Craftsman solidity of the main house, climbed the stairs that went up the side of the building to the apartment where her dad was staying, gripping the unfinished pine wood of a banister Keith had built a month ago when her ailing but unrepentant father had moved in. She banged on the door. "Dad, I need my iPad."

She heard paper rustling, a chair scooting back, and the painful sound of his breathing as he approached the door. She winced at the sound, wiping the pain from her face when the door flung open and her father stood there, waving her in. "It's in the john," he said. "Hang on a minute."

He trudged off, portable oxygen canister poking out of the backpack he wore, like the soldier humping through the jungle he had once been. "You could at least keep it out of the bathroom!" she called after him as she sat at one of the hardback chairs pulled up to a brown vinyl-topped card table.

Amber prescription bottles littered the table, their white childproof lids askew or off the bottles entirely. She had interrupted her father's breakfast—a congealing bowl of oatmeal sat before her, and a newspaper was spread in front of it. The twenty-year anniversary of the Murrah bombing was coming up in a few days, and the city was bustling with plans that took up the headlines. But not all the headlines. On the bottom half of the front page, she saw a thumbnail-sized photograph of her own face. She was wearing the black pearl earrings she wore when she needed to feel strong. Something about the pearls' improbable formation out of volcanic sand and the memory of the happy vacation she and Keith and Ian had taken to Oahu encircled her in the right kind of vibes when she was facing into bad ones. She wore them a lot lately. It looked like her dad had been reading about the town hall meeting she'd attended two nights ago, where she'd tried talking over a hundred Oklahoma City citizens all furious at Landon Energy's plans to drill close to the lake that provided most of the city's drinking water. It hadn't gone well. She'd wanted to melt into their mass and join them like the East German guards who threw down their guns and helped tear down the Berlin Wall. And she'd lost an earring.

The rasp of his breathing, as if the very air was scraping his windpipe, announced him before he reappeared with her iPad. Her father wore a pair of stiffly pressed jeans pulled up high over his gut, belted with a pewter horseshoe buckle she remembered him buying at a swap meet when she was a kid and a beige shirt with western stitching. The sleeves were pushed up, showing the mottled purple melanoma ulcers on his forearm.

"You know," she pointed to the device, "you can read the paper on that?"

"The real paper's more regular. Didn't know if I'd be able to get hold of your doohickey today."

"You mean steal it off my kitchen counter?"

He sat down in his brown leather recliner and grinned at her. She could tell he'd had his monthly haircut, high and tight, gray and bristling. Tubing ran from his nostrils, across his upper lip, and down to the oxygen canister on his back. Somehow it didn't make him look any more sympathetic. Maybe it was the way he wore all the paraphernalia of emphysema aggressively, like a badge of honor, maybe it was that he was smoking more than ever. She rustled around herself for loving thoughts and had just found a few when he said, "Looks like you're in some hot shit."

"Not me, personally. It's my job."

"That Landon Oil and Gas."

He called it by its old name no matter how often she corrected him. "Landon Energy is receiving a lot of criticism for sure."

"Guess you sold your soul to Landon *Energy*."

She glared at him. "It's work. You went to Vietnam. Did you like everything that job asked you to do? At least I haven't killed anyone."

"They ain't buying what you're selling, girlie."

"I love this from you, Dad. How many years did you spray chemicals for Big Ag? This is nice."

He pushed the lever on the side of his chair until the footrest popped out and the chair reclined. His hips slid sideways, and the tubing pulled at his face while he fixed her in a stony gaze. "I knew somebody would take you down a peg sooner or later."

She clasped her hands in front of her and looked down, inhaled and exhaled to the count of four. Where was that space between moments? Could she stay there? He seemed to want her to fail. He always had, yet here he was after so many years, and she was yearning for his approval again. "Dad, I'm just doing my job. I don't know what else to do."

"Up and quit."

"You sound like Keith now."

"Your husband's right."

Was he? She hoped not. He had compared her to tobacco company executives and climate change deniers in their furious fight they had while getting ready for bed the night before. "Easy for him to say," she said. "Easy for you."

"Good thing he gambles, huh? What would you blame your job on if you didn't have that to worry about?"

She closed the iPad and tucked it under her arm as she stood to go. How did he know about Keith's gambling? He could surprise her with his insights, even while she worried he was starting to lose it. Her concern took the sting out of his comment. "How are you feeling, Dad?"

"Half dead."

"That's half alive," she said in the chipper voice she'd used to cheer him up when she was little and he would come home from work and hole up in his room or spend hours in the backyard burning leaves in a rusty oil barrel, stoking the fire, talking to no one. She still couldn't believe he was here. Until a month ago, she had only seen him a handful of times since she was ten, and he had been an even worse father to her half sister. Instead of her mom, who was living in Savannah, Georgia, and to whom Edie would have happily offered her garage apartment, here he was, the man she'd longed for all her life, staying with her to be near the VA hospital.

He had been living too far away from the VA for proper treatment in the panhandle, where he'd flown a crop duster for the massive corporate cornfields that covered red dirt once known for blowing away. His emphysema was as likely to have been caused by the chemicals he sprayed over the fields for years and years as it was his cigarette smoking or the deforestation chemicals used in Vietnam, his lung cells the battleground of poisons from some of the twentieth century's graver missteps. No one was going to win, least of all her dad. Calvin Ash was on his way out. She leaned down and hugged him, startled by the boniness of his shrinking frame. "Don't forget to take your medicine. And call me if you need anything."

"Don't talk to me like I'm an invalid."

She shut the door and stood for a moment on the apartment landing inhaling. Breath. He was losing it, and it was taking his mind and memory with it. Breath was everything after all. Life itself.

After showering and dressing, she sat down on the couch and something jabbed her in the back. Reaching between the cushions, she extracted a Teenage Mutant Ninja Turtle action figure. Leonardo. She posed his arms akimbo and set him on the coffee table so he'd look ready for action when Ian came home. "Turtle power!" she said aloud. Resting her feet against the table, she opened the iPad on her knees. Instead of going straight to the meditation app, she checked social media. Eighteen emails. Four notifications on Facebook, six on Instagram, twelve on Twitter. The emails were mostly junk, plus one note from a mom in Ian's class asking for help with the class's upcoming Earth Day events, a message from someone in her Tuesday night AA meeting asking for a ride, and one from a reporter in Guthrie, a small town north of the metro, requesting a statement about an article in a national paper that talked about the loopholes insurance companies were using to keep from paying homeowners for damages due to earthquakes caused by fracking.

She hadn't read it yet, but she knew she would have to. She remembered waking up at some crash pad in Guthrie once, after a night of underage drinking, hung over with no idea how she got there. In the early hours before dawn, she had wandered around the old territorial downtown looking for a sign to tell her where she was. She gathered from the barbecue sauce caked beneath her nails that she'd been to a cookout, which explained the stomach cramps. She threw up in front of an antique store with a folksy name. That was Guthrie. Now it was being hit with multiple small earthquakes per day and everybody wanted to know what Landon Energy was going to do about it. Exhaustion hit her just looking at the subject heading. She'd have to gather her strength to respond to that one. Not now.

Twitter reported two requests to follow her, both by people she had hung out with in her Oklahoma City youth whom she had run into since she'd been back. She approved them. Then, Facebook: three further responses to a congratulatory thread she had contributed to yesterday about a friend's promotion, and one friend request. From—who? She slammed her coffee mug onto the coffee table and leaned forward, sure she had misread it. No. She opened the friend request.

She looked at the name again. Shock fogged her mind and she forgot to breathe. She read and reread the name on the screen. What? Delaney Travis?

4

EDIE

2015

Edie stared at the screen of her iPad. There was no photograph to accompany the name, just the generic gray silhouette of a female head that Facebook provided in lieu of a photo. Instinctively, she looked up at the photograph of Delaney she and Keith kept on the bookshelf next to the fireplace in a cluster of other pictures: Keith and Edie in their wedding clothes, the two of them with Ian a babe in Edie's arms on the beach in Fiji with Theron Landon and his extended brood, a family photo of fifth-grade Keith with his well-dressed parents against a fake autumnal backdrop. They kept the one of Delaney up, but neither of them could really bear to look at the photograph, which had been taken in Edie's old Honda on a day when the air conditioning worked. Edie's eyes habitually glided over it like it was a smudge or a hole, some familiar feature of the room she could ignore. But today, she looked. Her sister's smile stared back at her from under a blue stocking cap pulled over long, black braids, Delaney's wry eyes and dimples still hard to look at after all this time. Who would play a cruel trick on her like this? Who would pretend that Delaney was still alive? And why? Someone targeting her because of the fracking issue? But how could they know about Delaney? It was probably a bot or a scammer.

She confirmed the friendship request and went to the Delaney Travis home page. There were no posts—the page had only been created the day before. This Delaney Travis provided no information—no place of residence or age, nothing. She had four other friends besides Edie: three women who all lived in Abiquiu, New Mexico—Edie noted their names—and Keith Frayne of Oklahoma City.

Keith's gasp this morning. She had known there was more to it than his usual computer rage. Because it hadn't been rage, had it? His voice had trembled. Delaney Travis had sent friend requests to both her and Keith, and Keith had seen his first. But why, when she stood in the doorway and asked him what was wrong, hadn't he told her? A cold feeling crept over her as she remembered his face that morning, his Slavic pallor more pronounced than usual. He had lied to her face.

She walked to the front window and stared unseeing down the steep hill of their lawn and across the street at the 1920s Craftsman that mirrored their own. She wondered if he had lied to her about the Facebook message because his old instinct was still there. To be alone with Delaney. What a ridiculous thought.

Yet she remembered coming home from work and finding them naked in the kitchen, standing in front of the fridge sharing a postcoital carton of milk. He had shielded Delaney with his body although it was his body she was most startled to see, not her sister's. She had watched Keith grab an oven mitt to cover himself and follow Delaney, bare-assed and laughing, into her cave of a room. Edie knew, had seen firsthand the kind of single-minded ardor of which he was capable. Such wanting.

A brown UPS truck pulled up to a house down the block as she stood at the window. Those neighbors were always getting deliveries. Some shopping addict holed up in there, some lonely soul trying to construct a life through the little serotonin bursts that came with a new box to open, leaping one surge to the next and trying not to fall into the nothingness in between. It was how people lived—a matter of slot substitution for what provided the happy bursts: alcohol, gambling, shopping, sex, whatever. Like she had been with her drinking, like Keith and his gambling and the way he had been with Delaney, a way he had never seemed with her. Head over heels. Obsessed.

When Delaney vanished he had at first been unwilling to consider that she might have perished in the Murrah bombing. They had spent untold hours talking to police, rescue personnel, detectives, had run down every possibility, but when her jacket was recovered from the site, the green surplus army jacket decorated with Delaney's unmistakable collage of rock pins found sandwiched between collapsed concrete floors and ripped to shreds, he had begun to accept it, even though Delaney's remains were never recovered. As the weeks wore on and her name still did not appear on the list of victims, as the list was finalized and the building torn down, he had become paradoxically surer that she had died in the blast. Because what did it mean if she hadn't? Where, then, had she gone, and why? That way of thinking felt like madness.

Although Edie and Keith hadn't started dating until two years after the Murrah bombing, she had always felt like she was stealing Delaney's boyfriend. She remembered how little Delaney had seemed to feel for Keith, but Edie's guilt persisted. Their principal bond was shared trauma over the peculiar circumstance of Delaney's loss. Perhaps his need to salvage something had drawn him to Edie. Dissimilar as the half sisters were in appearance, they were still blood. She reminded him of Delaney. But this, she knew, said something pretty dark about her own self-esteem. Neither of her parents had cared much for her, but that was them, that was their stuff, their personality disorders and trauma, not anything to do with her. She had worked through all that. She was worth being with on her own terms, surely. And Keith loved her now. They had too much time and experience together for the memory of Delaney to be any sort of threat. She knew these things.

But he had lied to her face. Instead of looking up and saying, "I've gotten a Facebook friend request from someone claiming to be Delaney," what had he said? "Nothing—bullshit headlines." What had he been thinking? In that moment, her marriage triangulated, and she was the odd man out.

Edie stared at the Delaney Travis homepage on her iPad. *Who are you?* She felt pure longing for her sister, something she hadn't felt in a while, followed by jealousy that sluiced through her like a mudslide, uncovering her old self, the one who drank alone while Delaney and Keith made out in front of the TV, covered her ears with a pillow and tried to sleep while they had sex. She hadn't been that self-hating third wheel for a long time.

In one swift motion, she unfriended Delaney Travis. She didn't want Keith to see that she knew about his new friendship. She had been about to call him and hash out with him the possible meanings of this Delaney Travis character on Facebook—What do you make of it? Could this be real?—but his deception this morning introduced a shadow. She would wait and watch. She was good at pretending to know less than she knew, what woman wasn't. She and Keith, their lives soldered together in the heat of the Murrah bombing, had always, despite their troubles, been on the same team. But with the ding of a Facebook notification, the ground had shifted like a man-made earthquake.

5

KEITH

2015

Liberty 7s, that was his machine. Keith knew it didn't make sense to think one slot machine gave him any better odds than any other. Randomness—that was the only truth of slots, there was no skill involved, but his mind continually sought patterns and found them, sought systems, ways of beating the game. They always seemed to be there—a sign, a throb, runway lights you could see from miles away at night, even in the fog. It was a pattern he hadn't thought he'd see again after his last gambling debacle, his promises to Edie, and the mortifying lowness of his self-esteem in its aftermath.

It was true that he had dropped by this casino, Tornado Alley, just the week before. He hadn't gambled then, only strolled around, drank a Coke, and took a purely academic interest in its layout and setup, it being a shining example of the casinos that had appeared in Oklahoma after the passage of the State Tribal Gaming Act in 2004, while he and Edie were in London. He had been shocked at the scale of the thing. Tornado Alley was a Vegas-style casino the size of two Super Walmarts.

After dropping Ian off at school, Keith had driven back as if in a tractor beam and had already come within a couple hundred bucks of losing everything he had pulled out of the handy ATM machine at the casino entrance. The cash withdrawal was, in itself, a fatal one, since Edie would eventually see the withdrawal from their bank account. This fact had dropped him into a fatalistic binge state, his mind mostly shut down but running a ticker tape along the bottom that said something like, *if I'm going to lose everything it may as well be for more than a measly hundred bucks.* He had withdrawn again, and then again, and, still in a mental nosedive, he had come dangerously close to losing it all when he sat down at Liberty 7s.

Wanting out of his misery, he went right to the five-dollar spins, the highest bet on the machine. One, two, and three went like bones shattering in a body thumping down stairs—all but thirty bucks gone—but then four, just to finish off the bleeding corpse, and jackpot. The machine lit up. Next to him, a small, gray man in auto mechanic's overalls slapped him on the back. It was a modest jackpot but still a hit, and it had given him over half of his money back. His brain unseized and he came back into the room. Noticed the Eurythmics song ending and the Van Halen song starting. Noticed the smell of axle grease from the guy next to him and the overall stale funk of the place. For a moment, he felt on top.

His last disastrous gambling bout had been about a year ago when he had accompanied Edie to an energy conference in Bath, England. He had been looking forward to touring the Roman ruins but instead had wandered into a casino and lost all the money they planned to put down on a house for their upcoming move to Oklahoma. She had come out of her day of meetings to find him, finally, after hours of searching, at a blackjack table in nearby Bristol, his nails chewed to bloody stumps, his face shiny with the oily patina of panic he had visited and revisited over the course of many hours. Up, down, up, down.

She had found him at the table when he was down, almost wiped out, and she had demanded, standing at his shoulder, her voice shaking, that he cash out, that he stop right fucking now. He had done so—there was no ignoring her, no getting her to go away, he'd had no choice. But if he had stayed in the game, he would have come up again, that was what he couldn't make her understand. He would not have cashed out until he had made all their money back and then some. The whole point was to increase the down payment, not lose it! Buy low, sell high, right? She knew the stock market and understood that very basic principle, yet she had failed absolutely to understand his logic at the table that day. There had been no reasoning with her, and so the lump of cash they had planned to use on a down payment for a historical home in Mesta Park in Oklahoma City—her dream home, a home she remembered ogling from the back of her mother's shitty car—had evaporated. He knew it wasn't rational to blame Edie for the loss of their housing down payment, but sometimes he did.

"Keith!" A body crowded his periphery, and he turned in his chair to greet Brad Odel as his former classmate squeezed into the space between Keith and the empty seat of the machine next to him. "Twice in one week! I'm a lucky man!" Brad lifted himself into the empty seat, his legs dangling above the ground like sausages hanging in a butcher's window. He beamed at Keith, slapping his upper arm. Brad had been greeting fellow dudes in this way as long as Keith had known him, and that was going back to middle school.

Keith sighed. "B.O.! Hey!"

The other man scowled. "I told you, nobody calls me that anymore, Keith."

"How's it going, Mister Odel?"

"Living the dream, you know. Say, that's your wife I see on TV sometimes, right? Landon Energy?"

Keith nodded.

"Totally streetable."

Keith had to think for a minute, then remembered "streetable" as a term guys in high school had used for girls who were good looking enough to be seen in public with. As opposed to the other thronging masses of womanhood who only wanted to pleasure them in private with no expectations. Keith chuckled. A whole world of adenoidal male posturing opened back up to him with the word, which he hadn't thought of in years.

"My wife?"

"Yeah, dude. No disrespect."

"I'll be sure to tell her." Keith grinned, imagining Edie's response to being told that her presence on television as the vice president of a large energy company had garnered such high praise. Streetable. "What are you doing here bright and early on a Friday?"

Brad's florid face tightened up. "Same thing as you?"

Fair enough. He had run into Brad during last week's visit to this very casino and had determined that Brad spent most of his time here when he was between shifts at the furniture mall where he worked on commission as a shopper stalker. Brad pulled out his phone, tapped it a few times, and handed it to Keith. "Your number?"

Keith took the phone and typed his name and number in reluctantly. He didn't reciprocate the gesture. Why would he ever want to call Brad Odel?

Brad took his phone back and dropped it into the front pocket of his shirt. "The reason I was asking about your wife. The bet. You hear about it?"

Keith felt the same impatience to be away from Brad as he remembered when Brad would come huffing up beside him in the hall at school. There must have been a few moments of real friendship, but he couldn't recall them now. "The bet?"

"The earthquake bet?"

"How can you bet on earthquakes?"

Brad smiled and leaned close enough that Keith could smell his lonely body—meat breath, sour clothes, and God, could it be, unchanged since high school? That green bottle he kept in his console with his Tic Tacs and optimistic condoms? "Still wearing classic Polo?"

Brad flipped him off. He had a row of shrink-wrapped sticks of beef jerky sticking out of his breast pocket, and he took one out now, peeling it with deliberation. "Not on the earthquakes, per se. On when the energy companies are going to admit the connection between the earthquakes and the fracking they've been doing."

"Jesus Christ!" Keith looked up at the ceiling. "On when they'll admit it?"

Brad beamed. "Yeah, on the date. There's a range of dates, different odds according to what's in the paper day to day."

"And this is, what, you and some guys you work with? Small bets?"

Brad shook his head.

"Lot of money in the pool?"

Brad nodded with the exaggerated emphasis he had used in high school to indicate that, yes, he had weed.

Keith shook his head, dispelled the vista of risk that had shimmered into view. "Well, good luck, man. I hope you win big."

"That's the thing, Keith. I was thinking—you could win big, too, you know? You and me. Your wife must tell you this stuff, right? Comes home and talks about work?"

Keith closed his eyes as it dawned on him what Brad was suggesting. He remembered punching Brad in the face once, and the view from above of his friend lying on the basketball blacktop where Keith had knocked him. The fizzing contents of a dropped Dr Pepper can ran toward Brad's head like lava about to overtake a beach house. Keith had wanted to knock him out but stupidly couldn't stand watching the Dr Pepper soak Brad's hair, so he had pulled

Brad to his feet. His knuckles remembered the soft flesh of his friend's cheek, a sense memory with the urge to be repeated now. He closed his eyes to let the wave of violence roll over him. When he opened them, he let Brad see his fury. He had to, or Brad would keep needling him.

"Get the fuck away from me."

Brad shoved himself out of the seat like a cork from a bottle. His feet hit the floor and he rubbed his palms against his khaki jacket.

"Just talking, bro. Good to see you, okay?" He shook Keith's hand with a smooth, almost beatific expression. B.O. looked very happy. "My love to the wife. And the kid! You've got a kid, right? Love to him or her, too. If you change your mind, I'll be at Winchester Park this afternoon."

Keith watched his old friend walk away, hips before head and feet tipped outward like a character in the sort of cartoon they might once have watched together. What had just happened? He rubbed his face and stared at the bejeweled American flag decorating the sides of the slot machine. There was a betting pool on Landon Energy's making a public announcement about fracking. That was how far gone a conclusion it was around town that the oil companies were responsible. He wished Edie could've been there to hear that—to hear how thoroughly the natural-causes script she repeated for Theron fucking Landon was regarded as bullshit. But then, no, he wouldn't have wanted Edie there to see what else Brad had revealed: Brad had come there looking for him. Brad had taken the measure of him in their earlier encounters at the casino, had recognized a fellow sufferer, a degenerate gambler like himself, and thought Keith might betray his wife for a bet. Self-disgust settled over Keith like the concrete dust from the Murrah bombing that had covered his car. It had ruined the paint. Brad was disgusting, yet there it was, Keith could feel it tickling his insides like sexual arousal, the bet, the win, the big win, the nobody-would-ever-know.

He looked around the casino at the other gamblers in the padded chairs before the slot machines, most with one foot on the floor, one ass cheek in the seat, eyes glittering with intent, their heads cocked to watch their fates as they hit the bet buttons, one finger, again and again. They all walked a line characterized in the contradictory elements of their bodies' postures. Hope and seething need in the predatory eyes, the tautly held head, the tensile, rapid finger, while their overall hopelessness showed in their torpid bodies, the slow drags on the cigarettes that smoldered in ashtrays next to the bet button. It was noon on a Friday, after all. Didn't any of these people work? He thought he was probably the only gambler here who had ever bet overseas. Beijing, Lagos, and London casinos mixed in his memory. There was something about being smack in the middle of the country, in the floating stillness at the eye of the storm, that could make people who lived here see the rest of the world as unreachable, impractical. And unimportant. Maybe that was changing too, he thought it probably was, but it was one of the things that had bonded him to Edie—they had both seen that earth-bound provincialism in their families and friends and both had wanted out. And they had gotten out, they had traveled the world together. They were back now, though, where assholes like Brad Odel could find him.

He still didn't know how he felt about living in Oklahoma again. A reluctant nostalgia struck him at odd moments as he drove through the city. There were the smooth contours of the massive drainage ditch where he had skateboarded as a teen, the Dead Kennedys logo he and his buddy Aaron had spray-painted on its pale concrete side still plainly visible from the expressway. There was the IHOP he and his friends had been kicked out of for ordering late-night pancakes while tripping acid and doing unacceptable things with the syrup, the Baptist church where as a kid he'd eaten a lot of yeasty rolls and candied yams on Wednesday nights, the mall where he'd worked as extra holiday help at JC Penney. There was the old theater where he'd seen The Cramps with Delaney, watched her spew beer through her nostrils when Lux Interior, the lead singer, busted out his massive full frontal nudity. "Not real!" he had shouted anxiously in her ear while she laughed. "That can't be real!" The landscape remembered him, offering snapshots of his earlier life at almost every street corner. He had found comfort in that since returning home but no comfort today.

His and Edie's history stood strong against the wild hope that had fluttered inside him when he'd saw the Facebook invitation. Theirs was a trauma bond, started on the night they had sneaked onto the blast site in search of hope, and deepening through the years of grief, further soldered by standing together to try to prove Delaney should be counted among the dead. No Facebook invitation erased all that. Delaney had died in the blast, had to be the 169th unidentified victim. He would never forget when he and Edie claimed her concrete-caked army surplus jacket, pulled it out of a plastic bag, its rock pins crumbling in his hands. They had never understood why that wasn't enough to include her among the list of victims. Not that they wanted her there. They wanted her alive, but that wasn't possible, and so, the unsayable truth was just this: at a certain point, he had needed to believe that she had died. Because if she was still alive it meant that she had left him, had gotten out from under his love, rejected his story of their life together as he tried to tell it to her. Blown him off without a single glance backward, like somebody running for her life. Which would mean that she hadn't loved him.

As the emptiness in his chest yawned and widened, he looked at the red-white-and-blue neon 7s on the face of the slot machine. There was no reason to cash out yet. What if he stayed until he had doubled his money? What if the Facebook invitation meant Delaney was alive? If the residences of her few other friends on Facebook were an indication, she lived in Abiquiu, New Mexico, a site he remembered from a graduate school class as where a few small uprisings against New Spain had gone down in the seventeenth century. He looked it up on his phone. About a nine-hour drive from Oklahoma City, Abiquiu was in the mountains north of Santa Fe, near the Colorado border. If he could double his money, he could put back what he'd withdrawn today and fund a cheap trip.

He knew he should have told Edie about the Facebook invitation, should tell her he planned to go look for her sister, hell, should take Edie and Ian with him, but he couldn't. Feelings weren't his strong suit, at least not knowing what they were, so it was difficult for him to pull apart the threads of the rope tightening around his heart.

There was some need to protect Edie in case it was a hoax. He imagined her getting her hopes up, then suffering all over again when it turned out to be some asshole fucking with them, some former student angry about a grade or someone who had seen her on TV. There was also, dimly, his awareness of Edie's historical anxiety about his feelings for Delaney. He had tried for years to show her how much he loved her, but he knew Edie believed herself to be a consolation prize. Not his first choice. She struggled to see herself as lovable, could not fully undo the programming damnable Calvin had ingrained in her by leaving when she was a kid. It was always there, that feeling that their life was built over the rubble of his love for Delaney. That. And then, yes, an ancient part of him, the younger man he had been the morning of the bombing when he impulsively proposed to Delaney, not thinking it through, when she threw their future in his face and went off and died, maybe that guy was still there. Such strong threads, each of them, and so damned tight.

Why call it Liberty 7s unless that was a clue, his path to freedom? Hadn't he hit all his little wins every seven tries or so? He would push the button seven more times. Delaney was born in the seventh month, she had liked an all-chick punk metal band called L7, today was the seventeenth, and the town where she might be was known for events from the seventeenth century. A pattern. Dots that connected sevens to sevens, past to present, the living to the dead. He didn't believe in lucky numbers, but today was different, and today it was seven. If he started to lose, he'd cash out. He'd stop.

6

EDIE

1995

Edie came in the back door to Beryl's, the steak house where she had been working since her junior year of college. She punched in and called out a greeting to Reza, whose grocery bag of physics textbooks under the coat rack gave him away along with the Metallica blasting from the back of the cook's line. The other morning cook played country. Still dizzy from her hangover and the crazy noise that had shaken her organs, she began scooping buckets of ice from the icemaker and carrying them to fill the bins behind the bar. Reza pushed out of the walk-in freezer with an arm full of cardboard meat boxes and nodded to her. "Edie."

"Hey, Reza. Did you hear that?"

He shouldered by her, his dark arms pressing the boxes to his chest. They had dated for half a year and had only broken up the month before.

"That was a bomb, man." He shrugged the boxes onto a long stainless-steel counter. "You mark my word, some bad shits are going down."

She smiled. His English was basically perfect—his parents had sent him to the UK when the Ayatollah Khomeini took over Iran, so he had spent his teen years, when she was still a small child, speaking British English. There was only one chronic error to his speech, and it was invariably funny—he pluralized words that, in English, have their plurality implied, like hair and, although she had never thought of it before now, shit. What touched her was that he got the verb tense right. *Your hairs are beautiful. Some bad shits are going down.*

She watched him drop the heavy boxes onto a counter behind the cook's line. Maybe they could get back together. Then she wouldn't have to care about Keith pining over Delaney. Reza would finish his Ph.D. next year. He already had an offer to do postdoc work at Fermilab, the underground particle accelerator outside of Chicago. She could go to grad school in Chicago. She planned their future as she unlocked the liquor and began setting up bottles, stopping to find the remote.

The TV above the bar always greeted her with *The Today Show* when she opened in the mornings, but what she saw today was aerial footage of downtown Oklahoma City. Whatever had caused that loud noise this morning was big news—the local station was preempting the syndicated program. Helicopters circled a wide, smoking area. Edie thought of the column of smoke she and Keith had seen that morning, that she had watched blooming in her rearview mirror as she drove west to work. It was downtown, whatever it was.

Then she realized something. *The Today Show* logo was in the bottom corner of the screen. The voice of the commentator was that of the national morning show host, Matt Lauer. This was *The Today Show*. She was looking at downtown Oklahoma City on the national news.

"Holy shit," she said out loud.

The restaurant manager, Denise, hustled from her office, eyes on the television. "Is that it?" She smoothed the front of her slacks, pulled tight across her hips, and scooted onto a barstool. She pointed the remote at the television and turned up the volume.

"Do you know what's going on?" Edie said.

"It's not an accident," Denise said. "They're saying somebody blew up one of the government buildings downtown."

"On purpose?" Edie watched scenes of mayhem on the screen. Street scenes. People streaked through the bright April sunshine covered in blood. Edie looked out the long windows of the restaurant at the cool, sunny morning outside, then back at the television. Same sunshine. Same morning. Then the screen showed a fireman rushing out of rubble with a baby in his arms and Edie heard for the first time the name of the building. The Alfred P. Murrah Federal Building.

"The federal building? Is there just one federal building?"

Denise wiped a trail of tears across her cheek, her eyes fixed on the screen. "I never go downtown."

Reza appeared at the door to the kitchen. "Yes," he said.

"Where you go to get your social security card?"

"It's where I got my green card," he said.

Edie sank to all fours behind the bar. Her hands pressed into the black rubber mat, and she stared unseeing at the pipes under the sink. Delaney.

"Hey, are you—" Reza knelt next to her, the thick white front of his chef coat filling her vision. Her pulse thudded in her fingertips, in her temples. He tried to help her up, but Matt Lauer was saying "fatalities" and she dropped again to the ground.

Delaney could have gotten out of the building. Or she could have stopped somewhere for breakfast and not yet arrived when the bomb went off. Or she could have finished her business and left already. These things were possible. Or she could have been in the building.

Denise came around the bar, her hip joints popping as she crouched next to Reza. "You okay, darling?"

"My sister's there."

"Delaney?" Denise craned her neck. "Are you serious?"

"She lost her social security card."

"Again?"

Edie began to cry.

"Naah," Denise said, in a breathy rush. "That girl's never where she's supposed to be. Don't worry, hon, don't worry. Why don't you call home and see if she's there."

Denise was right—she had fired Delaney from this very restaurant for her lackadaisical notion of showing up for shifts. Just because Delaney had told Keith she was borrowing his Bronco to go to the federal building didn't mean it was true.

Edie dialed the phone at the corner of the bar. Denise and Reza watched her as she let it ring. A yellow pencil sat on top of the notepad for to-go orders, and she picked it up, furiously darkening the circles on the form they used to check off menu items as she braced for each unanswered ring. Then their machine picked up and she heard Delaney's voice: "We're not here. You know what to do." She put down the phone, shaking her head at Denise and Reza. Edie wondered if Keith had made the same call yet, if he had realized what was happening.

Denise picked up her keys and unlocked the liquor cabinet. She began pulling out bottles and sliding them into their spots on the lighted shelves lining the back wall of the bar. "I've got this," Denise said. "Why don't you go home and see what you can find out? I'll need you tonight, though. Be back at five."

Edie clocked out, jumped in her car, and drove like she had somewhere to go, but as she pulled into traffic, she realized she didn't know what to do. She was on South Meridian Avenue, a busy northwest street, only a mile or so from the airport. The Murrah Building was north and east. She could see the massive tower of concrete-colored smoke rising from the center of town. She would go there. Maybe Delaney was wandering around in the sunshine with a head wound like those other poor people she had seen on the news. She wanted to know rather than guess.

First, she stopped at a Texaco and bought a Budweiser tall boy. Her heart was going crazy, and she could barely breathe. She sat in her car in a parking space in front of the gas station and downed the beer in a few seconds. The news was on the radio—fatalities were expected to be massive. Of the 550 people working in the building, 300 were unaccounted for. And the child she had seen carried from the wreckage wasn't the only child. The bomb had been inside a Ryder truck that someone pulled in front of the lower-level entrance, directly below a daycare. People had just finished dropping off their children. A daycare.

Edie wept against the steering wheel. When she looked up, a couple of skater boys were holding their boards and staring through the window at the cashier's TV. At the pay phone, a woman in a business suit gripped the receiver and covered her face with her free hand. Edie went back into the Texaco and bought a twelve-pack. Usually she got ID'd, but the cashier was watching the news and barely glanced at her. She could probably have walked off without paying.

She headed north on Meridian and took the I-40 exit ramp that would take her east to the bombing site. She didn't know exactly where the Murrah Building was—she had held onto her social security card since she got it when she was a kid and had never had reason to visit the place. On the radio they mentioned Sixth Street. That was easy. On the radio they were also saying that the building housed a bunch of government agencies: the FBI, the DEA, the ATF and that was maybe the target. What was the ATF? The commentator explained—Alcohol, Tobacco, and Firearms. So, some antigovernment thing? She flipped through the radio stations. Middle Eastern terrorists, she heard someone suggest, the same people that had tried to bring down the World Trade Center in '93. It was all speculation. Their voices trembled, straining to maintain continuity in the absence of facts while the raw data poured in from the blast site.

She exited I-40 at Sheridan and made her way north up Walker to Sixth Street until a barricade prevented her from going any farther. She slowed to a stop, draped her bar apron over the open beer can in her cup holder, and unrolled her window as a distracted-looking cop leaned in and explained that the area was blocked off. "I want to help," she said.

"Miss, if you want to help, give blood. We're going to need a lot of blood."

7

AUGUST P.

1994

Settlers used to say only wild animals and wild people could survive inside these woods so I consider myself among their wild ranks for how good I got at crunching through that thick forest behind the compound, ducking and bending, snapping branches and yanking briars off my clothes. I spent a lot of time out there, as much as I could get away with, and knew it to be where anything the elders disapproved of went to stay safe. Whiskey, dirty magazines, marijuana, and me.

On that day, I was collecting cicada shells. I only kept the perfect ones, the ones where all their legs were whole, and the seam was intact along the back that had split to let the creatures out like taking off a coat. I used them as evil aliens in the battles I staged with my action figures. I had a Lando Calrissian, a Boba Fett, a one-legged C3PO, and some guy with blue skin from a different movie. Cicada shells are scary if you look at them up close, and they stick to things, like curtains and pillowcases, great for battle staging, plus they give the most satisfying crunch when you squash them, so I favored them and tried to get as many as I could in summer when they were to be found. I was fairly covered in them, had eight or ten stuck to the front of my shirt, when I heard the creak of a car hood come up and noticed the blue of McVeigh's pickup truck through the trees. He was staying in one of the trailers and had parked his truck in the dirt driveway along the side of it. I saw my chance to talk to him about the army.

McVeigh was bending over the open hood of his truck. I was nervous to come up on him out of the woods, so I snapped some branches and scuffed the dirt real loud with my boots, making plenty of noise over the steady thrum of cicadas to let McVeigh know I was there. I didn't know much about the fellow, but enough to know that there was something alarming about him—the stiff, protective body language of my stepdad Gary and some of the other men when I saw them talking to him told me to use caution, especially since McVeigh wasn't a scary-looking guy. The source of whatever it was that made the elders brace was something in his person that was hard to see but easy to feel.

McVeigh glanced up. He squinted, wiping his hands on a rag.

"You changing the oil?" I asked. I peered over the open truck like I could tell what I was looking at.

"Transmission fluid," McVeigh said. Up close McVeigh barely looked older than me, and he was kind of goofy looking, with jug ears and little eyes. In the sun, all the hairs on him glowed red—head, eyelashes, arm hairs. He was wearing a T-shirt with Abraham Lincoln's face on it. The back of it said, "The tree of liberty must be refreshed from time to time with the blood of patriots and tyrants." There was another quote, too, in Latin, about tyrants. It was a lot of words for a T-shirt, and intense ones—not what you expect on somebody's summer clothes—but I confess my memory of the exact quotation comes not from that moment but from the coverage of his trial. I guess he wore it to Oklahoma City those months later to set off the bomb. It must've been his favorite shirt.

I got tongue-tied. I smiled and nodded.

"You're the liberal kid?"

I felt like a hand had just squeezed my heart. I didn't know what the term meant, but for Gary and my mom, "liberal" was the dirtiest word you could hear so I knew to back away from it. "Shit no," I said. "I ain't a goddamned liberal!"

"Liberal's a town in Kansas. You ever been there?"

"No, no I haven't."

"I could've meant you're from there."

"Yes, sir. Is that what you meant?"

McVeigh let hurl a hatchet of a laugh. "Nope."

"Not how I took it, either." I was staring down at the car engine like it was the most fascinating thing I ever seen, but I was just scared to look up at him.

"Did you know you're covered with critters?"

"Oh!" I looked down at the army of brown translucent shells glowing in the sunlight. They gripped my shirt with their brittle arms and legs like I was their daddy. It did look weird. I could see that it did.

"They attack you all at once?" He grinned and reached for my shirt. He plucked one off and smashed it between his thumb and forefinger and I felt its death in the roots of my teeth. "I used to play with these," he said. "I'd pretend they were aliens."

I laughed and said me too, they're perfect. He allowed that they were, and for that moment he was my friend. We were boys together playing.

Then he said, "Aren't you a little old for that?"

"Could be." I wanted to ask him why he called me the liberal kid, but I wasn't about to. Something my mom said, probably. She was always calling me a pussy, and from what I gathered from context clues I thought they meant about the same thing.

"What can I do for you, boy?"

"My name's August."

"Why'd they name you after a month that's hot as the inside of an asshole?"

I did not know the answer to his question. I tried to smile. He laughed and told me his name.

"Well, sir," I said. "I was just wondering if you could tell me about being in the Army of the United States. Like, if you'd recommend it, all things considered." It was the second time I'd called him sir and this time it landed. I've never met a man who didn't start to like me right off after I called him sir. They think you must be a fine judge of character to recognize your betters so fast. It's like showing your butt with dogs. With the worrisome "liberal" comment hanging out there unexplained, it seemed called for.

McVeigh relaxed into one hip and smacked a mosquito on the back of his neck with the flat of his hand. He eyed me. "You thinking of joining up?"

My big sister, Malory, joined the army as soon as she turned eighteen and was living on a base in Germany now. Because of her and all the traveling she was doing, the army was my heart's desire, what I wanted most to do someday when I was old enough, but it crossed my mind that McVeigh was probably as antigovernment as the rest of them. I didn't know the right answer to that question, and I'd learned, being around there, that these old boys didn't really believe in everybody having their own ideas. If I said the wrong thing, God knows. I sensed that the best way to keep my balance in the conversation was to commit to nothing and get out of it as soon as I could. "Weighing my options," I said. "I don't know much about it—just curious."

He released the strut and let the hood drop with a bang that made me jump. "They give you guns, and they teach you how to use them. World-class weaponry and world-class training in how to kill."

I had never thought about the actual war part of the military. I told him about the weapons training I'd had just the day before, but he wasn't impressed, said the cheap Chinese ammo we had here was no better than firecrackers and those SKS rifles were some east-bloc nation's castoffs. The US military, he said, is the best of the best, where weaponry is concerned. "But," he said. "It'll cost your soul. What you need to be preparing for is the real war that's coming."

"A war?"

McVeigh stepped to the side of his truck and reached into the truck bed for a cardboard box about a foot square jammed behind the wheel well. He slid it down the ridges of the cargo area with one hand. Then he opened the back door and pulled the box close to him. It was sealed with packing tape that he pulled off with a loud rip. Inside the box were two stacks of red books. He lifted one off the top and handed it to me. I held it in both hands and read the title, in bold white letters: *The Turner Diaries*. I looked up at him. He had gone for the book and handed it to me like he was answering my question about a war, but I wasn't sure what to make of it. "I'm not much of a reader," I said. And I wasn't. The truth is, letters move around when I try to read, they jump lines and mix together, and I can end up getting meanings out of things that weren't there at all, and almost always missing the meaning that's intended.

"You'll read this," he said.

"I'll sure try."

"You'll read it," he said again, and the force in his voice was for sure this time. "You'll be a man soon, and you're a white one. Hell, you think you get to live here in this heavenly place and pay no price? When the war is over and won, places like this will have the only people left alive on the planet. You want a spot? You're going to have to earn it."

"H-h-how?"

"The book explains it all. What's going to happen and how. Start there. I'm going to ask you about it next time I'm here. I've got that book memorized, so don't try to lie. Lying's filthy."

I stop the picture here again and again. Had I picked up anything about McVeigh then? Had I felt he would murder all those people, all those folks going to work, those children, those tiny babies? Had the shadow of what he would do within months cast backward over that time and chilled the air between us? Sometimes, in the days and weeks after the Murrah bombing when McVeigh's face and news of the unspeakable thing he did was everywhere, it seemed to me I had felt something. But had I, really? Memory is tricky, and our minds can make us believe just about anything we want to be true. It's so scary, you know? How are any of us supposed to know anything?

8

ROBERT

2015

Robert didn't mind being called a conspiracy theorist. Most of the drivers he rode with knew about his interests, and if they didn't, it only took a shift or two in some parking lot in the Oklahoma City metro, sitting in the cab of the ambulance between calls, before he'd shared the gist of his thoughts. Most of them were too young to remember the Murrah bombing, so his tendency to talk about the event had gradually taken on a professorial flavor. Their ignorance was staggering and worrisome. His current driver, Blanca, was genuinely interested, though, which was a mercy. This morning she was asking him why more people weren't charged if Robert was right, and Timothy McVeigh had a lot more help than just Terry Nichols and Michael Fortier.

"I mean, not to doubt you, RT, but he confessed to doing it alone."

"Of course he did!" Robert could really get going on this particular aspect of the whole nest of hornets if he let himself. "He looks around and sees he's standing alone after everybody that helped him ran for cover. What else was there for him to do but make himself as big as he could? He was getting the chair no matter what. Die a pinhead fanatic who got used or die as a big evil mastermind? What would you do?"

"I wouldn't do any of the things he did," Blanca said. She turned the steering wheel slowly as they cruised the Tornado Alley Casino parking lot. She wore dark sunglasses, her black hair pulled back into a tight bun. She was about Robert's daughter's age, and he thought they might hit it off if he could talk his wife into inviting Blanca over for dinner.

On days like this, they might have to tend to some drunk who had fallen off a barstool and hit her head or passed out on the toilet. Sometimes there were heart attacks or injuries from fights. The great majority of casual visitors to the casinos, the people who could be entertained without triggering an addiction, came and went at night with few incidents, but gambling addicts were most of who was at a casino in the mornings on weekdays. Domestic arguments carried violently into the public space were common. How many bloodied knuckle bones had Robert bandaged after they'd smashed some addict's face in? How many addicts' broken faces?

The first thing he did when they stood by at a casino was ask his driver to cruise up and down the lanes of the parking lot so he could look down into the cars and make sure there weren't any kids frying or freezing in the backseat while their parent went inside. It was a worthwhile precaution, and he was certain he'd saved a few kids' lives by insisting on it. This morning's check had yielded nothing but empty backseats, or backseats full of belongings and trash piled to the windows, but no living beings. Not even any pets, thank goodness.

Blanca had brought the ambulance to a stop under a shade tree at the back of the parking lot. "If that's true, I guess I don't understand why more people weren't investigated."

Robert rested his ankle on his thigh and took a sip of coffee. "They were," he said. "From what I've read, a lot of people were looked into. It came down to a bird in the hand."

"A bird in the hand?"

"You know the expression, a bird in the hand is worth two in the bush?"

She laughed. "You are so old!"

"It means, take the sure thing. Don't worry about the stuff out there that looks better that you might not be able to get. McVeigh, he was the sure thing. And Terry Nichols, he was caught dead to rights, too. Have you really never heard that expression?"

"Maybe I have," she conceded. "All the other locos were—they were in the bush or whatever?"

"Right. And still out there in the bush, let me tell you. I've run across them online. You ask me, they're getting stronger. Now they got a Black president, and they can't stand it, Blanca. They faded into the woodwork after the Oklahoma City bombing, but now it's just a matter of time."

"Don't worry, RT. There aren't many of those people. They'll never really have any power."

He rustled in his seat. A tall, anxious-looking man wearing a T-shirt that said BIKINI KILL came out of the front door and loped across the parking lot, pressing his key fob. "I wish I shared your optimism. I hope you're right, but there are bad people out there. Look at that guy." Robert inclined his head in the direction of the pale, anxious-looking man heading for his car. "What the hell does Bikini Kill mean? It sounds like violence toward women, doesn't it? It probably is."

"Naah, Bikini Kill is just an old band. You need to relax, partner. The bombing was a one-off."

Being an ambulance driver had started his fixation with the Murrah bombing. In '95, he was back from the Gulf War, out of the army after getting his twenty, and floundering around doing odd jobs when he'd decided to be an EMT. He'd missed being of service, missed urgency, was jonesing for life-and-death stakes. His wife said he was an adrenaline junkie, but seriously, how did people go through life with these humdrum jobs? He had been in training when the Murrah Building was hit. He rode his first shift two weeks later, in early May, and it was still all anyone he worked with was talking about. Ambulances had converged on the site within moments of the blast on April 19th and spent an unimaginable day taking victims to all the city hospitals, filling one emergency room and then another, moving outward from downtown. In the days following, as the rescues slowed and then stopped, they idled in their vehicles and watched the recovery effort. He listened to their stories, watched their plunging sadness, their grim pride, and felt outside the veil of a great mystery. The more they said, "Be glad you weren't there, man," the more he wished he had been there—to help, regretting that he hadn't started his training earlier.

"This is a quiet morning, RT. You know what that means."

"Busy afternoon."

"You really do think there's, like, nests of locos holed up waiting to take up arms against the government?"

He turned in his seat to look at her. "I know it. I could tell you some things I've seen online. They're out there getting organized."

"What is it they want? What did McVeigh want?"

"A race war. He got his moves straight out of a book called *The Turner Diaries*. Heard of it?"

"I've heard of *Bridget Jones's Diary*."

He laughed.

"Not the same thing?" She grinned at him. "How would it do that? Cause a race war, I mean?"

"Oh, it doesn't make sense. I mean, he thought his likeminded wackos would rise up and help him finish the job once he struck the first blow. They'd get it. Like the date—April nineteenth was the anniversary of the showdown at Waco, and it was the day a guy who tried to bomb the Oklahoma City Federal Building in the early eighties was executed in Arkansas. There was some revolutionary war battle on that day. Lexington. The date was a dog whistle. He had it all worked out."

The need to be part of history. That need, at least, he understood. He had wanted to be part of the story in the moment. He had been piecing history together ever since. A compensation. If he could find one piece of the puzzle someday, *just one piece,* and set it in the puzzle, watch it click into place, even if the rest of the picture remained dark, even if no one ever knew, he'd call it good.

Blanca had opened a tin of Altoids and was holding it out to him. "All McVeigh's magical dates—it sounds like astrology."

"Does, doesn't it?" He took a mint. "People need patterns. And if they're not there, we find them anyway."

9

EDIE

2015

More people than usual were milling around the concrete courtyard in front of Landon Energy's entrance. Edie slowed her car and leaned forward to see, glad for tinted windows. She saw a television camera, no, two television cameras, bearing the logos of the local NBC and CBS affiliates. She saw an anchorwoman she didn't want to talk to standing between her and the front door, no doubt pursuing an update about Tuesday's rumored announcement before the weekend. She felt more fully alert than she'd been coming to work in a while—where was her fugue state? But facing media questions less than an hour after getting a Facebook invitation from so-called Delaney? She drove by and kept going, looping back to the highway before asking her car's computer to call her sponsor.

"What's up?" Kayli always sounded like she had been working out when Edie's call came in, and she usually had.

"I can't go to work."

"Who are you and what have you done with Edie? That girl don't stop."

"There's press outside. I know it's my job, but—"

"Not a grown-up today?"

"Not today." Edie told her about the Delaney message.

Kayli, who had learned the ins and outs of the Delaney story during the few months that Edie had been back in Oklahoma City, conceded the crisis. "I see that. I do. I wouldn't be about the fracking today, either. I'm about to chair the ten o'clock meeting. You should come."

Edie reached for a Big Book on the metal folding chair next to her. The chairs were set up in a circle in the middle of the square room. In a charmless corner of a strip mall shared with a check cashing business, a Goodwill, and a liquor store, the meeting space was used by a local nonprofit to feed homeless people every morning, so the long tables bedecked in seasonal tablecloths on which the free breakfasts were served were pushed to the walls of the room and the chairs circled for the meeting. Currently the tablecloths were pink, blue, and green with Easter eggs dotting their waxy surfaces.

The place looked cheerier during the daylight hours, and a mostly unfamiliar crowd filled the room. People in business suits or work uniforms, people on breaks. Edie usually attended Tuesday and Thursday nights, but she was unmoored and needed grounding.

After the bombing, she had felt as if time had started anew—After Delaney was AD. This postapocalyptic time scape had been her psychic domain, where she expected to live until she died. But now she didn't know where she was. Had time hit the reset button? Was a new dispensation announcing itself? Despite every indication that Landon Energy would need her to respond to an imminent announcement about fracking by the Oklahoma Geological Survey, she was here and not there. She wasn't at work.

Her sobriety had begun five years After Delaney, a hard bottom she had hit on a hungover morning when she could no longer give herself the usual self-improvement spiel in which she would treat the chronic fatal nature of her alcoholism like a bad habit—like she had eaten a pint of ice cream before bed or spent too much money on shoes, instead of courted oblivion. Worse, she had begun to remind herself of her dad. She had stood before ever-patient Keith and had groveled apologetically about things she had done and said while drunk and had understood better than she ever wanted to what the incorrigible Calvin had felt like in scenes such as this with her mother.

Above her, white ceiling fans circled lazily. The ceiling tiles were stained yellow from the years before the meeting went nonsmoking. Across the circle from her sat a familiar face from her regular meetings, August P., pulling on a limp forelock that hung at the front of his combed-back blond hair. It was James Dean hair, or Johnny Cash hair, which was funny given August's utter lack of swagger. She didn't know he came to the morning meetings. But why not? He was probably there every time they opened the door. He didn't have a regular job, at least she didn't think so. Instead, he devoted himself to lugging a huge wooden cross, with roller-skate wheels nailed into the bottom of it, around town. She hadn't noticed his cross outside, but then she hadn't been looking for it. He usually laid it down in the grass by the back fence at the rear of the parking lot because the group didn't let him keep it in the meetings, which were not religious, and people worried that a new person attending for the first time might get the wrong idea seeing August's big cross leaning against a wall. He gave her a shy wave.

She waved back. She took comfort in the eager way he leaned forward during the meetings, elbows on the knees of his filthy jeans, pressing on the moons of his ridged fingernails, an absorbed expression on his face as he listened while other people talked. The first time she saw him out on the road, his shoulder wedged into the right angle where the beams of the enormous cross intersected, his posture steadfast as he ignored the traffic that streamed by him, she had wanted to laugh at the literal-mindedness of the reenactment, but when she had realized the poor character trudging along the shoulder of the highway was August—August P. who poured the coffee at meetings, who beamed when he shook her hand, and whose idiosyncratic grammar filled her with vestigial memories of her mother's relatives—she had started to imagine the practical difficulties of his undertaking, began wondering if the cross gave him back pain, if the blue rubber wheel on the bottom often had to be replaced, where he kept it, and why he carried it. Now, after being back in Oklahoma City for seven months, she knew there was some terrible darkness in his past that led to his feeling eternally penitent. He said as much in meetings, alluding to his past without details the way you do when you assume everyone already knows the story. She didn't think they did, but they all seemed to trust him. Kayli hired him to stay in her house with her dogs whenever she went out of town, and another friend paid him to sit with her mother in the hospital during the day while she herself was at work. He was a welcome part of every group but always seemed alone.

As she silenced her phone and slid it back in her purse, a woman she didn't know took the seat next to her. Late twenties, in a Best Buy Geek Squad uniform, she smiled at Edie and seemed to want to talk. Edie turned to her and asked her name.

"Sandra," she said. "Are you on TV? The fracking lady?"

"The fracking lady?" Edie's voice rose in horror. "I guess so, yeah."

"Sorry, I know we're not supposed to—"

"It's okay."

"I wouldn't break your anonymity at any of the protests or anything."

"Well, thanks. I won't come to your place of work," she said, nodding down at the Best Buy logo on Sandra's shirt, "and reveal your secrets either."

"Great."

She thought that was the end of it, but then Sandra leaned over and said, "I'm sorry, just—do you really not think the earthquakes are caused by—"

"Of course I do. I'm not an idiot."

"This is a program of rigorous honesty, though, right? How do you get to stay sober when you're up there lying?"

She glared at Sandra. It was the question Edie woke and went to sleep asking herself every day. "I'm—I'm working on it. Progress, not perfection, right?"

The woman gave Edie a high five. "Don't let it take you down."

The unwelcome conversation had kept Edie from finding and talking to Kayli before the meeting started. Her sponsor opened the meeting briskly. Kayli sat cross-legged on her chair at the front of the room, fingers working the bottom of her yoga pants. Lately she was wearing a long weave that fell around the tattoos on her dark, defined biceps. She scanned the room and settled a significant gaze on Edie.

"How about you, Lady Bug?"

Edie registered her sponsor's nickname for her and searched for words across the blue low-pile carpet at the feet of the people around the circle. August P. rested his hands in his lap, one leg bobbing like a pump jack. "Thanks, Kayli."

She had learned not to tell people her theories concerning Delaney. When, in the past, she had tried to explain how her sister's death in the Murrah bombing had been unacknowledged, she could always see their skepticism, and she would shut down, unable to provide the details that would convince them. Sometimes she could tell they thought she was a trauma junkie, the kind of person who had to find a way to personally connect herself to any disaster. *My sister—well, half sister—she was in the blast—well, they never found her, but—no, really.* She couldn't bear to be misunderstood that way—she had known someone like that, a guy who had lived next door to her and Keith in London. His wailing and gnashing of teeth after 9/11 had taken on a special sense of entitlement because one of the people who died in the World Trade Center had worked in an office with his sister a decade earlier. He had always, with his gnawed fingernails and posture like a wilted question mark, seemed to be saying, "My sadness is deeper than your sadness." And maybe it was, maybe whatever sadness in him that needed to identify with external events in order to find a way of getting expressed was deeper than hers. But Edie had found him a turnoff and, watching him, had seen clearly how it was that nobody wanted to hear her Delaney story.

So she never talked about what had happened. But today she wanted to. Sandra's pointed question left her feeling defensive and explanatory. She wanted to hand out her argument, a bulleted list of the persuasive events in the narrative of Delaney's disappearance, show them all the inevitable logic of her conclusion, even if it couldn't be proven. She wanted to stand in front of the room, shine a pointer at a screen, and have them all follow along:

Delaney got up around 8:15 on the morning of April 19, 1995, and drove to the Murrah Federal Building to request a copy of her social security card.

She left at 8:40 driving her boyfriend's Ford Bronco.

The bombing happened at 9:02.

The Bronco was found parked in front of the Murrah Building covered in debris.

Delaney was never seen again.

Her jacket was recovered in the debris of the social security office, on the first floor front of the building, the office that sustained the most casualties, over 40 of the 168 official dead.

Without luck, they searched every hospital and morgue, filed police reports, and called everyone Delaney knew.

Then there were the further details, grisly, about the leg of the unidentified 169th victim. It had been mismatched and buried with the remains of another victim. The mistake was realized over a year later, the body exhumed, and the correct leg interred with the victim. It was that leg, belonging to an identified victim, that Delaney's DNA was tested against. Of course it had not been a match, while the leg of the still-unidentified victim, buried in the wrong grave for over a year, had been treated in the lab with some aggressive chemicals that made DNA testing impossible once they disinterred the leg.

But Edie still found it hard to allow these details into her mind, still resisted thinking of Delaney in terms of parts and remains. Her mind fuzzed out, a tingling white screen came between her and those hardnosed details, and she had no words. The people in the room all watched her, patient expressions beginning to give way to perplexity. She reached into her purse and pulled out a tangled ball of blue yarn left over from Ian's dream catcher, which she set in her lap and began pulling apart. "My husband lied to me this morning. But then I lied to him. At least, I wasn't straight—I hid what I know. Which is that he got this message and I did, too. I don't know why I did that." She looked up and scanned the faces in the room. "I—we—got a message from someone who died a long time ago."

Kayli wore a pained expression. Sandra looked like she was trying to make up for her prior invasion of Edie's privacy by looking away from the spectacle of Edie's discomfort. August P. focused on her, patient and encouraging as if she were in the throes of a bad stutter. She could see from the bored and uncomprehending looks of the other people in the room that she wasn't making sense. There was always someone in a meeting who was hard to follow, but it had never been her. Even when she was newly sober, suffering DTs in the community room of an eighteenth-century church near Highgate Cemetery in London, the only American and the only woman at her first few meetings, she liked to think she had strung together coherent sentences. But Delaney had been dead then, a tragedy that had never, ever made sense, but which, Edie realized now, had become an orienting focal point of her own identity. Her wound, her story. If Delaney were alive? She felt a longing for her sister that left her weak. But it couldn't be true. And Keith had lied to her. The room was overheated, and she could smell everyone in the circle, the sickening sweet smell of candy-flavored vape fumes, a medicated topical pain reliever, perfumes and colognes, cigarettes, hairsprays, and somewhere, from someone in the circle, a whiff of whiskey. She felt faint. "Sorry, Kayli. That's all I've got today."

"You're going to call me later?"

Edie nodded.

"Good idea."

10

KEITH

2015

Please, please, please, please, please. Keith had begged his mother on the phone, and she had agreed, in a voice heavy with disappointment, to meet him for lunch in an hour. Now he pulled his car up the steep driveway of his house, stopping by to change into a clean shirt. His shirt, his pants, even his jacket were soaked with the casino's stale air, which reminded Keith of the inside of a plane at the end of a long international flight, and his own ammoniac fear sweat.

As he swung out of the car, he noticed movement in the yard. The second-floor door to the garage apartment was open, and at the bottom of the external stairway, in Edie's daffodil garden, he saw the bent back of his father-in-law, the black backpack that held his oxygen tank making him look like a humped animal. What was Calvin doing?

"Good morning!" Keith called out, walking across the lawn.

He was still getting used to having Edie's dad around. He had never met the man in all his years with Edie until Calvin showed up last month and moved into their garage. Keith associated him with Delaney's recollection of first meeting him in a truck stop. Her mom, who had raised Delaney without help from or contact with Calvin, had died in a car accident when Delaney was seventeen. She'd gone to live with him until she turned eighteen. Edie had met her then, although she hardly saw Calvin, either, and had almost deleted without listening to his phone message telling her about her heretofore unknown sister and asking her to meet the girl. The disappointment of being Calvin Ash's daughter was a deep bond.

When Delaney disappeared, Edie had gotten no reaction from Calvin except that he had become even harder to reach in his trailer up in the panhandle.

What a destroyer he had been. Keith had watched Edie try again and again to overcome the conviction that there was something worthless about her that had driven her father away. Keith believed that all her considerable accomplishments had been to prove her value to the old man, and he had thought a lot about his own parents' love and his lack of ambition relative to his wife. His parents' regard was conditional in the opposite way—they believed he could do more than he was doing, could be more like they had been in their stellar careers. They were probably right, but so what? Would he be more driven, like Edie, if they'd treated him like he was incapable? Who could say if he would have risen to the insult. Gambling felt like some sort of compensatory sortie in a way he could only sometimes glimpse, a flash in the periphery.

Calvin was barefoot, wearing a yoked western-style shirt and his usual blue jeans with heavy starch, the rigid crease like a stick down the center of his legs. He hadn't brushed his hair, and it stood up around his head like the fluff of a baby hedgehog. Although he was younger than Keith's parents, he seemed much older, the clear plastic tube that ran above his mouth and into his nostrils punctuating the image of poor health he presented. His hands were gathered around a bunch of daffodils as he met Keith across the grass. "Hey, Boy-o!"

"Edie's daffodils," Keith said. He fingered the delicate yellow blooms.

"Think she'll like them?" Calvin's rheumy blue eyes shone up at Keith with uncharacteristic brightness. The old bastard was smiling.

"She planted them. I don't think she wanted them all cut down, though, man. You making a bouquet?"

"You know how they are. You gotta make them feel special."

"Who's 'they'?" Keith asked, though he knew the answer. He wasn't sure he could tolerate a parenting speech from Calvin Ash at the moment. Heat flooded his cheeks.

"Girls. Women."

"I've never known you to go out of your way to make Edie feel special, have to say."

Calvin waved a hand. "Listen, you can't spoil them. Look at her. She thinks she's some big shot anyway and I tried keeping her humble."

"Yeah, look at her. I guess you didn't stick around long enough to finish the job."

Calvin shrugged. "Just be glad you had a son and not a daughter."

"Daughters," Keith said, his voice tight. "You had daughters." He wanted to shove Calvin backwards, he wanted to drive him off their property and back into the wasteland he had emerged from. There was something missing from the guy. As low as Keith was feeling about the gambling relapse, contact with someone so much worse felt like a gift. He yanked the flowers out of the old man's hands. "I'll put these in water."

Her daffodils. Poor Edie. He had helped her plant them that fall, the two of them on their knees in the misting cold, digging holes, pulled along by her inexorable tropism toward renewal that pulled the whole family forward. He knew what she would say when she saw the bad haircut her dad had given the garden. *They'll grow back.*

What her father had said about her, she would never hear from Keith. It would go in that inner room, already crowded with the nights he had steered her toward safety when she was in one of her blackouts, with his stupid proposal to Delaney, with today's weird Facebook invitation, a room full of hurtful things there was no point in making Edie deal with.

Keith let Calvin follow him into the house. After he filled a mug with water and dropped the daffodils into it, he jogged up to his and Edie's bedroom. He found a pressed, white collared shirt and resolved to look legit for lunch with his mother. Turning the knobs on the shower, he wondered about Calvin. It had been breathtaking to actually hear the old man's feelings about daughters from his own mouth. Edie hadn't been wrong to feel he didn't care much for her, only wrong to assume it was her fault. Calvin usually seemed to have more mitigating layers to his personality. Maybe the loss of oxygen from emphysema was bringing on dementia.

Keith stood under the shower and let the hot water pummel him. Despair crept around the edges of his thoughts like necrotic tissue. Maybe dementia felt like this—when you can't control what your mind is doing. What hope is there when you watch yourself acting against your own interests and against your own will, compelled like an abductee with a gun to his head? If you can't control your own decisions, what are you but a rogue organism, a cancer cell bringing mayhem and death to its host environment? Edie didn't need this shit. Ian didn't. No one did. He slapped his palms against the wet shower tiles and leaned his head down, feeling the water pelt his neck. Christ, he had gambled again.

He simply had to beat it. He had to. Look at his life! It was good except for this. If he could excise the addiction, get clean and sober like Edie, truly have an entire mental shift and live on the other side of the struggle, then he would be golden. But the moment he thought he had it solved was the second before it pulled him under again. Edie had tried again and again to explain sobriety to him. "You're still trying to control it. That's the opposite of what works. Sobriety's like aikido. Step out of the way, let the blade miss you, let your opponent wear himself out." And other such inscrutable nonsense. It all made sense to her. It was as if she could pass through like vapor what for him were high, hard walls with no end. He shut off the shower and grabbed a towel. His mother would be waiting.

When he reached the bottom of the stairs, Keith heard the television and found Calvin stretched out on the couch, a hand tucked behind his head. He had arranged the pillows to prop up the breathing tank on his back.

"What are you watching?"

"There's a whole channel that plays old movies now. Nothing but."

Keith stood behind the couch and looked at the screen, recognized Joseph Cotton on a street in Vienna. "This is *The Third Man*."

Calvin wiggled his toes and tilted his head back to look at Keith. "Want to watch it with me?"

"I've got somewhere to be," Keith said. It was as if the tense conversation of half an hour ago had left Calvin's mind completely. "You've seen this, right?"

"Don't believe so."

"Right here." He pointed at the screen as a man at a café table read a book called *The Oklahoma Kid*. "I always seem to catch this scene."

He had watched this with the sisters, who showed him a lot of old movies at their duplex on Twenty-third Street. They'd force-fed him the Marx Brothers, the *Thin Man* films, any and all Hitchcock. The night they saw *The Third Man* he had been making out with Delaney through so much of the movie, he hadn't known what was going on in the story. Edie had lain on the floor in front of them, her hands under her chin, eyes on the screen, and had seemed not to notice him and Delaney behind her, but he knew now how it had killed her. When she told him, he had insisted they watch the movie together and had kissed her all the way through it. They'd missed the cemetery scene, they'd missed the Ferris wheel scene, and every other one except the *Oklahoma Kid* scene. He wasn't sure he'd ever seen the film all the way through, but he loved it, and somehow, through repeated exposure he had absorbed the story.

"Keep your eye out for Orson Welles," he said.

"Why? Is he hiding?"

"Just watch."

11

KEITH

2015

"Look around you, Keith." His mother waved a fork at the tables full of well-dressed patrons, their hair gleaming like precious metals above the white linen tablecloths. "You're in a room full of people, most of whom think the government has no right to do anything but round up poor kids to fight wars for their financial interests, but even they know fracking and earthquakes go together like tequila and lime. Even they want the oil industry regulated."

Warm baguettes appeared at the table with cold butter on a porcelain plate, brought by a waiter whose presence Keith barely registered. He and his mother sat at a small table along the back wall of the French brasserie, a quiet place set back from the road in the wealthy enclave of Nichols Hills. Art deco tiles lined the bar, and bright, abstract gilt-framed wine posters in fuchsias and yellows covered the walls. They had been sitting at this very table when he and Edie told his parents they were moving to London. He had painted a rosy picture, which he had believed, of his prospects in London academia, and his parents had toasted the young couple, their faces suppressing disapproval at his career path and his marriage. The whole moneyed environment felt like the claustrophobic gaze of parental disapproval.

Keith tried to settle in and listen to his mother, but he was itching to start his search for Delancy and desperate to cover his losses before Edie found out that he had gambled again. Gambled and lost, after the solemn promise to Edie never to gamble again. But his mother was in no hurry and she wanted to gripe about Edie. Normally, he'd be happy to shake his head over Landon Energy's official stance on fracking, but their fight the night before had exhausted his animosity toward his wife, and the Facebook invitation from Delaney had reminded him how much they needed each other. Right now, it was all just so much chatter, and his mother's schadenfreude over Edie's tight spot angered him. He defended Edie even though he had fought her over the same issue, even though he was there because he had just sucker-punched her with the gambling relapse she didn't know about yet.

While his mother pulled open her baguette, he watched her fine-boned capable hands, the blue veins standing high against the craquelure of her skin. She was getting old. Had she ever imagined she would still be bailing out her son in her midseventies? How did she see him? He doubted he could survive an unvarnished view of himself from her vantage point. She was his mother, but she was not sentimental, and not easily fooled. Eleanor Frayne had fought for civil rights in Oklahoma since the early 1960s, had stayed in one of the reddest states in the union and remained committed to social justice nonetheless. Her skin was thick, her mindset cheerful but bullish. She had no problem being the minority opinion in any room. She would say what no one else would say, and, deceived by her diminutive stature and beauty, people would find themselves holding their metaphorical entrails while she replaced her verbal sword. Before her retirement three years earlier, she had been the longest-reigning and best public defender in the city.

"Now," she said, "if the earthquakes had the good sense to stay out on those southern plains of ours, why, our neighbors wouldn't believe fracking had a thing to do with earthquakes. They'd think all the hullabaloo and science was just a campaign by a bunch of socialists trying to cripple a hale and hardy American-owned business."

Keith squirmed in his seat, feeling the embarrassment and pride he had felt all his life as her comments drew dark looks from people at the table next to them. She went on, oblivious, or maybe not at all oblivious, merely determined. "But those earthquakes have the temerity of rumbling under these people's property, shaking their chandeliers and sending cracks across their living room walls and the bottoms of their swimming pools. Threatening the whole city's water supply? They're not going to stand for that, no sir. Even that craven creature they've got in the governor's office is going to admit to the connection soon, or at least that's the scuttlebutt. I hear the Oklahoma Geological Survey will make an announcement next week. So these oil companies had better say, sorry, my fault, it'll never happen again, pretty damned fast. They should've already done it. Landon Energy should have already done it. And by Landon Energy, I of course mean your lovely wife."

"Mother, I know these things." Keith was in no mood to be lectured to by his mom, even on this topic, about which he agreed with her wholeheartedly. He wanted out of the small French restaurant, where she had told him to meet her when she had heard the noise of the machines behind him on the phone, She knew right away where he was and what he wanted. *Your father and I are not bailing you out again, Keith.* But she had agreed to meet him, which he took as reasonably hopeful, a rope dangling over the abyss that had opened up—that he had opened up. Only five hours had passed since he stood at the bathroom mirror brushing his teeth with Ian, the two of them humming like motorboats. Everything had been intact then. He hadn't checked Facebook yet. Delaney was still dead. He and Edie had fought about her job the night before, but he had woken determined to bring her close to him again. The money he had just lost was still sitting in his and Edie's savings account where it belonged.

His mother smiled at the waiter. The smooth edge of her chin-length bob seemed to underline her expression, its silvery shine an emphatic frame around her strong jaw and deep-set green eyes like Keith's. "I'm sorry to go on about all this business, but I figure you need schooling on the way things are. You were gone so long, and I know the lay of the land was different in London."

"Not so different," he said. "Except there they have the honesty to admit they have a class system."

She nodded agreement. "But you seem to have missed my point."

"I took your point."

"Well?"

"She says he'll acknowledge the earthquakes soon."

His mother's tinkling laugh rang out. "He'll acknowledge them. Like Theron Landon's bastard children."

Keith grinned. It was good to hear her laugh. "Yes, folks—the hairline cracks across your city. Dozens born every day."

"I guess 'fracking' and 'fucking' are too close not to make that joke. There but for a vowel and one negligible little 'r.'" She took a sip of iced tea and looked around the room.

"Mom!" Keith laughed out loud. "How's Dad?"

"Oh, he's good, good. He'd be here, but he's gotten himself ass deep into some old man's chess club. They play nearly every day. You should see him. Bobby Fisher, your dad."

"Ass deep, Mom?" He remembered his mother as more proper than she was. He could see his parents anytime he wanted now, not just during their annual summer visits to London, and was still getting used to it, relearning the full extent of their idiosyncrasies and establishing a rhythm with them.

"So." She concentrated on moving the croutons from her salad to the side of the plate. She never ate them but never remembered to ask that they be left off the order. "Speaking of ass deep?"

He looked down at the white linen napkin in his lap. "I'm really sorry."

"I believed you last time. Truly. I thought you were done."

"I thought I was, too. I really did."

"Out with it, then. Rip off that Band-Aid."

In halting language, unable to look up at her, he told her about his fight the night before with Edie, his need to show he could provide as much money as she could, the way he had withdrawn cash from the ATM and found himself in front of a slot machine like somebody sleepwalking. He wanted to tell her he needed the money to find Delaney, but he couldn't say it. He wanted to explain about his system, about Lucky 7s, but here, outside of the casino, the infernal logic of his belief in a winning pattern looked like daylight madness. It was, after all, a kind of madness.

"My God, what do you have to lose before you stop? You've still got a lot to lose, you know." She was sitting back in her chair, her arms gripping the sides like someone on a roller coaster. Her face was taut. "I'm going to tell you something and you'd better hear me. If you hurt my grandson, Keith, in any way, I swear to God, I'll become an enemy you don't want. I mean that."

"Come on. I would never let anything happen to Ian. You know that."

"You think you get to control the consequences?" She leaned forward and grabbed his hand. She whispered, "I spent thirty years downtown defending people against the pure shit set loose by their or somebody else's addiction. Better than half of my cases boiled down to somebody's addiction. Nobody meant any harm. None of them thought it could happen to them. You're not special. You're on a train that only goes one way, son. Goddammit." She turned away from him and covered the side of her face.

"I know," he said. He hated it when she spoke of his gambling as an addiction. She could lovingly reduce all of his thoughts and reasons to mere symptoms. There was no traction for him within that frame of reference. "I was fine until this morning. Then I got a message from Delaney."

"A message from—" She dropped her hand from her face. Her wet mascara dotted the skin below her brows. "Oh, for God's sake, Keith."

"A friend invitation on Facebook—"

But she was shaking her head. "I don't want to hear it. I do not want to hear one more thing about Delaney. God, I wish you'd never met those damned sisters. Heard from her! Well, why the hell not? I never really believed she died in the bombing. That was just you and Edie telling yourselves a story."

This was the first he had ever heard of any doubts. And she was misremembering. He could hear her telling him about the forensics experts she had talked to downtown, about the ways Delaney's remains could have gone unfound. His mother had in fact been their principal source of information from people she knew in the Oklahoma State Bureau of Investigation. He remembered having to stop her, unable to hear gruesome details. He stared at her for a long moment before he said, "I'm not sure if the message is really from her. I have to find out."

"So find out."

"Mom, I don't think you're hearing me. Delaney might be alive."

She waved her hands before her face like she was clearing away flies. "It's too much. All too much for me, I'm sorry."

"Delaney—that message—that's why I gambled. I wanted money to go find her. That's all I wanted."

She leveled a horrified gaze at him. "Oh, how did you get this way? What did I do wrong?"

"I need to know. I've spent twenty years trying to accept that she was dead. Edie has, too."

"And you couldn't think of any other way to get money? I know you're a pauper, but your wife is one of the most high-profile professionals in this town. She wouldn't loan you money for a Motel 6? Delaney's her sister—she must want to know worse than you do. Oh." She rapped the table with her knuckle. Understanding crept over her face. "She doesn't know."

"It all happened so fast. We were trying to get Ian off to school," Keith said.

"And so you want to find Delaney—why?—for yourself? So help me God, Keith—"

"It's some kind of fake, Mom. I'm afraid Edie might think it's real, get her hopes up. I don't want her to know where I'm going or why. That's why I wanted some—some invisible money to go to New Mexico."

Eleanor Frayne's shoulders slumped, and she leaned back in her chair. She pointed with her chin. "That Napa Valley print? I've always loved it. So bright and happy. I think it's the lavender. You know, the Victorians wore lavender for mourning? Interchangeably with black. I don't understand that—for me it's such a happy color. Don't you think?"

"I can pay you back, I'll pay you and Dad back."

He was wincing against the prospect of her anger, but she didn't raise her voice. Instead the life seemed to have gone out of her. She rubbed her hands up and down her arms as if she were cold.

"I told you no."

"Mom."

"No more. No more. We told you that last time, and we meant it. I'm sorry, but I'm not going to give you money to save you from having to be honest with your wife. That's ridiculous." She drew herself up in her chair like a marionette with a string at her spine. "Would you like a dessert? They've got the bread pudding. You always like that."

Case closed. She had moved on. Keith mirrored her movements, bringing himself up to the table and rearranging the napkin in his lap. "Yes, let's share it," he said.

He patted her hand. He felt momentarily numb, his whole soul like skin that takes a hard slap. Chastened and put straight. His mom had bailed him out plenty of times, a source of continual envy to Edie, whose parents had left her alone after she turned eighteen like cheetahs walking away from their offspring once they can hunt. She had pointed out to him often how lucky he was to have parents like his, and he knew it was true compared to hers, though he couldn't make her understand the pressures peculiar to his situation. Regardless, he was too damned old to have scenes like this with his mother. A bright clarity filled him. There was a Sanskrit word Edie had told him about after one of her meditation sessions. *Sankalpa.* It meant resolve, or intention, or something like that. Yeah, yeah, he had thought, a little dismayed to see Edie learning earnestly *how to feel her breath* from the whispers coming from her phone. But it was a good word for what he felt now. *Sankalpa.* A fitting mantra. It felt good to be in the truth again, to tell his mother what he had done and watch the menace dissolve as the putrid vapors hit the fresh air. He wanted to make everything right for everyone. To be the man he was supposed to be, that his family needed him to be. His mother was right to tell him no. He would get the money himself.

12

EDIE

1995

Edie told Denise she'd be back to work her shift at 5:00 but it was hard to imagine how she could be. All day long, she'd checked the hospitals, roaming helplessly in each emergency room like flotsam through the furor as ambulances pulled in and in and in from the bombing site. They were calling it that now—a bombing. The bombing. The Murrah bombing. It had a name. Something she knew about herself: she fainted at the sight of blood. She didn't want to create problems for the already-overwhelmed medical staff, so she averted her eyes from the wounded coming in on gurneys. She didn't try to see behind curtains. She waited in lines and at counters, filled out paperwork about Delaney, and in each hospital was told that, no, there was no Delaney Travis admitted. They referred her to the First Christian Church, where the medical examiner was setting up notification teams, a waiting room for families, and another area for press. All notifications would be faxed there, they told her. Go to the cafeteria on the north side and wait. Edie did, accepted refreshments from kind people, tried to listen, tried to talk, but the intensity level in the room was suffocating, and she balked at the idea of watching bad news roll in, watching other people get bad news, and waiting for it to be her turn. Going home and getting ready for work seemed impossible but also a relief. She tried to imagine who would be eating out that night.

    She went home in the rainy late afternoon and dressed for work in front of the television. Everyone they interviewed wore a rain slicker and stood under an umbrella speaking loudly into the rain and the roar of the generators under harsh artificial light. Edie's mind fingered and dropped images, possibilities, scenarios like reflections in a fractured mirror. Delaney, under crumbling plates of rubble, pinned, scared and calling for help as the day darkened and rain poured down. That was the optimistic picture. That was what she hoped for. That, or that Delaney wasn't in the building at all, that she had somehow been elsewhere when the bomb went off, but if that was the case, where was she? Why hadn't she called or come home? Edie ran her palm across the tops of nail polish bottles Delaney had left out on the coffee table, and then, in a spasm of frustration, swept them all to the floor. None broke, and she felt disappointed. Instead, they rolled around on their sides and settled against each other, one or two rolling under the entertainment center.

It was Delaney's television—the day they moved in together, Delaney had brought the TV in first, grinning in gym clothes with a bag of McDonald's breakfast perched precariously on top of the TV. She'd eased it to the floor, handed Edie a coffee, and sat down on top of the television, smiling and looking around. "We finally get to grow up together," she said.

Edie still kept hoping Delaney would walk through the door, and she didn't want to be gone when her sister strolled in with some offhanded, maddeningly thoughtless explanation of where she'd been all day.

But Edie had no choice. As she made her way across town to the steak house, the rain prompted atavistic thoughts, and she found herself attributing emotions to the weather. The sparkling morning had turned into a slate-gray afternoon, and the rain was heavy and relentless, coming down hard. Inconsolably, one might say. As if God was crying. Were we no different than our primitive ancestors when it got right down to it? Where had that ancient thought come from? Rain as tears, the entire natural world prostrate with grief.

As she waited on a red light at Twenty-third and May, she turned on the radio to hear President Clinton's speech about the bombing. God might or might not be crying, but at least the president knew what was going on. The relief she felt surprised her. He promised justice. Justice wouldn't change what had happened, but she felt it, the need to know who did it and to see punishment meted out, another primitive thought the day brought out in her. Edie's slow drizzle of dazed weeping rose and spilled over. She tried to keep her eyes on the red traffic light through her tears, and as she looked up she noticed that a man in a car that faced her across the intersection was crying, too, thick fingers pressed against his cheekbones. A teenage boy in the passenger seat wept as well. The driver of the car next to them, a blond woman with racing stripes running down the arms of her jacket, dragged the back of her hand across her eyes and glanced into the mirror to fix her makeup. Edie scanned the intersection, eight cars including her own. When the lights changed, there was a pause as everyone collected themselves and began to drive.

She shook her umbrella at the back door and clocked in. Reza was still there, only his torso visible to her from behind the line as the kitchen roared with Metallica and the rush and clatter of servers shoving dirty dishes across the transom at the dishwasher and pulling new orders onto trays.

"Edie!" Reza called out. He was sliding a bowl of French onion soup out of the broiler where he'd put it to melt provolone cheese. He gave the browned cheese an evaluative glance and slid the bowl onto the pass-through window. "Order up!" he yelled, yanking a ticket from a row before him and dropping it next to the soup.

Watching him, she tied on the black apron, slid three pens into the pocket, and grabbed her order pad. "That's the whole order? Soup?"

He raised his dark eyes to her. "People are sad. It affects the appetite."

"It's so fucked," she said.

"Fucking fucked," he agreed. "Some big cowboy yelled at me when I was getting gas. Acted like I was the one who did this."

"Oh, no," she said. "Are you okay? I heard them say Middle Eastern terrorist on the radio."

"Don't worry about me." He yanked down another ticket. "But I hope they find who did it fast, and I hope to hell it's not what they're saying. If it is, I'm out of here."

The restaurant, which typically served business travelers going to or from the airport and staying in the surrounding hotels, was packed. Ordinarily, when Edie arrived at work at 4:30, the cavernous, dimly lit place was nearly empty, its wood-paneled rooms and flagstone floors throwing back light and sound, standing ready for an onslaught of carnivores in business casual and high-end shitkicker duds. The teenaged hosts and hostesses in their black slacks would be leaning on the podium at the front, chatting while they rolled silverware, and the server who had worked the long afternoon shift would be sitting at the bar watching television and eating her shift meal while she counted her tips.

But today it was Defcon 1 when Edie walked in. The windows all around the restaurant were steamed, making it feel like everyone inside was underwater.

Bodies thronged the area by the front doors, crowding the hostess stand and lining up at the bar in wet jackets. The afternoon server was behind the bar pulling beers and trying to smile at customers as she shouted promises that the bartender would be there soon. When she saw Edie, she pointed at her and yelled. The crowd at the bar turned, and for a moment Edie had the feeling of being the target of a mob. She raised both hands in the air and yelled, "Hang on, people!" As Edie pushed the saloon doors that led from the kitchen to the bar, Denise hustled past with a case of Dewar's, her face red with exertion and her manager's computer card in her teeth. When she saw Edie, she dropped the card from her teeth to the top of the Dewar's box and shouted, "I need you clocked in!"

"I know!"

She set the box on the bar and grabbed Edie by the shoulders. "I'm sorry. Did you find her?"

Edie shook her head.

Denise squeezed her biceps. "Shit. Are you okay to work?"

"I need the diversion."

"Okay, then. Can you?" She pointed at the case and handed Edie a box cutter from her shirt pocket.

The whole world was here to cover the bombing. The customers were media, all kinds, from nearby Dallas, Little Rock, and Albuquerque affiliates to the major national networks and news stations, CNN, NBC, ABC, CBS. Even the big international stations were there. The BBC. Telemundo. Some had spent the day at the site; others had just arrived in Oklahoma City and were heading down to cover the ongoing rescue operations after they ate. Who did it? Every table of people speculated. Edie heard, "a yellow Ryder truck." She heard, "Jihad." She heard, "anniversary of Waco." She worked the bar and the tables in the bar, making drinks for her full row of bar customers, for all the other servers' orders as they came scrolling in on printed tickets by the bar register, then dashing out from behind the bar to run food to her tables, pick up plates, refill drinks, drop checks, run credit cards, and make change. She was drenched in sweat and didn't even notice the music, which tonight was the kind of new country that usually made her want to stab forks in her eyes.

With a large tray of steaks and lobster on one shoulder, she glanced at the clock above the bar: 7:30. Somehow the hours had passed, and she had been too deep in the weeds to think about Delaney, but now she plunged back into time, where the rain poured and downtown, at the bombing site, the body count climbed. Terror bolted at her like a figure through a doorway, and she flinched, her arm jerking the massive tray she had balanced at her shoulder. It began to slide. The butter tower that accompanied the lobster plates slid down the tray, the flame of its tea light candle flickering wildly as the ramekin of hot butter above it slid off its mount and into Edie's face. She dropped the tray, sending shattered dishes and ruined food across the floor.

Looking down at the mess, she braced for the usual jeers and cheers, the shouts of "Job opening!" But none of that happened. People looked up, but no one said anything.

A gray-haired woman in a red jacket who had been about to receive the lobster leaned back in her chair and handed Edie her cloth napkin. Edie wiped the greasy butter from her face as she apologized.

"It's nothing, hon," the woman said. "How's your face?"

Edie had been bending to pick up the mess, but she looked up. "It hurts. It's fine. How do I look?"

"Like you need a date with a makeup mirror and some pressed powder," the woman said.

As the evening wore on, more and more of the customers were rescuers and media coming from the Murrah site. Wet, shell-shocked, and exhausted, people were having dinner and much-needed drinks before returning to the ongoing search.

A new table, three men and a woman with press badges around their necks, ordered a round. As Edie dropped coasters around the table and set down their drinks, she heard one of them, a big, bearded man in a khaki vest, saying something about Vera Wrede. The fact that Vera Wrede and other anchors of the big news channels were there testified to the magnitude of the event. Oklahoma City didn't usually draw this kind of attention. It was still hitting Edie how bad the bombing was—they were calling it the worst act of domestic terrorism in American history. The bearded man said, "Before I rolled the camera she was standing there with the mic in her hand, and she says, 'What are we going to call this? How about "The Hillbilly Holocaust?"' She thought that was hilarious."

The woman next to him set down her napkin.

Edie, who had been waiting for them to finish before she asked for their order, interrupted. "Wait a minute. What?"

The cameraman looked up at her, an apologetic grimace showing through his beard. "'Hillbilly Holocaust.' That's what she said."

Edie's cheeks burned. The bearded cameraman continued, "Did you hear it, Jay?" A man across the table from him nodded. "No one could believe—my God. I covered Vietnam, but today we saw things—" He took a drink and raised the empty to Edie. "Another."

The youngest guy lit a cigarette. "How about that interview she did with the police chief?"

"She asked him if he thought the Oklahoma City Fire Department could handle it," the woman said. "I think they aired that, too."

Edie should have moved on—they weren't ready to order, and she could feel the impatience of her other tables needing her attention, could see drink tickets tumbling from the ticket machine at the bar, people on the barstools peering around to find her, and servers coming to pick the orders up—but she was choked with fury. Hillbilly Holocaust? She felt her heart beating in her neck, the skin tight on her face. Her jaw muscles ached.

She felt a tap on the back of her thigh and whipped around.

"Any time now, girl." He was a young guy, leaning back, tipping his chair with the toes of his Nikes. Looking at him full in his doughy adolescent face, she realized she should have ID'd him. She placed him as younger than her, a good bet he was underaged. She capped the ashtray at his table and asked to see his ID card. Barely-21 took umbrage. "ID? Are you crazy? For me?"

She smiled at him. Her jaw muscles were killing her, tense as though she had been chewing rubber all day.

"You already served me."

"If you'll just show me some proof of age, I'll be happy to bring you another."

He stared at her. Dark calculations wheeled behind his eyes. "I'm for real, you'd better hurry. Some of us are ready for a drink. It's been a bad day, in case you didn't notice."

Edie gripped the tray in her hands. She closed her eyes. Delaney would know just how to handle a guy like this, Edie had seen her do it. What would she do? She would laugh. Delaney would understand that a guy like this wants to be taken seriously and to laugh at him is a gut shot. Edie could imagine it—if she laughed, this guy would crumple, regroup, and probably get out of there in a hurry, tabbing out with a flounce, stiffing her on the tip, calling her a bitch. But she wasn't Delaney, today least of all. She couldn't laugh. She just couldn't. Instead, she said, in a tight, prim voice she hated, "It's a busy night. I'll be back for your order when you've had time to produce ID."

He laughed at her. "I bet you're not twenty-one."

His friend at the table chuckled along with him. Then, on the TV above the bar Vera Wrede appeared, looking irritated in the rain with the Murrah Building behind her lit up for ongoing rescue work. The network's catchy title for the bombing appeared in the chyron below Wrede's face: *Terror in the Heartland*. To think someone had worked on that title, batted options around a conference table. Better than Hillbilly Holocaust.

The other bartender had finally shown up and was behind the bar popping beer caps and sliding fresh drinks to the customers in front of him. He turned his attention to the tickets the servers were waiting on and glanced up at her, shaking his head. She strode back behind the bar and took off her apron. She pushed her receipts, credit card slips, and cash into a drawer and said, "I'm so sorry, Saul."

"Hey!" he said. "Edie, no!"

She broke into a run. She heard his voice behind her, as she pushed through the swinging saloon doors into the kitchen, past the line where waitstaff and cooks faced each other, shouting over "Fade to Black," past Reza at the drink station chewing ice, past his look of alarm, past his voice calling her name, past the time clock and the laminated announcements from the US Department of Labor, past the handwritten notes on cocktail napkins of employees wanting to pick up shifts or give shifts away, out the heavy back door, and into the cold rain.

13

EDIE

2015

"You want my opinion, Edie? I think you're being paranoid."

Edie looked at her friend, framed by the sun's glare on the plate-glass window behind her. Fiona Bolton had never been a good listener. Not ever, not in college when they first knew each other, and not now. Their years apart hadn't improved Fiona's capacity to absorb and think about other people's problems. It was why Edie liked to talk to her. Her friend missed most of what Edie confided in her, which gave a coffee date with Fiona something of the benefits of stepping into a confessional. She could unburden herself and know Fiona would never repeat any of it.

"You're probably right."

Now, though, Fiona's failure to grasp what she was told made Edie want to stand up and pour coffee all over her friend's long brown hair. Her dead sister had sent her a Facebook request. No response to that. What Fiona had heard was Edie's insecurity about Keith's feelings, her fear that he might be planning to take off and find his old flame. The tawdry part.

"It's not jealousy, it's—"

"Big news, I know. Look, I don't want you to get your hopes up, okay, hon?"

Edie gazed at the coffee rings on the filthy table Fiona had chosen and tried not to think about her hopes. "You don't think it could be her?"

"Are you serious right now?"

"But, I mean, what if—"

"There's no chance, okay? Not even Delaney can come back from the dead. Anything short of that I wouldn't have put past her, but not this. Don't forget, I knew her."

Edie did tend to forget that fact. She and Fiona had been tight when Delaney showed up in her life during her freshman year of college, and they had tried being an awkward threesome for a while before Fiona took a gracious step back and let the newfound sisters devote themselves to one another.

Fiona emptied a sugar packet into her cappuccino and took a sip. Her big brown eyes reminded Edie of pleading puppy cartoons, liquid pools of persuasion that made her occasional insensitivity a continual surprise. "First time I met her was after that Chainsaw Kittens show down in Norman, remember? Your dad had just told you two about each other. It might've been the day you met. She was sashaying around with the lead singer's boa around her neck. At least she said it was his. It looked better on him."

Edie laughed. Fiona's affront at losing her to Delaney back then still showed up sometimes, although Delaney was gone, and she and Fiona had been friends for ages now. Fiona had even visited Edie in London a few times.

Edie looked at her watch. They had planned to have coffee before the Delaney situation happened. Her reason for meeting Fiona at this closet-sized Starbucks off the Broadway Extension was to tell her again and in person that she couldn't give her any breaking news about Landon Energy's plans for her city blog, *All the Red Dirt*. It seemed to have a growing readership, but there was some magic number of hits or subscribers or shares or something that Fiona was aiming for, at which point sponsors would begin throwing money at her. She had worked for years for the city paper, had quit and founded her blog in a fit of pique, and was going to have to crawl back to her regular paycheck if her blog didn't gain major traction soon. This was part of what made Fiona such a bad listener—she listened with a filter on, and anything that wasn't pertinent to the issue she wanted to write about was strained out and responded to with vague musings. "Mm hmm. Right, right."

Edie tried again. "It's more than—"

"I know, I know. You're already under so much stress with the fracking farrago. You must be about to pop. Do you know, I actually felt a little nervous about meeting you today?"

Edie almost admired the way Fiona could flip the conversation back to what she wanted, just like that. "Nervous? I'm one of your oldest friends."

"Don't worry, I absolutely have your back. If anybody recognizes you and starts to accuse you of being an oil industry whore, I'll—"

"Fiona!"

"I'll explain it to them. People, I guess they think you believe what you're saying for Landon since you are—since you are saying it." Fiona shook her head in bafflement. "But they don't know how it is for you. Your little boy and your sick dad and your gambling addict husband. That stuff is real."

"Thank you. It is, yes." She knew she was being insulted, but she didn't care. Fiona seemed to think shaming her would give Edie the solution to the work problems she hadn't seen yet by going over and over them.

"How's the gambling? He still clean?"

"I don't know."

Fiona's eyes widened. "You don't know?"

Edie didn't want to explain that just moments before, while she waited on the barista to make her espresso, she had opened her banking app and checked their daily balance. It was lower than it should have been. Keith had made several small ATM withdrawals that morning. It was a pattern she knew.

"Well, you got your man. Be careful what you wish for, right?" Fiona had devoted more time to Edie's problems than she usually did, but enough was enough. It was time for the conversation to move on. "Now, speaking of, I haven't told you about Zack. He's from Montana."

Edie settled back. Unlike her friend, she found it restful to lose herself in other people's problems. "Oh, goody! Tell me about Zack-from-Montana."

"Well, he's a—guess what?"

"Cowboy?" Edie aimed pistol fingers at her.

"Yee-hah!"

Fiona fetishized cowboys. Edie had tried suggesting the idea that doing the same thing over and over expecting different results was a form of insanity, but Fiona didn't hear. Hers was a genuine problem with reality, and its results were predictable as one of her elusive lover boys getting bucked from the back of a bull. But Fiona's conversation was always entertaining, and it would allow Edie a brief respite from worrying about fracking. And the high probability that Keith was gambling, another genuine problem being served up by reality.

14

KEITH

2015

Lunch was a humiliation. Back home, Keith was relieved to find that Calvin had finished his movie and gone back to his apartment above the garage. Keith sat in his study gazing unseeingly at a Google Drive folder full of ungraded papers. He opened one, read the first paragraph, wrote a long comment about its lack of focus, and deleted it. Who was he to tell anyone about focus? It was like he was a painting of a decent guy that a hand reached up and smeared right before his paint finished drying, again and again. He'd been almost dry this time, his features set, his colors rich. He had almost been that decent guy for good. Now he was back to the squalid split-screen of a brain that would get through the weekend acting like a good dad and husband on one screen and worrying Edie was going to check the balance in their account before he could win back what he'd lost on the other. Damn his mother! He knew it wasn't fair to blame her, but she could have easily helped. Now, uncertainty ruled. The money, Delaney. Even his marriage, impossible though that was to think. Maybe all he'd ever wanted was a sure thing. He opened the sobriety calendar app on his phone. Today was his 378th day of being gambling-free. Except it wasn't. He deleted the app. Then he sent a message to "Delaney Travis." Or whoever. *Who is this? For God's sake.*

He paced the ground floor of the house, taking long, loping steps, unable to concentrate. He stopped before the photograph of Delaney they kept on the bookshelf. He picked it up and gazed down at her smiling face. *I'm just not sure I love you that way, Keith.* She had patted him on the shoulder like a buddy. They had just had sex. She sat up, the ribbon of her spine twisting as she reached for her clothes on the floor. She was smiling, but she had chilled the instant he uttered his intentions toward her, and he could feel her hurrying to get away from him. *Try to be cool, okay? Marriage? I'm twenty years old. That's way out there, Keith. Way out there.*

How had he responded? He'd been angry at himself, humiliated and hurt, and had wanted to argue. Had he pouted? He couldn't remember, but what he said was nothing to be proud of, nothing mature. Nothing he'd ever want Edie to know about. She didn't know he'd asked Delaney to marry him the morning of the bombing, and she never would. Some humiliations were best kept private.

Delaney had jammed her bony feet into her smelly black boots and asked to borrow his Bronco for an errand. *I'll be back before you have to go to class.* She bent over and ran her hands over their clothes on the floor until she found his jeans. She thrust her hands into the pockets and yanked out the keys. Twirling the key ring around her pointer finger, she eyed him for his answer. And he said yes, take it, because if she was borrowing his Bronco, she couldn't have just broken up with him, which was what it otherwise felt like. The fact that she had his vehicle meant they were a couple and she'd return and hand him his keys and he'd go off to class and they'd table the marriage discussion for another time. He had rushed her. She felt put on the spot. Okay, but to his way of thinking, their thing was a sure thing, and for her not to see that? *Later, dude.* Her final words to him. Not honey or babe or sweetie, but dude, the cool distance like the flat of her palm on his chest, backing him off.

Thank God he hadn't gotten what he wanted back then. Keith didn't let himself think too much about fate, because the uncomfortable fact was that he was much better off having married Edie. Edie was a great girl, they had a great life, and he loved her. A marriage to Delaney would have been brief and heartbreaking. He knew this. So it was good how things worked out for Keith in the long run, but you couldn't think such a thought without feeling like the dirtbag of the century, because it was the bombing of the Murrah Federal Building that had jackknifed his fate in such a way. What it had done to the fates of 169 other human lives, including Delaney's, not to mention the lives of the hundreds of survivors and the thousands directly impacted by the loss of people they loved—that was senseless tragedy, pure wretched carnage, and any positive effects were dross. No, thinking about fate was a dead end that he avoided.

His phone rang in his pocket. He liked to keep it in the thigh pocket of his black cargo pants so that it was on his lap when he was sitting down. Now he fumbled with the button on the pocket, only half interested in answering. It wasn't Edie's ringtone, nor the one for Ian's school, and he wasn't sure who else would be calling. He had plenty of old friends still in town that he kept meaning to reconnect with, but he hadn't done so yet. "Hello?"

"Bro!"

Keith put his free hand on his hip and looked up at the ceiling. "Brad?"

"Hey, what are you doing right now?"

"Working."

"I didn't know you had a job."

Keith grimaced. "I do have a job. Several, in fact. Interviewing for a better one next week."

"Yeah, seeking employment is a job for sure. The shittiest one. I hate my job, but I hate the idea of looking for a new one even more. Plus, my job has its upsides. Easy to get away for my side projects, if you know what I mean. Hang in there."

Small talk? Keith wandered into the kitchen and flung open the refrigerator door. Yogurt and more yogurt. Little kid yogurt for Ian with pureed vegetables hidden in it, low-fat sugar-free almond milk yogurt for ever-vigilant Edie. He grabbed a jar of kalamata olives from the door of the fridge and slid it onto the counter. "What's up, man?"

"You know that machine you were on today? Liberty 7s? I see what you mean about it! After you left, I jumped on for a couple spins. Hit a jackpot on the second go."

He popped an olive in his mouth. "No shit."

"Six grand."

"Six grand?" Keith laid his forehead against the refrigerator. "Six thousand dollars? Brad, do you know how rare that is? What am I saying, of course you do."

"I kind of feel like I owe you a cut."

Keith raised his head and spit the unchewed olive into the sink. "It doesn't work that way. You know it doesn't." It always felt to him like it should—everyone who played the slots knew the proprietary feeling you got for a machine and the sense of being robbed that came when someone hit a jackpot at a machine you had just abandoned, having poured all your money into it. But it didn't work that way.

"I know it, bro, I know it, but I kind of got the feeling you took a hit this morning, and, I don't know, I guess I missed your sorry ass. It's great to see you! We go back, you and me. Maybe we're getting old, but that shit feels important to me now. I mean, you knew my mom. Remember my mom?"

A short-haired woman with severe eczema on her arms and face who Keith had rarely seen out of her nubby blue La-Z-Boy. He knew she'd worked in some office and took care of Brad, but Keith had always seemed to come over in the late afternoon when she was relaxing, always with a newspaper, working on sets of numbers in a moleskin notebook, pencil in her teeth. He had liked Mrs. Odel. He'd even read to her for a couple of weeks once when she was sick. She had a sing-song voice. "Hello, boys! Nuke some nachos if you want! There's a jar of jalapeños if you can take the heat." She was sweet. Keith said so.

"She was. She passed last year, dude, can you believe that?"

"Oh, man. I'm sorry. I didn't know."

"Some stupid infection she got in the hospital. They were treating her eczema—you remember that? It was kind of gross." Brad's voice trembled on the edge of real emotion. "Some stupid infection got to her heart."

Poor woman. Who had she been? Someone strong enough to keep her disappointments to herself and present a kind face to her child. Death was so secretive. Or maybe life was. Another inscrutable human here and gone, like that. Poor Brad. "Damn, I'm sorry."

"I'm headed up to Winchester Park right now. Me likes the ponies. Want to hang out? I got to share a little wealth with you, man, only fair. Don't say no."

"I'll be right there."

Keith grabbed his keys from the kitchen counter and trotted out to the car, then backed down their long, steep driveway. It was 1:30 and he didn't have much time before picking up Ian, but if Brad was really offering to loan him money *right now*, money that he could deposit this afternoon to replace what he'd lost before Edie found out he was gambling again? He had to do it. No way B.O.'s sudden largesse was about the good old days or even the fact that Keith remembered his mother. It was about the bet on Landon Energy's fracking announcement, presumably. It was amazing what you could lay odds on. If it was someone else, he might worry, but Brad? You couldn't worry about a guy whose initials meant body odor. He had always claimed to be part of some Okie gangster clan, that was the sort of ludicrous fantasy he had of himself, so it was easy to see the sort of flattery he required. Keith could handle Brad Odel and be nice to him in the deal.

His Spotify channel was on something like "Surprise Me!" And it did, sending through his car speakers a Junior Brown song he hadn't heard since he first met Delaney sometime in the spring of '94, about a year before the bombing. Junior Brown had played VZD's, a local club, and it was the next morning when Keith laid eyes upon Delaney for the first time.

He saw her paintings before he saw her. They were on display in a diner off Northwest Expressway in Oklahoma City where all the hungover punk rockers went for huevos rancheros on Saturday mornings. Keith was one of them, his head pounding. Coffee. Conversation—he was with two other guys, geeks like him who knew music but not how to get girls. They were dissecting the show they'd seen the night before at VZD's. Junior Brown, one of those country music anomalies who attracted the indie crowd, a non-Nashville independent who jumped genres and went straight to the roots music that was a big part of punk. That kind of stuff was having a moment because of *Pulp Fiction*. Everybody was in love with rockabilly and the Dick Dale surfer sound, and Junior Brown was part of that mix. He had a voice like a basset hound baying from an unpainted porch.

Peter, the more cheerful of Keith's breakfast companions, a little guy with a spree of black hair that he wore like Robert Smith from The Cure, was singing, "You're wanted by the po-lice and my wife thinks you're dead."

You had to like stuff like Junior Brown ironically, that was key, so landing hard on the country diction, delighting in the hard diphthong in "po-lice!" was part of the charm of debriefing after a show like that. Keith got sick of all the attitude, though. He wanted something he could like fully, without pretending it was quaint or funny or a sideshow. Newly hung paintings occupied the walls above each of the six booths in the restaurant, each about two feet square, each vivid and inscrutable, and he noticed the purples and mustards of the one above the condiments in their booth while his friends talked. Its paint rose off the canvas thick and dimensional, like Van Gogh's. Up close, the painting seemed abstract, splashes of color, but as his eyes slowly adjusted, he saw it in fact had a subject. It was the hood of a car, a long purple sedan, with the sun either rising or setting behind it and some figures in the background, maybe people, maybe buildings. The figures had blurred edges, as did the car, and the sunlight filled the space between the solid figures like water flowing around rocks.

Keith thought she was the server at first. She was standing in front of the table, and his friends barely noticed as they dug into their eggs like a litter of puppies, but when she didn't say anything, the unexpected silence caused them to look up. Her eyes were on the painting. She didn't seem to see them.

"Hi?" The round freckled face of Keith's other friend, Ben, flushed with annoyance as he looked up at her. It *was* a little annoying, this chick standing like a zombie at their table. Keith could tell that Ben was about to be a dick about it, but he took her in and softened his tone. Delaney's long black hair looked about halfway to dreadlocks, matted and tangled in that studied way that lets you know she's not actually a homeless person. Bright black eyes, her skin a sickly greenish cast with too much makeup over acne-scarred cheeks and red lipstick. Ben was an insecure guy who was hypersensitized to any situation that let him act superior. Acting superior was his greatest joy, part of why their conversations about music were so heated. He was clearly on the alert now for an opportunity.

Looking at Keith and Peter like *watch this,* he said, "May we help you?"

Who knows what he thought she was going to say? That was always Ben's problem; his need to feel superior brooked no forethought. Otherwise, he'd have known she had a reason for being there and he would end up looking like an asshole for talking to her that way, but he couldn't help himself. It was the reason why Ben was a virgin. He was probably one still.

She brought her gaze down to them and smiled. "What do you think about that sorry painting?"

They dutifully turned their heads and gave it a good looking over, like students in a class. "It's out of control," Keith said. He'd had a single art history class in his undergraduate curriculum, so he thought that gave him the chops. "That sunlight's just too much and everything else in the picture barely holds its shape. But that seems on purpose, doesn't it? Which means it's not out of control at all."

He turned and gazed back up at her to find her watching him with a look that drew him up short. In retrospect he understood it was need, unvarnished need for his comprehension of her work, but at the time he only knew he wanted someone to look at him like that always.

He said, "Why do you call it sorry?"

Ben had gone back to eating his eggs, and Peter, shy unto muteness when sober in front of a woman, was watching Keith with admiration from behind his wall of hair. Keith chuckled remembering it, startling himself with the sound of his own voice in the car. He had been the alpha in that little group, a low bar, but he'd be lying to himself to say it hadn't felt good unexpectedly striking gold with this girl while his loser friends watched.

"I just need to put a price tag on that one. May I?" She lifted one hand and her gray flannel shirt fell back to show her fingers, tapping together like she was playing castanets. Neon orange stickers with numbers written on them balanced lightly on her fingertips. "Sorry to bug you guys while you're eating."

"Oh. Oh, I see." Keith stood up and let her slide across his side of the booth. He noticed for the first time that the T-shirt visible beneath her flannel was streaked with paint. "It's yours." She tapped one of the stickers onto the lower left-hand corner of the painting. The sticker read "$100."

She turned and smiled at him over her shoulder. "It could be yours!"

He bought it, obviously. A hundred bucks. Would you change your own life for a hundred bucks? You might if you didn't know what was coming.

PART TWO

SEARCH

All day, news helicopters cruised aloft
Going whatwhatwhatwhatwhat.
She pours me some boiled
coffee that tastes like noise,
warning me, once and for all,
to pack up my troubles in an old kit bag
and weep until the stones float away.

Denis Johnson, "The Incognito Lounge"

15

EDIE

1995

Edie was drinking a beer as she made her way up the walk to her front door. Was rage a symptom of shock? Fuming over Vera Wrede and the guy who wouldn't show ID beat thinking about what had happened that day. She knew it wouldn't last, but right now she liked the way it simulated focus and kept feelings at bay. It took her a second to realize someone was there, sitting on the concrete top step, protected from the rain by the roof. Delaney?

She stopped. "Who's there?"

"I didn't mean to scare you, Edie."

"Oh, hi, Keith."

"Wow, you sound disappointed."

Of course she was disappointed. For a moment, Delaney was back from wherever she had run off to that day; she'd lost her key again, she needed Edie to let her in, and the bombing downtown had receded from their personal sphere. But no.

Edie hurled her open beer at him, nailing him on the shoulder. "What the fuck, Keith? I thought you were Delaney, didn't I?"

"Ouch!" He rubbed his upper arm. "That hurt, dammit. May I come in?"

She stepped onto the porch out of the rain and set the twelve-pack down on a blue cement plant holder, squashing the desiccated tendrils of a dead bougainvillea hanging stiffly over the sides. Delaney had tried all the previous summer to keep it alive, misting it, sunning it in the mornings and bringing it in before the afternoon sun scorched it, but the weather had done it in. "A hundred miles to the south," she'd been told at a gardening center. "Those semi-tropicals will survive." Here, it could get really cold. Edie watched the crisp veiny membranes of dried leaves fall and skitter down the porch, disappearing into the rainy night. She said, "I didn't know you were here. Where's your Bronco?"

Keith stood up and held the screen door open while she fumbled for her keys. "Delaney borrowed it, remember? My parents dropped me off."

"Oh, shit, that's right! Is it down there?"

"I don't know." He stepped into the house as she turned on a tall halogen light that leaned from its midpoint like a drunk. The air was stuffy, redolent of old fast food and still laced with the *nag champa* incense Delaney burned constantly. "We don't know—that's the thing. We don't know where she is."

"If she was in the Murrah Building, then the car is there, but you know her, she's probably partying somewhere. Maybe she made up with our dad? I left a message with him," Edie said.

"So did I, but it's unlikely. She hates the guy."

Edie shrugged, conceding the point. "She could be anywhere, is all I'm saying. Remember that time she quit her job and drove to Kansas City to see some concert? She was gone for three days!"

"She didn't even invite me."

"We could go downtown." She patted the shoulder she had hurt. The need to console him had overcome her, and, like the rage storming her body moments before, its energy flushed the shock from her system. She leaned into it, her mind fixing on the issue of Keith's Bronco. "If the car isn't there then we'll know she wasn't in the building. Proof positive!"

He twisted his heels like an impatient toddler. "Be real, would you? It's the crime scene of the century. Of the history of the United States of America. You think they're going to let us just waltz in?"

"There has to be a way. It's a whole area of the downtown."

"There's massive law enforcement. It's all closed off—yellow crime tape for blocks. We can't get down there."

"How do you know?"

He dropped onto the couch. "I already tried, okay?"

"Let's try again."

He looked at her. "Edie—"

"We'll go under the tape. Or over it, whatever. It's just yellow tape. Once we're in, who's to know we don't belong there? It's dark and it's rainy. On TV everybody at the site is wearing rain gear. Do you have anything?"

He shook his head.

"Delaney and I bought ponchos last fall when she was hell bent on getting those daffodil bulbs in the ground. Remember? We put them all in upside down." She grinned, for a moment stepping into the past where Delaney cursed and jammed her spade into the soft mud. "She was so mad when we figured it out. Hang on."

He pointed the remote at the television and flipped through the search and rescue coverage while Edie dug through her and Delaney's closets, looking for the rain ponchos. She found Delaney's easily—it was one of the only items hanging in the closet, most of Delaney's other clothes being on the floor or draped over a red chaise longue. Her own was hanging neatly in her closet with her other outerwear, where it was supposed to be, as all of her clothing was. The reek of margarita, steak, and butter from the lobster tower she had dumped down her face and shoulders at work that night enveloped her when she stripped off her work clothes and stepped into the shower. Bottles of shampoo and conditioner were still toppled into the tub, and the sink was still full of toiletries from the morning blast. She put everything back in its place and showered quickly, leaving an empty bottle in the shower caddy. When she was finished and dressed, she pulled the black rain poncho over her jacket and jeans.

Down the hall, voices from the television conveyed tragedy before she could hear what they were saying. Their hushed circumspection sometimes took on a querulous edge, as if they'd had it with this all-day drill and wanted to hear it was all a mistake. The news from the blast site was too much to take in, and it kept coming. Would for days, weeks, months, years. There would be reflective moments later, but right now, the newscasters sounded fried. So was Edie. She walked into the living room and tossed Delaney's yellow poncho onto his lap.

"Are you ready?"

"The death toll is up to a hundred and thirteen," he said, pointing the remote control at the television. "Vera Wrede interviewed the fire chief." He flattened his palms against his knees and pushed up from the couch. "The way she talked to him? I don't know. I don't think I like her."

"You're a good judge of character."

A few minutes later, they were in the car. Edie turned south on Twenty-third Street, heading down Broadway. Blackness with a single glowing center greeted them where the city should have been. "Downtown is gone!" she said.

"They've turned off the electricity. It wasn't safe," Keith said. "That lit up area, that's it."

In the passenger seat, Keith unfolded his rain poncho and wrestled with it. He pulled it over his head without taking off his seatbelt and had to free himself and start over. It was bright yellow, like that of most of the rescue personnel, which they agreed was good camouflage.

Edie parked in the big, empty parking lot behind the First Baptist Church of Oklahoma City, a red brick building that covered most of a city block several blocks north of the Murrah Building. The tall, stained-glass windows of its sanctuary had been blown out, and from the sidewalk, they could see the shadowy ceiling of the inside of the church, unprotected. Glass crunched beneath their feet and covered the grass, jewel-toned shards glittering like an ocean under moonlight. It was dark, and it was raining, but light from the site bled down the streets and alleyways like a spreading infection. A helicopter thumped overhead, and somewhere close by a siren wailed. A police car appeared from an east-west road a couple of blocks down and drove toward them. They ducked behind a billboard advertising a bail bondsman and waited for it to pass.

"We've got to be careful," Edie said.

They peeked out from behind the sign and continued on, dashing from parked cars to dumpsters to recessed doorways to stay hidden. They headed east and could see the glow of the Murrah site rising several stories into the purple sky, rain falling through the wide column of light. At the corner of Tenth and Broadway they encountered the perimeter, yellow tape stretched out of sight to the south and west. Another police car crawled slowly by, and they dashed behind a stand of bushes. On the other side of the barrier, they saw figures on guard.

Keith said, "I feel like a criminal."

"Let's go this way," Edie said.

They ran, vulnerable to the sudden appearance of any cops, until Edie saw a space between two buildings with no guard visible on Sixth Street. They lifted the yellow tape and were inside the innermost perimeter. Edie felt like a criminal, too, ashamed for intruding into the work of dying that had gone on there, private and unexpected, for intruding into the taut and fragile headspace of the rescuers, people far out over a mental tightrope held up by a sheer sense of duty who dared not look down into the deep space stretching beneath them.

She feared that deep space, too, feared what she might be about to see, but she couldn't step back. Edie hated ambiguity, although it surrounded her, always. She was the kind of person who characteristically said, "Give me a yes or no answer," and that's what she was looking for tonight—she was drawn forward by the promise of closure. They would have a look around, they would satisfy themselves that Keith's Bronco was not down there, and they would go home and wait for Delaney to return from whatever wild-hare adventure she had taken today. Closure—was there any stronger need?

Painting their kitchen yellow one weekend, Edie and Delaney had talked about the need for definite answers as their brushes rolled up and down the old gray walls of their rental house. Delaney had expressed the opinion that no one really wanted closure, because it was death. What we want, in her opinion, was for everything to stay open-ended forever. It was the anticipation we couldn't stand. If we could disable the need to know, all would be well. "Sure," Edie had said, pausing her paint roller in its vertical course. "But we can never do that."

Keith and Edie rounded a corner, and the building came into view half a block away. "God!" Keith grabbed Edie by the shoulders and turned her into his chest. She stayed there for a second, her eyelashes brushing against the wet plastic of his poncho, but then she pushed away from him and turned to look.

They had seen it on television a hundred times that day, white and torn and crumbling, like a layer cake that someone has gouged apart with bare hands, but there was no comparing the reality to the screen image. Depth made the sight hard to take in. The visual field regressed into the bowels of the building, into exposed rooms and dark crannies behind overturned desks and dangling potted plants. What looked like crumbs hanging from cake on television were car-sized chunks of concrete in real life, straining to fall toward the crater in the middle of the building. Despite the rain, the building still appeared to be smoking. Was it steam? Whatever it was, it gave the wet concrete debris the look of a live animal, a being whose entrails steamed and strained to fall even farther from the shattered shell of the body that had held them.

Edie tried to pick out where the floors had been, looked into the rooms imagining the fate of a tender human body among all that hard matter. Delaney could be in there right now. Right there, under hundreds of tons of wet concrete and rebar. She bent over and vomited. Keith rubbed her back. When Edie came up, wiping her mouth with the bottom of her poncho, she understood that Delaney was in all likelihood dead. Closure. What a primitive thought it seemed to her now, the idea that reality might conform to the human mind's need for symmetry. There would never be closure.

"What floor was the social security office on?" Keith asked. He had turned away from the sight of the building and had to repeat himself so she could hear him over the loud hum of a nearby generator.

"I don't know." Her teeth were chattering.

He looked at her with concern. "Hey, we don't have to do this," he said. "We can go back."

Faced with the building, lit up like the middle of the afternoon, the list of the known dead seemed sure to rise. It was a big building. It had been full of people. The fatalities were up to 126, they'd heard on the radio right before they parked the car, and for a moment Delaney's fate seemed lost in the vastness of the event. Even if Delaney was home when they got there, this had still happened. "Come on," Edie said.

They walked briskly toward the building, moving through groups of fast-moving people wearing ponchos and other rain gear, FBI and ATF logo omnipresent. Police cars, Red Cross vehicles, and news trucks crammed the space. A crane towered overhead. The building seemed to be writhing. As they approached she understood that it was crawling with rescuers, people moving inch by inch through the rubble, looking under every piece of debris. They were approaching a parking lot off what had been Fifth Street, the street that ran in front of the Murrah Building, and she began seeing cars, flipped and disfigured. Some looked burned out. Some looked melted. All were covered with a layer of cement dust, now wetted to mud. She nearly stepped on a big man sitting on a curb weeping with his back to her. She became more and more convinced that they would be stopped soon and arrested.

Picking his way along, Keith said, "We'd better get out of here."

"Let's head south," she said. "It might be easier to get out on the other side."

He nodded and pushed ahead of her.

She kept her eye on his back, and they went a little farther west, looking to dodge south when they passed the building. She followed Keith as he crossed the street, weaving in and out among overturned cars and emergency workers, but suddenly she was rushing in to him, putting out her hands against his back. He had stopped. She stepped up next to him and saw what he saw. She couldn't make out the green paint under the thick wet layer of concrete dust, but the boxy shape was right and in the jagged corner of the shattered windshield she could see Keith's student parking sticker. Edie put a hand on Keith's arm.
    "That's it," he said.

16

KEITH

2015

Keith saw the stadium lights above the horse track first, before the rest of Winchester Park came into view. On the east side of town, where I-44 and I-35 intersected, it was easy to reach and hard to miss. The impulsive nature of gamblers being well understood by casino owners, horse tracks and casinos always seemed to be designed with dedicated exits off major thoroughfares, no winding through long distances or making many turns in which to doubt the risk/benefit analysis you were making on the way to the casino once your mind had already caved to the allure of risk. No, a quick turn and you're there, and the parking lot, an ocean of concrete bigger than some small towns, prevents you having to drive around looking for a place to park and changing your mind in the process.

He couldn't get Brad's fracking bet out of his gerbil wheel of a brain, as Brad had surely known he wouldn't. Because it was a sure thing. If Edie told Keith when Landon Energy was going to make an announcement about the fracking and he then bet on it, there would be no way to lose. He went over it and over it in his mind, but he couldn't see a single way he could lose. She tells him the date and he lays a big bet on that date. She announces, and they win big. Kapow! A sure thing. If this were the stock market it would be insider trading, he could see that, sure, but this wasn't the stock market. This was some low-level local bet. Invisible. It was too bad, really. He wasn't going to do it, but it was tempting.

He had been to Winchester Park plenty before he and Edie moved to London, always alone and without Edie's knowledge, and then it had been an unlovely, utilitarian horse track befitting the feeling of grimy subterfuge that attended his activities, the sort of place you could imagine seeing Charles Bukowski tipping his plastic chair against a beige cinder-block wall with his betting sheets and his cigarette and his stiff drink on a Formica table, but since the State Tribal Gaming Act passed in 2004, the place had undergone a change to keep up with the nicer, newer places run by the tribes. Now it was as bright as Tornado Alley. He pushed open the front doors into a sensory onslaught of light, color, and the chaotic sounds of hundreds of machines all making come-hither noises, a full-service casino with the slot machines lined up like cars at a dealership. Apparently, no one at Winchester Park had gotten the news about smoking. It was a thriving habit there, happily indulged by a good portion of the people Keith passed. He strode through the smoke-filled blue neon room looking for Brad's fat back and beginning to have the sorts of doubts you're not supposed to have in those places.

Keith had already gambled and lost once that day. The money he'd withdrawn that morning was supposed to be seed money for a modest win to finance his search for Delaney, but now what? Edie had given him an ultimatum the last time in Bath when he lost the large down payment for their house, her face baffled and enraged, and he knew she meant it. He had made every promise he could think of and had believed them all. Never again, you have my word.

How could he have seen this friend request from Delaney coming, though? It was impossible to ignore and impossible to pursue without hiding the fact from Edie. He was surprised that she hadn't gotten one, too, but she'd have said something if she had. All the more reason to suspect it was bogus and to protect Edie from the emotional fallout. If she saw that Facebook page with Delaney's name on it and falsely got her hopes up? No way. He couldn't watch Edie go through it. At least if he had to suffer lifting the seal on his memories of Delaney only to slam it back down after all, he could comfort himself in knowing he'd shielded Edie from the blow. He'd take a trip Sunday—he hated to lie to Edie, but he'd tell her it was research, whatever, and he'd take a quick trip to New Mexico and find out what the hell was going on. He'd be back before his job interview on Tuesday.

He felt a slap on his shoulder and looked to see that Brad had floated up beside him, scanning the horizon, his body language calm and proprietary. "The smoke getting to you, dude?"

"I thought we had a law about smoking indoors? This place is worse than Tornado Alley."

Brad shrugged. "Exceptions have been made for the casinos."

Marveling at his friend's instinctive deployment of the passive voice for a situation no one wanted pinned on them, Keith followed Brad's assless, hulking shape out of the cavernous room. His friend kept up a constant line of patter as they rode an escalator to the top of the racing stands. *Remember that time you dropped a roach in your dad's car? Remember that beautiful girl with scoliosis in Spanish I?* Outside, the bright April day shone on the mostly empty seats, and the indistinct boom of the announcer's voice vibrated the walls. Horses ran on the track below them, small in the distance. Brad held open a door and stepped inside a private viewing room with a wall of glass that looked out over the stadium. Plush armchairs filled the center of the white-carpeted space with a bar in one corner where the neat back of a small woman leaned over the counter. He couldn't tell what she was doing.

Keith stood awkwardly in the doorway, as reluctant to enter as Ian had been on his first day of preschool, hugging Keith's leg for all he was worth against the barrage of screaming toddlers. Ian! What time was it? Keith stood in the doorway and watched as Brad grinned at him from inside the room.

"Keith, I want you to meet Louise. Louise, this is my good pal I was telling you about."

He had half an hour before he needed to drive across town and join the constipated line of cars waiting to pick up children in front of the school, each with its construction paper banner containing a child's name obediently slid onto the dash. Still standing behind the bar, the woman had turned around. Keith thought she was an employee of the park when he first noticed her, someone there to make drinks and maybe turn in a food order. But as soon as she faced him, he could see she was not there to serve. More the opposite.

Louise gave a little wave, manicured nails squared off like hammer heads. "Nice to meet you."

She didn't give a last name. Her eyes were wide set, dramatically made up, and she had a bony nose in a heart-shaped face. She wore a burgundy leather jacket fitted tight to her small frame and the kind of stiff, dark jeans that weren't his idea of jeans at all but some sort of weird formal wear, tucked into tall, fawn-colored boots. Keith thought she looked younger than him, but the gravitas of her expression made him think otherwise. Tiny and hard, she reminded him of a former ballerina he and Edie had met at a Landon Energy party in London.

Brad wore an expression more cautious than any Keith had ever seen on his face, a wary set to his features that Keith hadn't thought his old friend was capable of, and it told him that he was in the presence of someone Brad didn't want to upset. Keith took a deep breath. Someone had smoked in here and someone else had tried hard to rid the room of the smell. Had anyone ever died in this room? A stray thought, a strange one. He imagined a bloodstain scrubbed and new carpet laid. But no, this was a room for a family to watch their quarter horse run or a company to treat its employees to a day at the races. Nothing to fear here, and maybe the carrot at the end of the stick would be worth it. Louise's presence could indicate real money, could mean this Landon Energy bet could have a big pot. That was the feeling he got from Brad, who stood next to Louise like she was the rightful queen of France. It was amazing how you could vibe a guy out like it was yesterday when you used to run around with him. Brad probably thought the same thing. Keith stepped inside and closed the door.

"Louise, it's a pleasure." Keith offered his hand. The tips of her nails scraped the underside of his wrist, and he could tell she was gripping for all she was worth, trying to convey strength and purpose and all those winning traits a strong handshake supposedly indicated. From wherever the truism about a strong handshake came, the notion was so exhausted it now conveyed its opposite. He'd met tons of successful people at Landon Energy social events in London, and he noticed they never bothered to exert the slightest energy in their handshakes. Someone who tried to take your arm off, on the other hand, was probably trying too hard. Surprising that he was someone she wanted to impress.

"I feel like I'm meeting a celebrity," she said.

"Me?" Keith scratched his chin.

"I've seen your wife on the news, I think. Isn't that your wife? Landon Energy employs half this state, practically."

"I don't know about that," Keith said. "It's a big company, though."

"She's something else."

He didn't know what that meant. "Yes, she is."

Louise dropped lightly into one of the chairs. The dark leather settled around her form. She rested an elbow on the arm and smiled up at him. "Now, she's in PR, right? Pretty much the face of that company these days. Which can only be good—God knows nobody wants to look at Theron Landon's ugly mug. Face of a junkyard dog. All that money and he still looks a mess."

"She's a VP." Keith said it with pride, but he was uneasy. Edie didn't need to be the topic of conversation. The idea of Louise and Brad watching her on television and thinking how they could use her infuriated him.

Brad took a seat next to Louise and, looking at Keith, tossed his head in the direction of the empty chair next to him. Keith stepped closer to the chair but didn't sit. Now he was looming over them in a way he could see that neither of them liked.

"Well! That's something, isn't it? VP!" Louise had to tilt her head up to look at him. "And here I thought she was just a pretty face and an expensive hairdo."

Keith smiled. "Quite a bit more." What was it Edie said about women who said sexist stuff about other women? A special room in hell.

"Stay a while, Keith." Brad patted the seat next to him.

"I have to leave in a second to pick my boy up from school."

"You're leaving?" Brad's face reddened.

"Duty calls, I'm sorry."

"I thought we might talk about when Landon Energy and the other big oil companies are going to drop this silly façade and admit what we all damned well know about these earthquakes." Louise stood up and moved closer to him. "I reckon the person who knows when that announcement will happen could do very well for himself."

"Lots of assumptions in this bet of yours," Keith said.

Louise tilted her head. "What do you mean?"

"Don't you have anyone in the other oil companies you can have this talk with?"

"Other people are running those bets. Landon Energy is mine," Brad said.

"Like you're the bookie?"

"It's a big chance for little Brad," Louise said.

"What if it never happens?" Keith said. "There may never be an announcement. Have you met Theron Landon? I know the man pretty well, and I have to tell you, he doesn't eat a lot of crow. Not that I've ever seen."

Louise stood back up and gave him an impatient smile. "I think he will," she said.

Keith shrugged. He did, too, but that was none of her business. "Think what you want. Landon's rich enough to live in his own little dream world. If he wants to pretend the earthquakes aren't happening, that's just what he'll do."

"Until there are consequences. Until he starts to lose money."

"He's got a lot of that."

"Look, I think we're all going to make a lot of cash when you tell us when this announcement is going to be." She opened her hands like she was tossing confetti. "That's what I think."

He looked down at the white carpet. His hands shook. He was furious—at this stranger trying to throw some redneck grifter bullshit on him like she read it in a manual, at idiot Brad, who was and ever would be a fucking fool, and at himself, mostly at himself, for being there, for gambling again, for the whole degenerate bag of shit he carried around and couldn't seem to help jamming his hands in up to his elbows and smearing the contents all over his life.

"I can't do this," he said. "Can't do it." He stepped back and rested a hand on the doorknob. Calm settled over him as soon as he said the words. He had done the right thing. He had beat the insidious voice of the gambler in him, and he had acted like a good man. A husband, a father, an honorable man who would not, could not sell out his wife to win a bet. He saw Edie, Ian, and his mother with trust in their faces and his dad looking up from a game of chess and giving him a good job nod.

Louise laughed. She turned to Brad, who had stood up, too, and was rocking nervously like he was winding up for a pitch. He said, "I get it, you know. Sure. But think about this. Will your wife believe you?"

Keith dropped his hand from the door. "What?"

"When I talk to her about your help with this bet—do you think she'll believe you when you say you weren't involved?"

"I beg your pardon?" Keith lunged for Brad. "When you talk to her?"

Brad jumped back but persisted, talking steadily. "Betting on your own wife is dirty, dirty, my friend. I always knew you were scummier than anyone realized, but I got to say this surprises even me. I pity her, you know? Like I have a moral obligation. Feel like she needs to know."

"You son of a bitch."

"Don't be mad at me for trying to make you rich, bro."

"I said I wouldn't do it. No."

"And he said he'd call your wife," Louise said. She rubbed the squared-off tips of her nails against the pads of her thumbs. "I could also call the press, give them an anonymous tip about Edith Ash from Landon Energy's plan to profit off the fracking she's been denying."

It was an ambush. Keith thought about Black Cloud and his people camped on the Washita in 1868, defenses down because they had signed a peace treaty that General Custer pretended not to know about and massacred them anyway, thought about Kit Carson at Adobe Walls in 1864 watching the tribes he thought he could scatter come over the hills in greater number than he knew they had, right at him. History showed that the moment you felt you had things under control was the moment you got it good from the direction you weren't looking. And they say a Ph.D. in history is useless.

Keith thought of the hole in his and Edie's savings account from the money he'd lost that morning. Liberty sevens—what had he been thinking? And since his arrival at Winchester Park, Brad hadn't given him any share of the jackpot he had supposedly won that morning. Of course the Liberty 7s jackpot had been a lie, Keith could see that now. If Brad did call Edie—and he believed the sonofabitch would do it—she would think he'd bet that morning's ATM withdrawals on the Landon Energy announcement, just as Brad was claiming. The missing money would look like proof.

He would lose Ian. His whole life. He gazed out the wall of windows at the sun shining outside. The rumble of the horses came up from the ground, and he could see from the way people crossed the green lawn to lean over the white fence at the edge of the track that this race meant something.

"All we need is for you to tell us when the announcement will be," Louise said softly.

"I'm telling you I don't know." He fell into the chair next to Brad. "I can't tell you what I don't know."

"You'll find out, though," she said. "Surely you will."

17

AUGUST P.

1995

If I were any kind of hand with a weapon, the German fellow that ran security for the compound might have wanted to keep me around, but I weren't. I have a startle reflex so strong it startles others, my distance vision is fuzzy, and I breathe loud when I run, or at least that's what they told me. The daily hard times they gave me finally came in handy, because when I lit out without a warning one night in February, nobody seemed too surprised. When I found my mother in the kitchen after dinner that evening and told her I wanted to go live with my dad in Tulsa, she didn't even look up from the soapy water her hands were in. "Course," she said. "Go on." She glanced up, her face pink from steam, and gave me a sad smile. "Thank you."

"For what?" I said.

We were in the wood-paneled kitchen built off one of the white polyurethane bubble buildings the elder had erected when he first founded the place. Other women were bustling around us, glaring at me like I was displeasing the Lord as they moved up and down the counters drying dishes and putting away the cooking supplies. I don't know if another male had ever been inside that kitchen. It was steamy and smelled of warm bodies and boiled cabbage, with the cold night coming in from under the sink and around the edges of the small windows. Not yet six o'clock, it was already dark.

She reached one soapy red hand out of the water and patted me on the cheek. The water was hot on my face, then a patch of cold when the air hit it. "I know you can see how hard your being here makes it for me." She thought I was leaving so she could fit in better. It was just as well. She might have noticed I looked scared, but if she did she thought she knew the reasons why.

"I love you, Momma."

She picked up a big dirty ladle from the dishwater, then lowered it back into the soapsuds. "I know," she said. "You're my sweet boy, August. Take good care of yourself."

As I stared at her, I felt something in my throat like a lock. I would have told her what happened in the woods if she'd asked why I was leaving, but she wasn't going to. How could I tell her? The look of relief on her face made me happy for her. I didn't want to let her down.

What had happened, I was out in the woods late in the afternoon when the sun was almost down and the night air was sharpening. Rambling is all I was doing. Gathering myself before I had to head back in for dinner. It wasn't the season for cicada shells or anything I could think to search for. I liked the woods in all seasons, even then, when the trees were gray and bare. I liked the shadows and the carpet of leaves the gray of turned meat, the fallen limbs and the stalks of wildflowers dead where they froze, upturned faces stiff and dark, like some kind of witnesses silenced. You could hear the animals better in winter, their light steps snapping twigs in the underbrush. I was alone there, free there, safe there.

I had stepped too close to some brambles and was trying to separate my sleeve from the row of thorns holding me in place when I heard a sound that wasn't an animal. A high, soft sound drew my attention to a small clearing I knew about twenty feet or so ahead of me and to the right. I could always tell deer slept there by the shapes on the matted grasses, but the sound wasn't a deer. I yanked my sleeve away from the bramble and walked toward it. Afraid I'd come upon a couple trying to be alone and get my ass kicked, I couldn't decide if I should try to walk quietly so they didn't hear me, walk loud so they would, or walk normal so they'd think I hadn't heard them first. But I didn't have a chance to settle on a choice when suddenly, there was a streak of something bright flying through the brush in front of me. Light catching, wheat colored. Long blond hair.

A mermaid in the woods? That was my first image, but a second later the blond hair was suspended from a bramble, stuck and hanging. "Fuck!" The person who had been under the hair spun around, and I saw a woman with red lipstick that turned out, once I really looked, to be Phil Carey, one of the new bank robbers. He was just a couple years older than me, but he had come there as a soldier, not as somebody's kid, like I did.

I reached out and yanked the wig out of the brush. It came away with stickers in it. I turned it over in my hand. Mesh on the bottom held the hair in place. The hair was slick and surprisingly heavy. Phil was eying the wig and eying me, wiping the lipstick off with the back of his hand, wiping his hand on the bark of a tree. One thing I'm good at is knowing when someone is about to hurt me, so I dropped the wig and I made to bolt. As I turned, Phil shot a what-do-I-do-now look at a spot a dozen or so feet away. That was when I noticed the other new bank robber, Roger Scott, standing next to a tree at the edge of my peripheral vision. He was wearing a camouflage hunting jacket and a bill cap pulled down low over his forehead. We formed a triangle, the three of us. "I didn't see anything," I said. My breath fogged the air. I said it loud enough for them to hear me but soft enough so they'd know I wasn't trying to draw attention. "You don't have to worry about me. I'm leaving."

I hadn't had time to think, but that wig and that lipstick? On Phil, a man? Well, I knew the Elohim folks. I saw them once interrogate a gal with brown eyes about her origins, wanting to know was she secretly "of the mud people," which is what they called folks who weren't white, and who they believed had no souls. I saw them make Phil and Roger surrender their watches when they first showed up because they didn't believe in clock time, only used a sundial because it was of God. The worldliness and vanity of that wig and lipstick would've gotten my mom in trouble, any of the women, but Phil? My gut reaction was to danger, the way a kid in a normal community would react if he came upon a loaded gun. Phil would be put down mean for wearing that stuff, so he was going to put me down mean for seeing him. Phil, he had been okay the few times I'd met him before and so was Roger, but I couldn't count on that to save me. "I swear I'm leaving in the morning. For good."

Phil looked at Roger and Roger looked at the wig. Good enough? For a second, yeah, it looked like maybe we could all sneak back to our quarters and I could disappear in the morning like I promised but it weren't to be that easy.

"We'll say it was yours," Phil said. The lipstick left a pink stain on his mouth that looked like a bruise. He had a body like an upside-down triangle, broad shoulders and skinny hips. His scrawny legs looked like roots dangling off a plant in water, but his arms were big and tough.

"Two against one," Roger said.

"We'll say we saw you out here in a blond wig with red lipstick on like some kind of homosexual. We'll say you wanted to suck our cocks."

"We're going to Tulsa tonight," Roger said. "In an hour. You're coming with us."

"Two against one."

It was math even I could do. "Okay," I said. Back on the compound, I threw my clothes in a bag and said goodbye to my momma. My stepdad, Gary, was off somewhere so I didn't have to explain anything to him.

Phil and Roger were coming out the door of their trailer when I showed up. Phil took my bag and tossed it into the backseat of Roger's blue Chevy. His face was clean of cosmetics. I almost doubted what had happened out there in the dusk, but they were still working on getting rid of me, so that was proof enough.

"Get in back," Phil said.

Roger, a big boy, slid the driver's seat all the way back so there was no leg room for me on his side. I got in behind Phil. Phil and Roger put on their seatbelts in unison, like a mom and dad, which struck me as funny, given all these folks didn't believe in. Not clock time, not American money, or any other people on the whole wide earth but themselves, but seatbelts, yes. Guns and seatbelts. Unfortunately, I started laughing. Nerves, I guess. I mean, I did think they might be taking me somewhere to kill me. I couldn't stop. I held my hands over my mouth, but my chest shook. I just couldn't help it.

Phil whipped around in his seat and glared at me. "What in the hell's so funny, freak?"

"Nothing," I held my hands up. "Sorry." I saw Phil had a handgun pointed at me. I quieted down.

The security team stood around the entrance and unchained the cattle gate for us. I could tell by the looks on their cold white faces in the headlights that they couldn't make any sense of the three of us together, me and Phil and Roger, but those two acted like they had serious business and I tried not to give away that I was scared. I didn't know how scared to be, and there was a big part of me that was glad to be getting out of there. Since my mom and Gary brought me there the year before, I'd wanted nothing else. If I could survive the ride with Phil and Roger, I'd be free to live my life away from Elohim City, or at least that's what I thought at the time.

The backseat was damp and smelled like a garage. I pressed my fingers into the seat and smelled them. Engine oil. I was sitting in a big stain. We rode without talking for the first hour, blasting punk rock music that they said was their band they'd been in back east. It was a lot of noise and bad words. The sixty-minute TDK cassette case on the dash had a swastika inked on the label. "What instruments do y'all play?" I asked, but nobody said anything until we got to some little gas station near Tahlequah where we stopped to pee. Outside the restroom door on the side of the building, Roger said to Phil, "Think they'd sell to us?"

"Shit, who cares? I'm ready to hold the place up for a goddamned Coors."

Their eyes met and they thought together. "We shouldn't," Roger said. "Pappy didn't sanction it."

"I want a fucking brewski," Phil said. "Even if it is this low-point Oklahoma bullshit."

"Let's try buying it first. Maybe they'll sell to us. Who looks older?"

I realized Roger was asking me. "Oh, older?" Neither one of them looked like a grown man to me, not any more than I did. But then I thought of something.

"Y'all are wanting to buy beer?"

Phil tilted his head to the side. "What was your first clue?"

"It's just—well, I could get it for you."

They laughed and both crossed their arms. "Go on," Phil said. "How you going to do that, Mister Fixit?"

I patted my back pocket and took out my cloth wallet. I pulled back the Velcro and found the only ID I had. It wasn't mine. It was my dad's, an old Oklahoma State ID with the bottom edge clipped to show it wasn't any good anymore. When his license was suspended for DUI, he'd had this nondriving state identification card instead, and when he got his license back, he gave me this ID so he could send me out for beer. I did look like him, though nobody would believe I was thirty-nine. Most of the time, though, it worked. Roger and Phil looked at the ID, then at each other, then at me, and then there was something like joy in Phil's eyes. "Do it!" he said. "You do it, and we won't kill you. How's that?"

Roger looked surprised. "Hey, Phil, that's—you sure?"

"Two cases. Can you buy us two cases?" Phil took out some bills and shoved them in my hand.

I nodded. Killing me, it was for real their plan. To hear them talk about it out loud sent me into a kind of mechanical state, no feelings, moving jerky like a robot as I walked up the sidewalk and yanked open the glass door. Bells jangled. The music inside was a girl singing *let me see you go back, let me see you go forth*. Go back, I wanted to. The beer cooler was fogged and I had to open every door to find the regular Coors they wanted with the tan cans the color of a white person's skin. I wondered if that was why they liked it. There was that lock on my throat again and I sincerely feared I would have diarrhea right there. At the counter, the girl working looked about my age. She was making friendship bracelets, braiding together a bunch of neon-colored threads while I took out the ID. She snorted when she looked at it. "Yeah, right."

"Listen," I said. I was ready to tell her about the neo-Nazis outside who said they were about to kill me if I didn't get their beer, and probably would anyway. I worried for her, too, and wondered if they'd look in the door to monitor my progress and see her dark skin and decide a holdup with a shooting was the better path after all.

"You think I care?" she said. "That beer's nasty, though."

I handed her the cash. "Thank you."

When I came around the building with the two cases of beer it was like Phil and Roger turned into my best friends instead of my would-be murderers. They whooped and we all jumped in the car and they downed six beers between them, I swear, before we were fully merged back onto the highway. I watched the dark world outside and thought of all the places they could kill me. Every exit sign seemed like my own headstone. I wanted my mom. She had thanked me for leaving. When would I see her again?

Inside the Chevy, the beer had changed things. I had solved a big problem for Phil and Roger, and they were deep in their drinking. I flashed on my dad and how surprised he'd be to see me. Under normal circumstances I wouldn't want to drop in on him and had no guarantee I'd be welcome, but I didn't care a fingernail about family problems right then. Family problems sounded cozy compared to riding with these two. "My dad's place is on the east side of town," I said. "Almost to Broken Bow."

"Why didn't you live with your dad to begin with?" Roger asked. He had little eyes in a big face and he was peering at me through the rearview mirror. His hands were on the steering wheel and I could see he had letters tattooed on his knuckles, but not what the letters spelled. I was okay not knowing.

"He's mean," I said.

This made them laugh. I wasn't sure if it was okay to laugh along with them, so I just listened, my funny bone having gone still on me. "Mine too," Phil said and laughed some more.

"Same here," Roger said and patted Phil on the hip. Phil glanced up at him and they both smiled. "How old are you?" Roger asked.

"Me? Sixteen, just turned sixteen." Out the window, the billboards were all for Tulsa, with exits coming up in the next ten miles. I could see the glow and the skyline up ahead as we came west.

"I was sixteen when I got involved with the cause," he said. "Remember?" He glanced over at Phil.

"We were playing a concert at a bar in Philly," he said. "These geezers had a band and they thought it made them look like bigger deals if they had an opening band so they got us in and let us play."

"You know Justin? He gave us a copy of *The Turner Diaries* and told us about this place." Phil turned to look at me. "About Elohim. We wanted to be part of what's coming."

I didn't need to ask what was coming. I had been struggling my way through my own copy of *The Turner Diaries* in a panic that ol' Tim would be back to quiz me before I got it finished. He hadn't been around in a few months and I was on this part close to the end where Earl Turner flies a biplane into the Pentagon. He figures everyone will blame it on Black people and that will start a race war that will wipe out everybody but Earl and his white friends. You'd think it would be easy to prove the dead guy in the plane was white, but maybe they figured he'd be too crispy. "I know about *The Turner Diaries*," I said. I had already discovered that it could come in handy around these folks, that just holding it was sort of like being in disguise. I could walk through the compound with my head down and the book tucked under one arm and nobody would ask me where I was going. Sometimes I'd even get a pat on the back or a friendly nod. Even my mom acted glad to see me reading it. She hadn't read it herself, though, and when I told her about how it said that females thinking they were people, not women, was part of a mass psychosis, she looked off and seemed a little surprised.

Phil narrowed his eyes at me like he was trying to tell if I was for real. "You read that?" he said.

"Sure," I said.

"We never read it. If I read a book, that's going to be the one, though."

Roger said, "You may be called on to do your part one of these days, you know."

"So I been told."

"We've all got to do our part, buddy. You got an address for your old man?"

We reached my dad's apartment complex in another ten minutes. It was horseshoe shaped and four stories high with sidewalks that ran along outside the entrances. I was glad for all the open front doors and the people getting in and out of their cars when we pulled up.

Phil got his gun out again. Roger slammed the car into park and turned around. He said, "What did you see in the woods today?"

"Not a thing," I said. I could read Roger's knuckles now. They said, "YOUR NEXT." He nodded at me and Phil waved like, "be gone," and so I grabbed my bag and slid out of the backseat, shutting the door behind me and standing on the parking lot until they backed out and drove away. I could smell the engine oil on my pants. Then I started to laugh again. It's a bad trait, that nervous laughter. Weren't nothing funny.

18

EDIE

2015

Theron Landon liked to walk and talk. Looking back over their years working together, Edie could see that most of their walking meetings had contained significant disclosures. These command performances—in which, rather than walking a few steps down the hall from her office to his, she was to meet him at some appointed outdoor locale—had something more to do with his paranoia about being recorded saying anything revealing of the inner workings of either Landon Energy or himself than any love of nature or sudden enthusiasm for getting his heart rate up in the late afternoon. Today he'd told her to meet him on the far west side of town, on the dam at Lake Overholser.

She drove past a row of lakeside mansions—stuccoed, gated, and evocative of old Hollywood or new Santa Fe—and pulled into the lake's east-side parking lot. The old dam rose before her, a buttressed concrete structure with a wide walkway across the top and a red-shingled building perched on its east end that held the water works. Built during the first flush of urban planning after Oklahoma's early twentieth-century statehood, the enormous steel gears of the dam's mechanism reminded Edie of *Metropolis*, of old movies in general, full-moon assignations with gangsters stepping out of shadows, dames in shiny evening wear falling screaming down the seventy-foot sides into the waters of the reservoir. They could have met somewhere comfortable. She could have had an espresso and air conditioning. Theron's flair for the dramatic was a pain in Edie's ass more often than not.

His white Porsche Cayenne was already parked at the front of the nearly empty parking lot, its red security light beeping from the dash. She shut her car door and stood on the blacktop looking for him. A pair of runners trotted by on the sidewalk in front of her. A lone fisherman sat in a lawn chair under a tree, his line cast into the shady waters, and a group of kids on in-line skates swooshed by. Lowering her eyes to the steps leading up to the walkway across the dam, she saw Theron's block-like form, broad shoulders, squat legs, and the wide, angular cranium that had inspired Ian and Keith's snickering nickname for him, "Lego Head." His stiff gait, made awkward by a Vietnam War injury that kept his right knee from bending, made him easy to spot. She thought of calling to him but instead watched him go, gleaning from the tension in his body that she hadn't been wrong about the severity of the news he had brought her here to discuss. Silver head down, he took the stairs like a criminal climbing his final scaffold.

Upon beginning to work for him when she was twenty-six, she had been surprised at how quickly he had learned to lean on her. What it was about her that he trusted so instinctively she didn't understand, but her loyalty to him now, despite the untenable spot he was putting her in, had everything to do with gratitude for the faith he had shown her. She wanted to return his trust with trust. At least she would try. There was no way to minimize how his esteem had changed her self-understanding for the better. He had taken her in with the openness of a child after their first meeting at the London offices in 1998, asking her point blank, "Do people know about Landon Energy?" The open look on his face had changed her stature in the world and in her own mind. Her perceptions could change someone else's reality? A big, global reality? She truly might not have to tend bar again. It was the first time in the three years since the Murrah bombing that she had forgotten for a moment about Delaney's fate. Instead, she had considered his question. "No," she'd said. "Not like British Petroleum or Conoco. Not like the big names."

He had raised his chin and looked down his stub of a nose at her, a gesture impeded by the parity of their height. They were eye to eye. For a moment he seemed angry. Then he had grinned and said, "See, I didn't think so. Those dipshits." He pointed into the now-empty conference room where they had just met with the rest of the PR team of which she occupied the bottom rung. "They keep telling me we're a household name."

"Do you want to be?" she asked. "I'm not sure of the benefit, sir, unless you plan to move your energies from exploration to retail. Gas stations?"

He shook his head a quick no and looked out the window. Their offices were in an artless glass office complex in Battersea with a view of the twin smokestacks of the Battersea Power Station rising dark and stern above the rooftops. Edie knew she would never look at them without expecting to see the flying pig from the cover of Pink Floyd's *Animals* hanging between them. She doubted the old smokestacks created any such association for Theron Landon. She pegged him for a country music lover who pretended to appreciate opera. She had been right, as she later found out.

"Do you know who E. W. Marland was?" he asked.

She shook her head.

"No? I thought you were an Okie, young lady. The Marland Mansion? Come on."

She feigned familiarity with the name. "Right, the Marland Mansion!"

"I mean, you just mentioned Conoco."

She assumed this character had something to do with the founding of Conoco and made a note to brush up on her historic oil barons. "Is he an inspiration to you, sir?"

"To a point, to a point. I like how he did business."

After that day Edie learned everything about E. W. Marland that she could, a little surprised that Landon had taken such a dubious character as his hero. From then on, when she needed to nudge Landon, she could usually deploy a Marland reference to get him seeing things her way.

She might need one today. Smoothing her hair after a gust of wind, she tried to remember any stories of Marland admitting wrongdoing and changing course and how admired he had been, sir, for his forthrightness, and how his business had boomed as a result. Yes, it would need to be pure fabrication, but she needed a story like that because this meeting had to mean the moment for the mea-culpa fracking announcement had come. A pre-crisis circling of the wagons, you draw their fire, Miss Edie, and I'll cover you from under my wagon. In other words, you give a press conference reading this statement about Landon Energy's mindful and changing relationship to fracking, and I'll watch it from my office TV.

She felt a buzz from inside her purse and withdrew her phone. *Home soon?*

Meeting with Landon. Could be awhile. I'll keep you posted.

There was a long pause as she watched the ellipsis dance on her screen. Was Keith writing a manifesto? She waited, and finally a single line appeared: *Can't wait to hear about it.*

She typed. *U will. U2 eat w/out me.* Then a string of green vegetable emojis for their ongoing food battle with Ian.

Will do. Hopeful?

Fingers crossed.

WWEWM do?

She sent a smiley-faced emoji. *What Would E. W. Marland Do?* Keith's refrain when she was in doubt about how to handle her unpredictable boss. He was usually right. It usually helped. But the sweet normality of their exchange slipped away as Delaney's Facebook invitation and his ATM withdrawals filled her mind.

Theron had reached the midpoint of the promenade and was gazing down the steep concrete backside of the dam. Most people would stand on the other side and look out at the lake. Landon's choice seemed to typify his particular business genius, how he had found oil in the Leneer fields, a vast area that stretched vertically up the western haunch of Oklahoma where many had tried and failed to drill. Don't look where everyone else is looking. Look behind, look at the underpinnings. He turned and finally saw her as she came his way. He put up a stiff hand. It was how he waved.

The long walkway across the top of the dam was made of metal grating that caught the heels of her shoes as she stepped onto it, reaching for the railing. She struggled to find her footing and tried not to look down at the water rushing under the grate. The manmade lake reminded her of another one in the Wichita Mountains in southwestern Oklahoma that her father had flown her over in a Cessna for her tenth birthday. He'd shown her a WPA village under the water and then, swooping above the jagged mountain range, had pointed out the round shaft cover of an abandoned Spanish mine. Edie's imagination filled with riches and pirate treasure, but her father had assured her it was empty. He'd grinned at her through his mirrored aviators, squeezing her skinny thigh. *People don't abandon valuable things.* He left for good a week later and his confident assertion had come to seem like a converse explanation of why he'd left her.

She joined Theron Landon and they stood shoulder to shoulder for a few seconds gazing into the dark waters of the spillway below the gates of the dam. Enormous catfish glided through the greenish depths, and the heads of turtles dotted the surface. Facing them across the water on a sandy embankment, a group of ten or twelve people fished at the edge of the water. Children ran around playing, and a couple of campfires were roaring big enough to be visible in the sunlight. Immigrants up from the border, she guessed. They must have just arrived. Soon they would have apartments and jobs—Edie remembered the team of Guatemalan dishwashers she had worked with at Beryl's, six of them in an apartment, uproarious teenagers having the adventure of their lives. If one of them was too drunk to work another would fill in, counting on management's indifference to their actual identities and racist inability to tell them apart. They were probably homeowners with kids in the local schools now, like her.

"They're catching their supper," Theron said, nodding at the people around the campfires "That's not sport fishing, that's not catch and release. That's dinner." His voice sounded admiring. "My dad used to say catch it or starve. Haven't thought of that in a long time. Catch it or starve."

He was going to get sentimental if she didn't redirect him. He wasn't one of those anti-immigration nuts, mainly because he admired the work ethic of the Mexicans he'd employed in the oil fields, but he was entirely capable of standing there looking down at those people, admiring their efforts to stay alive Wild West camp style in the middle of a twenty-first-century American city, and never connect his philosophical admiration to an impulse to help. All roads led to an opportunity to stand in awe of Theron's own rags-to-riches life story, the child of a couple of small-town store clerks who had risen to such prominence.

"This must be important," she prompted him.

"State of Oklahoma's putting up a new website Tuesday. This Tuesday—in four days. It's not about tourism, Edie."

Then their dynamic kicked in, the conversation unrolling with a pacing both knew how to anticipate, like swing dancing with a partner whose stride length you knew. "You know how much I donated to that fool's campaign?" he said. "She made goddamn promises, but here we are. She's going to issue a statement."

"Also on Tuesday?" If the governor, who was known to ask people to pray for the oil companies, was taking these steps, the pressure building up must be truly oppressive. All those little earthquakes were leading to one big shake-up. There was no morality to her change of heart; that was one thing Edie was sure of. This was pure political survival.

He nodded.

"What changed her position?" Edie asked, but it was like asking why someone facing into a hurricane would scramble for dry land. Oil and gas and its allies in state government were the last people on earth to admit what had been popularly understood for at least a year, and trying to hold their position against all known facts and daily earthquakes in the hundreds was like defending the Alamo, with no heroic connotations.

"Damned OGS is releasing a statement."

Finally. The Oklahoma Geological Survey had been the last breakwater, allowing oil and gas to keep going, to pump as fast as they could months after the United States Geological Survey released its findings concluding that the wastewater injections used in shale fracking operations were almost certainly causing earthquakes. Oklahoma's GS, its scientists bewildered to find themselves under political pressure, had resisted the national conclusions as long as they could. Apparently even the fear of Theron Landon and other prominent oilmen's wrath, which was considerable and had been made known to the individual geologists responsible for these decisions in ways that Edie did not want to know about, was now the lesser evil. The scales had finally tipped. Any longer and the entire Oklahoma Geological Survey would have lost all credibility in the scientific community.

She had to fight to keep a smile from her face as relief coursed through her. Keith would be so happy when she told him. "So you're changing policy on the Leneer sites?"

He looked at her like she was crazy. "The Leneer fields are my life's work, Edie."

"Wait. Then what are you saying?" She pushed her hands through her scalp and stared at the group fishing below them. She throttled her anger, knowing that he would shut down and dig in if she was too critical. It wasn't the way to maneuver him. "A slowdown, then, a gradual shift back to good old vertical drilling?" She let her voice rise at the end. Just asking a question.

He smacked his lips like he had just eaten a bad clam, something he did to show disgust. "I know you're on the people side of this business, Edie, but I thought you knew more about the science than that. Vertical drilling can't get anything out of those shale layers—the veins are too thin. Horizontal drilling's the only way, and we've got to dispose of the wastewater. If there was another way I'd take it, but fracking *is* the other way—I spent damn near my whole working life looking for this solution and I won't be told I can't use it now. They can all go to hell."

"Theron, the wastewater. We've got hundreds of quakes every day in a state that didn't have them before."

"This fuss about contaminating the drinking water is just plumb ignorant. People don't understand how far below the water table we're injecting the wastewater. Hell, there's no risk, or not much."

"But the earthquakes are real. There will be consequences you can't anticipate. The minute a house falls down, a bridge goes out, someone dies—"

He waved his hand impatiently. "The idea that I want to hurt anyone! You're my public relations. How are you letting this happen?"

"I can repair your reputation if the fracking stops. Over time I can craft a whole new identity for Landon Energy, especially if we move into clean energy, but not while the wastewater injection sites are still going. People don't take to being collateral damage. That's a term that makes everybody think of Timothy McVeigh and what he said about the kids he killed. You do not want that comparison."

McVeigh's name shook him. "Come on, now. Never once has it crossed my mind to hurt anybody. Never once! I'm just following the oil."

"Nobody thinks you set out to hurt people, nobody thinks it's premeditated. The earthquakes—who knew that would happen? But it's the fact that the human cost doesn't count at all for you that's hard to defend, Theron. That you didn't consider the effects and that now, knowing the damage, you still don't stop. It's profits over people. I've told you about this."

His face had turned red. He squeezed the wrought iron railing until his leathery freckled hands blanched. "What will we do?"

There it was, the trust and need she had first seen that day in the Battersea offices. Finally. She placed a hand on his shoulder and turned to him, facing into the sun in the western sky. She spoke low but firm. "Let me announce ahead of the governor and the OGS. Monday morning. Monday, Theron. Beat them to the punch, make it look like they're following your lead. *Upon careful consideration, Landon Energy has decided to curtail its wastewater injection operations until safety concerns can be assessed.* That's all! I can word this so you don't have to have the details worked out yet."

"No." He shrugged away from her. "If this is the hill I'm to die on, then so be it. The Leneer is mine. After the money I've made for this state? No. No announcement. Forget it—we'll fight them."

"Oh, Landon." Her jaw muscles tightened. She knew she would cry if she didn't watch it. "Think about when Marland let his company merge with Continental. He felt defeated—you know he did—but look what came of it. Conoco, for god's sake."

He looked at her pityingly. "Now that's no kind of parallel."

He was right—it was weak. "What are they doing over at Devon and Sand Ridge? Chesapeake?"

"This ain't a neighborhood association, Edie."

"Okay. Okay, we'll need to give your geologists a chance to—We'll need—"

"Are you with me?"

"I—" He was watching her closely. She leaned against the railing and looked out. The late afternoon sun cast long shadows from surrounding cottonwoods across the camps below, making the fires visible. A long row of fish impaled on a stick lay across one of the fires. If they were a little closer, she'd be able to smell it. She thought of Keith's disappointment in her. Like one of those tobacco company reps, he had said. God. But what about her disappointment in him? He hadn't gambled in a year and that was about as long as he'd ever gone—she should have heard the clock tolling midnight. The message from Delaney had proven too much for him. He was fragile, and if Edie was unemployed? "I am. Yes, okay? I'm with you."

He nodded like he had never doubted it. "I'll see you Sunday morning."

"What's Sunday morning?"

"The Murrah bombing anniversary. We need to be there."

"I—" *I can't go there. I won't go. I can't stand it.* She clasped her hands before her, nodded, looked down through the metal grating at the dark water churning beneath her. "I'll see you there."

19

DELANEY

1995

I hate waiting. I hate waiting for my own paintings to dry—that's how bad I am. I hate waiting rooms; I hate taking a number; I hate the shitty gossip magazines on the tables and the people all around me with their butts sliding in the seats and their rustling and their bored faces resigned to the wait. I stand holding the heavy glass door to the social security office, taking it all in—the place just opened, I mean *just* opened, it's 9:00 sharp, and already all these people are here and finding seats, everybody hoping to beat the crowd and get it over with. The fluorescent lights are still flickering and buzzing to life, service reps are still opening their stations, walking to their chairs blowing on their coffee and looking over the rim of the mugs at the crowd like pool players lining up their shots, sizing up the difficulty level, the overall mood. One of them is smiling, peaceful like she just came in from a morning run and is looking forward to helping all these folks, but she sees me in the doorway and grimaces, already deciding that I'm going to give her grief today.

I'm not. I'm just here for a copy of my social security card, easy-peasy. I've done this twice before—I always lose my purse so I know about the paperwork and the wait before my real card comes in the mail. I just need that receipt that says I ordered one, so I can work tonight. No receipt, no shift. An older gentleman with wavy gray hair hands a magazine to his wife. It's got Howard Stern's ugly mug on the cover. The woman looks at it and makes a face. Her husband grins and I'm with them, no gossip rags for me, so I turn and walk out of the social security office. I'll need something to doodle on if I'm going to have to sit there. Even a pencil and paper, anything so I can draw.

I stride across the building's downstairs lobby, smiling at people as I go because I feel badly for how I affected the social security worker just now. After all, why not be cool? The morning sunlight is blocked because an asshole in a yellow Ryder truck has pulled in front of the glass doors like it's moving day at the Murrah T. Federal Building or something. People skirt the truck on their way in, rushing because it's 9:01, and they're officially a little late for work. There's a G-man-looking dude in a tight black suit who I figure for one of the Secret Service or DEA guys with an office upstairs. This building is full of those types. They all look so uptight, which makes it almost a moral imperative to flirt with them. Square boys are hard to resist—that's what got me interested in Keith at first. This one sees me and holds the door open, the yellow side of the Ryder truck outside framing him like a canvas. He wears a not-so-patient smile on his handsome face that tells me *anytime now*, so I try to hurry. In the doorway I stop and touch his arm and smile up at him. And he blushes! What a sweetheart. Score one for me today.

20

EDIE

2015

She looked down at his bare chest stretched beneath her, still panting. His arms were behind his head on the pillow as he watched her, naked astride him. "Look at you," he said fondly.

"Look at you."

Early Sunday morning sunlight splashed across the yellow sheets, Egyptian miracles made with some impossibly high thread count she had treated herself to the previous spring. It had been not long after his last—or so she had believed—gambling binge, and the sheets had felt like a vote of confidence in their future, a private avowal to forgive and go forward despite it all. He reached up with one long arm and traced the contours of her breasts. "How long until Ian can make breakfast?"

Edie laughed. "Be careful what you wish for."

Above them, they heard Ian's small feet hit the floor and cross his bedroom. They both stared at the ceiling. "He'll play for a few minutes," Keith said.

She leaned down and stretched herself over him, feeling his spent penis slide from her, semen spreading warmly between them. Her head rested below the rise in his collarbone. The sudden crush of secrets between them had given their lovemaking an intensity that startled them both. She was so furious about the gambling, so hurt and confused about the Facebook invitation, and so terrified of just about everything coming her way that her body had been a bottle of storms. In England she said she'd leave him if he gambled again and had meant it. You couldn't share a life with someone who could, at any moment, be lying to your face, unraveling the thread of your life as you wove it. But she couldn't think about it now, and if her alcoholic mind was good at one thing, it was compartmentalizing.

"He just said hell no, huh?" Keith said.

"Ian?"

"God help us! No, Lego Head."

"Right. I could not bring him around. He was hung up on premeditation or something. Seemed to think that since he didn't *mean* to cause the earthquakes, he should be given a pass to keep drilling. Made no sense."

"You've got to admire the guy, though."

Edie fitted herself along his length, her head against his shoulder. "Do you?"

"You know what I mean. His monomania, that tight focus of his, it has its good side."

"It's a good work trait, I suppose, but I'm surprised to hear you say it." Since she told him about her meeting with Theron at Lake Overholser Friday afternoon, Keith had been stuck on it, returning again and again to the ins and outs of Theron's stance. *Could he do that? Just refuse? Just hypothetically—when would the announcement be if she were going to make one?* "A couple of days ago you compared him to tobacco company owners denying that smoking causes cancer."

Keith crossed a leg over his bent knee. "It's true. He's denying the science even though he knows it's right. But knowing the man as we do, it's complicated."

"Like how?"

"Like his focus on finding oil. Those stories of his about working as a land man in Louisiana, knocking on doors, running from dogs and shotguns."

"You mean trespassing?"

"I guess."

"You're just all over the place, aren't you?" She pulled the top sheet over them, and he reached up to help her. "One minute Theron is the great evil and now all of a sudden you're living and dying by what he's going to do."

His hands stilled just for a second. She rolled over on her elbows to look at him and there it was, his tell. Every gambler has a tell, he had taught her that, but what he didn't know was that he had one and that she could read it. He'd freeze for a heartbeat pull his lips into a tight line, and momentarily widen his eyes. The tell meant he was hiding something. Well, she already knew. The Facebook message. The mysterious cash withdrawals that surely meant gambling. If he didn't bring it up today, she would. But it would be so much better if he told her himself. Why didn't he?

He turned onto his side and cradled his head in his palm. "You really expected him to change policy when the heat got bad enough."

"It's what any reasonable person would do."

Keith nodded, lost in thought. "Now you think—what? There will be no announcement? No change?"

"I can't put words in his mouth. I can't dictate company policy. Oh, but Keith, the speech I could write. I could pivot him to wind turbines in two graceful sentences. We could become part of the solution."

"This is hard on you." He said it gently, but she could tell his mind was elsewhere.

"The worst part has been feeling like you disapprove of me." She laid a hand on his shoulder. "If you're okay with it, then I can get through this. I'll hate it, but I think I can do it."

"I'm not okay with it, but I'm okay with you." He looked her full in the face and his urgency scared her. There was the tell again. Twice!

He picked up his phone from the end table and glanced at it. "In two hours it will be twenty years."

She grabbed it. Seven in the morning already. She had to get up. Theron expected her at the twenty-year anniversary service at the Oklahoma City Memorial. She would rather do almost anything else. Keith had a text from someone named Brad Odel. The first line was visible. *What's the news, dude?* Brad Odel? Maybe a fellow historian? But, "dude"?

She handed Keith his phone. "Twenty years ago this morning I was showering and you were at the door to the bathroom asking me if I was okay. I was so glad it was you there that day."

He swung himself out of bed and pulled on a pair of gray sweatpants draped over a chair. "You never told me that."

"What?"

"You were glad it was me. As opposed to someone else?"

"Oh. I only meant it as a compliment."

"Yeah. You preferred me to the other guys she saw."

"What? No. I don't know." How had she let that slip after all this time? "Never mind."

He put his hands on his hips and looked down. "She was seeing other people?"

"You weren't exactly exclusive." If he was feeling wounded about Delaney's promiscuity, he could think a minute before he asked her to comfort him.

He was still looking at the floor. His woundedness infuriated her and she said, "You didn't know that when you asked her to marry you?"

His head shot up. "What?"

"It was the last conversation we had. She came out onto the porch griping about your proposal." She stood up and wrapped the sheet wrapped around her with a swoosh. "She was pissed."

"I didn't know you knew." He watched her. "You never told me."

"*You* never told *me*. Like you didn't tell me about that Facebook invitation you got Friday."

They stared at each other across the bed.

Finally she said, "You didn't think I got one, too?"

"No, I guess I—Edie, I thought if you'd gotten one you'd have said something."

She laughed. "I would've, but I saw you had gotten yours and didn't say anything about it, so it looked like you were going to keep it a secret."

"Just until I found out if it was real." He sat back down on the bed. "Fuck, I'm sorry. You talk about the unexpected—I can't wrap my head around it."

She sat down next to him. "Some mean hoax, right?"

For a moment they sat in silence. It was what she had wanted since the Facebook invitations came in—to think about them with Keith.

"Has to be. Probably. But we need to find out," he said. "I tried messaging. No response. It can't be her, right?"

They stared at each other. She said, "Whoever it is—looks like they're in New Mexico."

"Let's all go. You, me, and Ian."

"I have to stick around for work," she said. "The governor's announcement and the state website go up on Tuesday. What about you? Isn't your interview for the tenure-track job on Tuesday?"

"I can be back in time."

"Don't you need to prepare?"

"Yes?" He rubbed his forehead. "But what are we supposed to do? Put a pin in it? Oh, Delaney might be alive? Let's look into that when we get some spare time."

"Keith, go today."

"After you get back from the memorial."

"Why don't you and Ian come with me to that?"

He shook his head emphatically. "At 9:02 I'm going to be doing something fun with Ian."

"Help him finish his dream catcher," she said.

"I'm going to explain to him about cultural appropriation and tell him the history of dream catchers in Native culture like we agreed."

"Okay, good. The version for seven-year-olds."

"Of course."

"I don't want to go to this thing." At 9:02 she would be standing with hundreds of other people at the memorial observing a moment of silence for all of those who lost their lives. For the first time since the night of the bombing when she and Keith sneaked onto the site, she would be there. And for the first time since the night of the bombing, she wasn't certain Delaney had been in the building.

21

AUGUST P.

2015

The sky looked smudged. It was a gray, chilly morning, and the crowd looked gray and chilly, too, like creatures molded out of wind. People at the memorial were crowded in tight, but still folks near me tried to give me a wide berth because that cough of mine sounded like something they didn't want to catch. The insides of my lungs hurt. My throat was swollen near shut, my eyes burned, and my body lacked power. I wanted to lie down on the green grass at the top of the hill between all those legs facing the memorial and rest. Don't cough drops help this? I needed some cough drops.

    I weren't the only one with a broken clock from that day, I could see. Look at all of us, wanting! Thousands of folks there, all hoping for something from that day. We wanted for it to have never happened, but we knew that couldn't be so we came to remember. What helped was knowing I weren't the only one hung up about it. I was on top of the rise between the bombing site and the museum. It was a natural elevation, but it felt like the bombing site was lower because the earth was blown away. There was a grandstand set up where the boundary of the Murrah Building would have been, right where the front entrance would have let out onto the street. Right where the yellow Ryder truck carrying the bomb pulled up and parked, if I weren't wrong, which I could have been. I'd been wrong about so many things going on the day of the bombing, so what did I know? The podium was X marks the spot with seats flanking it full of dignitaries. Former President Clinton and that tall fellow who runs the FBI, state governors and Oklahoma City mayors past and present. The back wall of the Murrah Federal Building was behind them, a gray concrete shell with holes where the rebar was wrenched out by the bomb, and glass-bottom chairs that glow at night fill the green lawn where the building was, one for everyone that died. They tried to put them in the areas of the building where the victims were found, so the little chairs from the day-care center were front and center. The eternal pool shone ahead of them, a glassy rectangle of water running the length of the building where 5th Street used to be, representing the minute when the bomb went off. 9:02. On either side of it were the monoliths called the Gates of Time, bronze entryways like brackets that say 9:01 and 9:03. The pool between them was the space of eternal 9:02. Throw a penny into 9:02, if you think it will bring you luck, but why would you think that? Not this water, not here. Toss your lucky penny in the fountain at the mall or one of them fancy casinos, hell, your own bathtub, but not this pool. Personal luck is not what this pool was in the business of, no indeed. Not just curiosity or civic duty on all those faces, either, but long-suffering and grief. Not as bad as the day of, not as bad as that, nothing could ever be, but still it was there, hardened and smooth like scar tissue, willing to take solace in what was offered that day. Needing something.

Always I felt like I could help somehow, it was why I was there. But what could I do, a man who couldn't do much of anything but stay sober one day at a time and roll a cross the size of the Lord's up and down this city's highways? Those are two things I did every day, and that day I was there. Sometimes I thought I was nothing but a guilty conscience, like a sponge. The ceremony began *we come here to remember* and while the talking boomed out over the crowd I looked at faces, one by one, row after row, each face the front door to a whole timeless, spaceless soul—ain't it something? I saw familiar people, a clerk at Walgreens with a Wonder Woman tattoo covered up with a coat that morning, this red-headed lady who was the counselor I never called like I was supposed to, and a short Black guy with gray hair that was my landlord about ten years ago, who evicted me for crying. *Nobody can stand listening to you boo hooing all the time, man. Can you cheer up a little?* I couldn't, and he was nice about it, but he said I was bringing everybody else down. It was a small apartment complex, only four units, and I was in the middle, so everybody heard. I didn't blame him. Jimmy, that was his name. He even helped me find the place where I was living, a little house on a patch of grass, my own homestead smack in the middle of the city. Oklahoma City was funny like that—here and there were pockets of early settlement inside the city limits, lone farmhouses left from when there was nothing else here, now hemmed around by restaurants, car dealerships, and neighborhoods of spiffy brick houses with brick mailboxes to match, all alike.

I didn't see anybody I wanted to talk to until I caught sight of Edie A., that poor gal from my meetings. Oh, but she looked unhappy! Her little face was tight and pale and she was looking around like she wanted to run away. She was down near the front to one side, close to the entry that says 9:03.

When she saw me it took her a second to figure out where she knew me from. When she did, her face broke open in a real smile that warmed me to my toes. She patted my arm. "August, how are you?"

"That's the blackest suit I ever saw," I said, and she laughed and looked down at her outfit and brushed a sleeve even though there was nothing on it. "Do you have any cough drops?"

She tapped her lips. "You know what? I might." Into her big black purse she went, sifting through Lord-knows-what-all and coming up with a little thing wrapped in white and yellow paper. "It's sugar-free," she said. "But better than nothing. You need real medicine. You know not to take Nyquil, right? That stuff's like 120 proof. Have to reset your sobriety date if you get into any of that. Check the labels."

I unwrapped the cough drop and popped it in my mouth and thanked her. "Why are you here?" I asked.

"Work," she said. "My boss told me I needed to make an appearance, but I don't see him anywhere."

"Is that all?"

"What do you mean?"

"Did you lose someone here?"

She winced. "August," she said. She stared off into the reflecting pool. Then she looked right at me, her eyes wet. "I lost my sister. Half sister."

"I'm sorry. What was her name?" They were going to be reading the names of the victims soon, and you could see their pictures and read about them in the museum. I was curious to learn about this half sister, full gone.

"She's not on the list of the victims."

I thought about that. What that would mean for Edie. A sister gone from the world and missing from the list of the dead, lost in a hole like a black roar tunneled down Edie's very center. Crumbling edges she'd have to step around for the rest of her life. So this was Edie's sadness. I knew it was a mighty one. No words came to me. I doubled over, coughing.

She pointed at a spot behind me. "We found the SUV she drove over there. And her jacket," she pointed to the middle of the memorial, "was recovered over there. I always knew she died here. Knew it. But now? I don't know. Maybe those people who told us they couldn't count her among the dead were right not to. Maybe she's not a victim."

"But you are."

"What?"

"You are."

She looked confused. "I never thought of it that way."

I took off in another coughing fit and started to sway. I felt her hand on my back and the other one on my arm.

"Come on, August." She led me through the crowd and down the steps of the monolith out onto the street.

"Where are we going?"

We walked alongside the chain-link fence on Harvey, covered in pictures of the victims, signs and teddy bears and T-shirts. It had been put up around the search and rescue operation before they tore down the remains of the Murrah Building and built the memorial. There were old photos in waterlogged laminate, sun-faded ribbons, and big signs covered in signatures of school children sending their sympathies. There were new things, too, necklaces and flowers and cards. People tended it like a grave. Edie pointed at an ambulance parked across the street by the Jesus Wept statue and pulled me toward it.

She knocked on the passenger-side window and a dark-eyed man with salt-and-pepper hair opened the door and stepped out. He had heavy eyebrows and strong forearms. He was familiar to me.

"Hi, folks. Can we help?" Then his eyes lit on me and I could tell he knew me, too.

Edie looked at his name plate and said, "Robert, could y'all take a look at my friend here? He seems pretty sick."

"You bet." He looked me up and down. "How you doing today, August?"

Edie watched with surprise. Squinting up at Robert, she said, "You know him?"

"This guy? Everybody knows August." He glanced down at her. "We've come across him a few times, haven't we, friend?" He always lifted his voice when he talked to me, like people do. "How's your ankle?"

He had set my ankle when I twisted it in a posthole off I-35 one afternoon, and he'd given me a bottle of water once, on a hot day. Another time, during a tornado watch, he and his partner took me home, slid the cross in the back of the ambulance, and let me ride back there with it.

His partner came around the side of the ambulance with her hands in her pockets and told everyone her name was Blanca. She remembered my name, too.

"What's going on today, August?" she said in her soft accent.

Edie told them about my cough, and they opened up the back of the ambulance and let me sit on the bumper while they checked me out. Then they told me to lie down on the cot inside and put an oxygen mask over my nose. "Pneumonia" was a word they said a time or two and tried to talk me into letting them take me to the hospital. I didn't want to go.

Edie looked down at me, pushing her hair behind her ears. "What have you got going on that's more important than getting well, anyway?"

"Lots," I said. "I have a lot to do." People didn't understand that. Edie didn't, I could see. There are more tasks than the ones they pay you for. There are higher callings, louder screams, tighter vises. I had a schedule to keep.

"St. Anthony's is two minutes away," Robert said. His eyes were on a monitor they had me hooked to. "Your vitals are stable, but you need care, my friend."

"Care?" I pushed myself up on my elbows. "Who cares?"

I thought that was funny, but something about the comment sparked a change in Robert. His face set and he looked me over with floodlights for eyes. "August, are you safe?"

"Safe?" I opened my hands to take in the space around us. What could be safer than the inside of an ambulance?

"What I mean is, are you thinking of harming yourself?"

"Oh!" I sat all the way up. "Gracious no. Heck, I just don't like hospitals."

I wasn't telling the whole truth. I surely do think of setting down this heavy burden sometimes. Of course. But I don't deserve a rest, not yet. Robert believed me, though, and smiled. "Glad to hear it," he said. "I don't like hospitals, either, but hey, think of the free food. You know they've got ice cream?"

"No kidding?" In that moment, I felt Robert's big presence, unavoidable, like we were tumbling down a hill in the same barrel. He had one of those past-and-future faces, the kind where you can see the little boy he was and the old man he will be in his now face. We could hear the memorial ceremony still going on, booming voices in the distance. The tone was heavy, the pauses long. I reckoned they were reading the names of the dead.

"August, you'll just get sicker if you don't work on getting better." Edie was talking to me but looking across me at Robert and Blanca. I felt ganged up on. She kept reaching out to touch me and then pulling back, holding her arms around her waist. "Deal with it now or deal with it later, when it's worse and will take more time out of your schedule."

That sounded true enough, but I still didn't want to go, and I told them as much. Blanca made me sign something that said I understood if I died it wasn't their fault, Edie and Robert singing a danged duet about rest and antibiotics. What finally convinced me to let them take me to the hospital was listening to those two wrangling with each other over who was going to take me home, Edie saying she could take me in her car and Robert saying, no, no, we already know where he lives. They should have let me walk off on my own, but they weren't going to do it. I felt ashamed to be such a problem, I thought it would easier for them if I just laid back and let them take me where they'd be free of me and feel like they did the right thing. "I do feel pretty low," I conceded.

Robert's big ol' eyebrows shot up. "Yeah? I hear you. Okay. So." He nodded at Blanca like a director saying action. "Let's get to the hospital."

Edie looked lost for a minute. "I guess I have to go," she said. She looked at me like I might tell her what to do, and this time, she gave into her impulse and laid a hand over mine.

"Your fingernails are pretty," I said. I haven't been around women too much, except at meetings, so their ways are impressive to me. I watch their hands, on their laps, tapping their phones, and touching their faces, some with nails gnawed to tatters and some with these fingernails like paintings.

She gave a short laugh and turned her hand to look at them. They were see-through shiny like water.

"You can follow us," Robert said.

Edie seemed more than happy to leave the memorial ceremony early and turned up at the hospital before they even got me checked in. She brought me a big hot chocolate in a to-go cup with whipped cream melting under the lid. "You want me to let people in the group know you're here?"

I told her no; I didn't want anyone going out of their way for me. I didn't plan to stay there for long.

22

KEITH

2015

The cold, cloudy morning had given way to a warm afternoon. Keith kept his sun visor down, dark-tinted Ray-Bans on, but it hardly made a difference to the penetrating rays tickling the back of his skull. This was the sun as Delaney had painted it all those long years ago, a brightness that overtook every object in its way, like one of those old public service clips of a nuclear bomb ripping through a neighborhood, mannequins in housewife costumes blown to smithereens, their white arms and legs breaking apart and flying at the camera. He had missed this sun. It served the whole planet, sure, but there was no light like this in London, not ever. And he had missed these open roads, too. Hundreds upon hundreds of miles of straightaway, following the dotted line over the curve of the earth. The optimism he felt having the Facebook invitation out in the open was vast. Traveling with Edie's blessing, under the flag of family, fueled him with virtuous purpose. Only then, after his spirits rose, did reality kick in.

The weekend had been one of the worst of his life, starting with his afternoon at Winchester Park. As vile as he felt about betting on his wife, they had him over a barrel—she would leave him if she found out he had gambled again, and the truth was that if he could win back the money he'd lost before she noticed it was gone, it would save his marriage. Save his marriage! Wasn't that a good enough reason?

But he felt like hell, more hellish still with Edie's revelation that Theron Landon was refusing to take the high road with the upcoming OGS statement. Now not only had he lost his self-respect by agreeing to supply Brad and Louise the insider information they wanted for the fracking bet, but *it wasn't going to work*. When you sell your soul for an expedience, you expect the goal to be met, at least, right? But Landon Energy would make no statement. He wouldn't win the money back that he'd gambled, Edie would notice the missing money soon enough, and his marriage would be over. He would be shunted to the periphery of Ian's life, a sad dad who saw his kid on weekends.

He knew he had underestimated Brad. He'd Googled the Odel family. Turned out it wasn't so much the Odels as the Zabels, Brad's mother's side, that he needed to worry about. Brad's sweet little mother had been a world-class handicapper for her brother, Stanton Zabel, a gangster everyone in Oklahoma had heard of. Keith thought about the rows of numbers in her moleskin notebooks, the paper spread out to the sports pages, and felt stupid for never understanding. They'd gotten started as bootleggers in the 1870s, selling in the Unassigned Lands, where alcohol was outlawed long before prohibition affected the rest of the country. Louise was probably Brad's aunt or cousin or something—someone watching over him for Stanton.

Keith heard a noise and realized he was crying. Weeping into the silence. When had he ever driven in silence? The thousands of songs in his phone all seemed wrong. He couldn't think of the soundtrack for moral disintegration.

He thought of the talk he would give if he made it to the final round of job interviewees, on the Medicine Lodge Treaty, and he wished he was at home working on his PowerPoint presentation instead of blasting due west on I-40 trying to get to Abiquiu before the sun went down. He might be restored, returned to his best and truest self if he could spend a day in his research. He was a scholar, after all. A geek, an unworldly creature with the worldliest of addictions. He longed for a day in some western history archives, quietly hunting for hidden connections in the tangled threads of history, smelling the old papers and the wood oil, leaning close to old sepia-toned photographs with his magnifying glass and pressing microfiche under glass plates to read the nondigitized documents of a not-so-long ago time that America had already almost forgotten. A little over a century and it was ancient history.

In most other parts of the world, a hundred years was recent, a layer of topsoil on the historical past that stretched out behind them. But here in the land of eternal newness, even the 1995 bombing of the Alfred P. Murrah Federal Building was already starting to leave the collective unconscious of his countrymen. Edie had come home from the twenty-year memorial service with a story of overhearing a couple about their vintage telling their kids about the bombing. They may as well have been at a Civil War battlefield, as remote as she could tell it seemed to the kids. "I know we're getting old," Edie said. "But it wasn't that long ago. I still have the boots I wore down to the site that day. Still wear them."

They had been standing in the kitchen maneuvering around each other making lunch. Ian was at the table admiring his dream catcher, which was really coming along. The tiny plastic Star Wars figures Keith had suspended from the bottoms of the strings spun in the light when Ian held it up and asked, "Can we make one for Nana and Papa?"

"Sure," Keith said. "My folks love anything you make them." He poured iced tea into glasses and said to Edie, "I've got an idea for a paper. I want to look at the Supreme Court decision *Lone Wolf versus Hitchcock*. It was—"

"Fine with me." She usually liked hearing his disquisitions on the evils of Manifest Destiny, but she had been distracted ever since she came back from the memorial service. Grief was cyclical; that was the truth. She'd probably be this way all day. He cupped her shoulder in his palm and looked down at her. "You're okay?"

"I'm all good."

"What was it like?"

"Sad."

She looked like she had eaten something bitter. He knew this look and knew, also—they had talked about this, agreed—some experiences were beyond words and it was best not to bungle them up with inadequate descriptions. So: sad. Message received.

"I ended up helping this odd guy from my group. He was so sick, like hacking up a lung, and he didn't seem to realize it."

"You sure you're okay?"

"Seriously. I'll be better when I know what's at the other end of that Facebook invite. No matter what it is. You hear me? I want the truth, whatever it is."

"I promise. All the details and all the moral support."

She reached for her open yogurt container on the counter and ate a spoonful. "Isn't that a funny phrase? Moral support. Sounds like fortifying a weak wall. Like my morality needs shoring up." She shrugged and dug her spoon into the plastic container. "I think it does."

Not hers. Ian, who had been listening, tapped Keith's leg. "Here, Daddy." He held it up and looked through the web of string in the middle.

"Your dream catcher! For me?" He reached down and hugged his son. "Look what you made!"

"Don't lose it."

"I'll guard it with my life."

Now Keith glanced at the dream catcher sitting atop his overnight bag in the passenger seat and smiled. He wanted to hang it on his rearview mirror, but they had neglected to loop some of the string over the top to hang it with. Hardly a gas station in this part of the country was without its stand of dream catchers for sale, so next time he stopped he'd buy one for its hanger and attach it to Ian's. The idea of his son's bright handiwork catching his own jumbled dreams appealed to him, as if Ian were keeping him safe on this journey. Had there ever been a time when he knew less about what he'd find at the end of the road? Not even close. He could tell a class a few things about Abiquiu's thousand-year-old indigenous settlements, its Spanish colonial past, and the years when it was the trailhead for the trade route that linked Santa Fe to Los Angeles, but of the contemporary town he knew nothing. A Google search suggested the town was little more than a travel center and a small bed and breakfast on a scenic road in the Jemez Mountains of northern New Mexico. On the Delaney Travis Facebook page, two other friends were listed. One was the manager of the gas station in Abiquiu. The other listed Ghost Ranch as her place of employment. He had long heard of it—an artist's retreat of some sort right up the road from Abiquiu. It had something to do with Georgia O'Keeffe, the painter. Adobe churches. Big vaginal flowers. Negative space.

"She's a painter." He spoke under his breath, an obvious fact about Delaney but one he'd never considered in the context of her as a possibly living person. A series of associations rose like an illuminated trail before him. Delaney was the one who had first told him about Ghost Ranch. Generations of artists visited for the desert light and landscape. She had wanted to go there to paint someday, talked to him about it at a Mexican restaurant in Norman one night while they were drinking margaritas and eating chips, Georgia O'Keeffe prints lining the turquoise walls. She pointed to the one hanging next to the bar, ringed with a string of red chili pepper lights. It showed a giant detail of the inside of a dark purple iris. "She did that one at Ghost Ranch."

Keith cocked his head, studying it. "It's a vagina."

"It's an iris."

"It even has a clitoris."

"Stamen. It's the stamen." Then she smiled, rolling up a flour tortilla. "Yeah, it's totally a clit."

Had Delaney been at Ghost Ranch to paint? Was she there now, holed up in the high desert mountains like a latter-day Anasazi, like Georgia O'Keefe, sketching cow skulls and steep red cliffs? "My God," he said, pounding the steering wheel with the flat of his hands. "If she's alive, she's painting."

From inside the black leather overnight bag on the seat, his phone rang. He was passing a semitruck at the moment, surging past an enormous photograph of Tyson breaded chicken fingers that decorated the truck's long white flank. He unzipped the bag, fishing around for the phone and wishing his car stereo was Bluetooth enabled like Edie's. Eyes on the road.

"Hello?"

"There you are!"

"Hi, Brad."

"Edie says you're on vacation?"

Motherfucker. Called his house. "Quick road trip. I have some work to do."

"Well, I'm glad I caught you. What's the word up at Edie's office? I damned near asked her myself, but then I remembered you said you'd do it."

Ah, motherfucker. Brad the dipshit, he of the can-you-write-my-report-for-me-dude-I'll-give-you-a-joint pedigree, was trying to be clever. Keith gripped the steering wheel with such force, his wrists hurt. "I asked her about it." And then it occurred to him that telling Brad that Landon would announce on Tuesday was plausible enough that it might get him out of trouble. He could tell most of the truth. "There is some scuttlebutt."

"Tell me."

"Word is OGS will publish a report on Tuesday. The governor's going to say something, too."

"Day after tomorrow?"

"Tuesday morning," Keith said. When the governor's announcement came on the morning of the twenty-first and Landon Energy didn't respond, he'd act as surprised as Brad. No announcement? Sorry, dude. "Edie says Tuesday. April twenty-first is your day."

"That's when Landon will make a statement?"

"Near as Edie can tell." Lying to Brad felt great.

"I knew it!"

"Pretty exciting stuff."

"You wouldn't lie to me, would you?"

Keith laughed the laugh that would have accompanied a back slap if Brad were in the car with him. "I can only tell you what I know, man. Could I be wrong? Sure, but if I keep asking Edie about it, she's going to know something is up."

In his this-dime's-all-seeds-and-stems voice, Brad said, "Where did you say you were going?"

Keith was in the unpopulated western part of Oklahoma where wind turbines loomed over the fields on either side of the highways, their colossal blades slicing the wind. The landscape was beginning to change from grass plains to desert. Ahead, the hills turned to mesas and bushes gave way to prickly-pear cacti. "Ghost hunting."

"What?"

"Look, I told you what you wanted to know." His voice conveyed none of the fear he felt.

"Okay. I'm going with your information."

"Here's to that."

"You'd better not be meooing with me, bro."

23

EDIE

1995

They needed blood. All the local stations were posting addresses of new Red Cross sites set up across the metro for blood donation. Edie had woken up the day after the bombing hungover as she had ever been and had sat huddled on the couch, drinking a beer. Soggy notes scrawled in her own drunken hand covered the coffee table. She'd been writing to Vera Wrede, writing the network, protesting the "Hillbilly Holocaust" thing, apparently. Drunk and angry. She'd written all over the blue airmail envelopes she'd bought for her overseas graduate school applications. Some of them were already addressed and stamped, useless now. A different brand of beer can than the one she'd come home with was there, too, meaning she'd driven again to get more beer. "Oh, man," she said aloud. Her blackouts were getting worse.

She turned on the television, and watched the ongoing coverage of the search and rescue operation and the search for the perpetrators. There was a theory that it was someone from the Middle East, and the Middle Eastern students who attended the local universities were on the news protesting their innocence. They were terrified of being blamed, assaulted, killed. Edie picked up the phone and called Reza's apartment. She knew he was probably at work, but she left him a message. "Hey," she said, her voice hoarse with the first word of the day. "I hope you're safe. I'm sorry about all this—I'm watching the news."

For the rest of the world, those not missing someone, the search for who did it was everything. She knew it was important, but all she could focus on was that Delaney had not slept in her bed. She and Keith had gone down to the bombing site for a yes or no answer, and they had gotten a yes. Yes, Delaney had parked in front of the building and Keith's car was still there. The mute message of the ruined Bronco was deafening.

Edie held the notes close to her face and squinted. She couldn't read her own writing. Just the word BITCH, underlined and in all-caps, was legible. What sort of life was this, where attempting to piece together her lost hours was like retracing the steps of a total stranger?

She stood up, determined to help somehow. She swept everything on the coffee table into the trash, took a shower, and drove to one of the blood donation sites.

The line of people waiting to donate blood snaked around the building like wound dressings, a couple of hundred people deep. Edie stood in line with the others, shuffling forward. People were grim but friendly. After almost an hour in line, she felt a tap on her back. The woman behind her was short and thickset with gray hair pulled into a ponytail.

"Yes?" Edie turned and smiled at her.

The woman stepped very close. Without introduction, she looked fixedly at Edie and said, "My first husband was an alcoholic. He would drink at night and in the morning, he'd shower and eat breakfast put the night behind him, but the thing is, the alcohol was coming out of his pores. I could smell it. He thought people couldn't tell, but everybody could tell." She inclined her head toward Edie until their foreheads almost touched "I don't mean to intrude, but I hate to see you wait in this line all day. They won't take your blood, honey."

Edie stared at the woman, formulating a response, preparing to protest, but her brain was too scrambled to mount its usual defenses. She yanked her arms out of the woman's gentle hold and ran, away from the line, into the parking lot, and into her car, where she sobbed against the steering wheel. She rubbed her forehead back and forth against the steering wheel, crying, making resolutions.

The next day, Timothy McVeigh was all over the news. He had been picked up for a routine traffic violation heading north on I-35 right after the bombing and was in jail in the small town of Perry for firearms violations during the traffic stop. While he was in the backseat of the state trooper's car, he took a business card out of his pocket and left it on the floorboard. It was for a munitions surplus store in Wisconsin. On the back of the card, McVeigh had written, "Will need more TNT—$10 a stick."

Reza was apologetic when Edie walked in to work to find the kitchen crew celebrating. He pulled her into the walk-in. "I know there's no good news for you. I don't mean to seem so happy, it's just I'm glad to have the target off my back."

"I get it."

He pressed his palms together and nodded. "Thank you. It's good they got the bastard. That's going to help with the healing. And I'm so glad he was white—I'm sorry, but . . ."

"I understand. I do. If it had been someone from the Middle East, God knows you wouldn't have been safe. I wonder what this guy's story is. What's his name?"

"Timothy McVeigh."

"Don't you wonder what he thought he was accomplishing?"

News about McVeigh's Desert Storm military background, his white supremacist beliefs, and his involvement with the Patriot Movement started to come out as the search continued. For days afterward, she couldn't reach Keith. Not until a week later, April 27th, did he finally call.

"Where are you?" she asked, cradling the phone under her chin. It was late at night—she had just gotten home from work and was unbuttoning her shirt.

"I dropped all my classes," he said. "I had to get out of town."

"But they haven't found her yet," Edie said. The list of casualties continued to climb, and days had passed since they had found anyone alive, but the search was ongoing. The Murrah Building remained lit up at night, the search moving forward twenty-four hours a day.

"I'm in Colorado."

"Colorado?" Tears sprung to her eyes. He had left the state without saying goodbye to her. She had felt so close to him the night they searched the bomb site for his car, she had imagined he cared about her. Not like she did him, but at least as a friend. That had been all in her head, though. He hadn't even thought of her as he left town.

"My parents have a time share in Breckenridge. I'll be here for a while, Edie." His voice sounded flat and far away.

"But everything's still happening," she said. "That police officer we talked to said she'd call us back. They're still searching for survivors. Your car—"

"It's ruined," he said. "Everything's ruined."

Edie walked into Delaney's bedroom and turned on the light. Canvases lined the wall, and one painting was still on an easel. The bed, a box spring and mattress lying directly on the wood-planked floor, was unmade. A Bud Light bottle and an empty coffee cup sat next to it. An unopened bag of peanuts lay atop a book split open at its spine. *Portrait of an Artist: A Biography of Georgia O'Keeffe.* A digital alarm clock, its green digits glowing, told her it was nearly midnight. "I'm so sorry, Keith. I know you love her." She narrowly avoided referring to Delaney in the past tense. They weren't there yet, not quite.

Edie had been waiting for the moment when Keith discovered that Delaney wasn't faithful to him, hoping that the poor sap would snap out of it then and realize Delaney didn't share his feelings, would go on and find some nice woman commensurate with his capacity for devotion—herself, to be exact—but now she would never tell him the truth. To say something now would be nothing but cruelty, and there had been enough of that visited upon them for a lifetime. It wasn't her place to ring the changes between them, and the truth would come out, anyway. She had given her word, and so she kept quiet and listened to him quietly weeping on the other end of the line.

Finally, she said, "Breckenridge, huh? I bet the mountains are beautiful."

"It's dark right now."

"How long do you think you'll be gone?" she asked.

"I don't know," he said. "Maybe a long time."

"Well, so—" She switched off the light to Delaney's room and closed the door. "Take care of yourself."

"You too, Edie. I'll look you up when I'm in town."

24

KEITH

2015

Keith had been driving a few hours and was near the border between Oklahoma and the Texas Panhandle. He stopped to fill up at one of the big travel centers with multiple bays on two sides, one group for trucks and the other for citizens on the road. It felt very much like a trucker's universe that grudgingly tolerated the visits of other people. After filling his tank he went inside with Ian's dream catcher jammed in a pocket to see what he could find to hang it with from the rearview mirror Also, for the restroom and a cup of crappy coffee for the road, maybe some junk food for dinner.

He passed fried fast food, all the same golden yellow color, leathery hot dogs turning on spits under orange heat lamps, rows of candy and nuts, beef jerky and protein bars. What was whey protein, anyway? They sold ball caps—Oklahoma City Thunder, camo with a deer inside a bullseye, This Is How I Roll with a large cinnamon roll on the front. USBs and headphones, car jacks, motor oil, audiobooks—he spun the rack looking for something he could listen to and found instead action stories with "Vengeance" and "Kill" and "Lethal" in the title, quasi-religious self-help titles featuring "Purpose" and "Overcome" and "Angels." And yes, dream catchers in all sizes and colors, including one the same blue as Ian's with a looped hook he could easily remove and attach to Ian's so the tiny Star Wars icons could swing from his rearview mirror and help the force be with him.

The wide, tiled corridor to the bathroom led on to a shower area for truckers and a "movie theater," a place for truckers to wank and God knows what. All that he had heard about Oklahoma highways being grand central station for sex traffickers was more than believable here. Were there any mute, terrified girls lurking by the fountain drinks, anyone clearly being shuttled from spot to spot? He wanted to save someone! Heroic acts soared across his mindscape,

I will get you out of here, hide in my backseat, I'll handle these guys, I can take you to the authorities, we will notify your parents. It was just a travel center, but he was glad Ian wasn't there, glad Edie wasn't either. Much as she would resist being thought of as a vulnerable person, sometimes she was. Beyond the so-called theater, another door with an opaque glass front bore a sign that said "GAMES." Under the bastardized country twanging from the speakers, he heard the familiar beep and swoosh of a casino, including the unmistakable heraldic measure that sounded from Liberty 7s every few seconds, like gambling had something to do with winning the Revolutionary War. Games? Slots, more like it. He peeked in.

2 5

KEITH

2015

When he came out of the game room—the casino—it was dark. Hours had passed. He was parched and starving. He lurched up the beige-tiled hallway past the restrooms, through the truck stop, busy with dinner-hour stopovers, people lined up at the Subway counter, shifting foot to foot, getting bags of food to go, people sitting in the plastic booths that lined the front windows chewing and staring out across the concrete, their body heat fogging the glass. Children pressed their faces to the counter glass before the line of sandwich ingredients as an exhausted-looking teenager with a pierced septum and clear plastic gloves on his hands putting shredded lettuce on and taking it off a sandwich as a child changed her mind.

Keith moved through the space like a smear across a canvas, like a drunkard lurching outside into the dusk. A strip of gold marked the horizon as the night came over the sky like a closing eyelid. He stumbled to his car. The car roared to life, and he pulled it around to the exit ramp, jumped onto the highway.

West. In the ruins of his life, in the bottom where the air pressure drove his skull against his brain, he drove straight west, his eyes fixed to the vanishing point where his headlights cut the darkness, pushed it back and ate it, and he knew that what he had just done in the gas station casino was out beyond the headlights' reach, in the dark and the cold of the desert. Beyond what he could forgive himself for. Edie, she would be done with him, and Ian—Oh, God. Keith drove without intention, the thought of Delaney alive in New Mexico a remote abstraction that could only matter in his old life, the life he knew before he walked into the gas station casino and tried to win back the money he had lost. He drove without music and passed the state line into Texas.

A little while later, he flew past an exit he recognized. He'd taken it once when he was in graduate school and had been reading about the two battles at Adobe Walls and decided to find the battlefield. That trip had ended with a burger and shake in Borger, Texas, and no sense of where he'd missed his turn. He was surprised he hadn't thought of the old battleground before now.

Adobe Walls had been a stop on the Santa Fe Trail, and the fight was over Native raids on settlers along the trail. Satank, a signer of the Medicine Lodge Treaty, was part of the earlier battle, heading up a Kiowa/Comanche coalition of fighters. At the fight ten years later was Quanah Parker, whom Keith could never think of without remembering reading Parker's biography to Brad Odel's mother.

Now here he was heading on much the same route, bypassing Santa Fe and heading a bit farther north to Ghost Ranch. Trying to matter in this landscape, holding to the importance of little human plans and schemes against the unblinking indifference of geologic time, and vast open space, was difficult. In high population areas like London, human history could seem deep and long, from Stone Age tribes to the Romans to Anne Boleyn to Winston Churchill to David Bowie with all infinity of art and politics crowded in between. What people thought and did mattered a great deal, and evidence of how much it mattered was everywhere from the books you picked up to the buildings and roads all around you, but out here in America's vast middle, all of that was temporary, the eye pulled outward and up to a scale that relegated human activity to impermanent surface action like graffiti scratched on billion-year-old stone.

Still, he was human and the human scale was where he lived, so he blinkered the vastness and kept going. People problems were usually a relief against the dehumanizing scale of historical time, but not today. His self-made mess was too big. Even the plague of earthquakes wrought by the oil companies could seem small against this land and sky, but not the gambling. It was bigger than him, bigger than anything. And it would take everything unless he could put things right.

He took the next exit and doubled back to the exit that would take him to Adobe Walls. The journey was longer and darker than he imagined, through Pampa and Borger to a turn on a wind-cleaned road, passing only one set of headlights along the way, to a historical marker standing alone out in the absolute middle of nowhere. Eventually he got there. The wind blew sand against his skin as he used the flashlight on his phone to read the information on the large granite sign. The sand and the wind were so bad that he grabbed his sunglasses from the dash of his car and put them on in the dark to protect his eyes. Give it long enough and the words on the marker would be sanded off. Longer still, the marker would wear away like the wind-carved wall of a canyon. Why were time and death his business? They had been his preoccupation even before becoming his profession, guilt over the time he spent with history's dead and the easy way he connected with them compared to the living a part of his makeup for as long as he could remember.

He turned slowly, taking in the area and remembering reading at some point that the actual site of the Adobe Walls battles was a little way off from the marker, the location of the marker coming down to a practical question of land ownership or something. That was good, because he could make no sense of this site as a battlefield of choice. There was no cover anywhere, no advantage in any direction. On another day he'd have learned the exact location and spent the day finding it and figuring out the likely positions taken by the combatants in the two historical battles, but not today.

Before he gambled, the day was supposed to have been about Delaney. His favorite dead, the one he thought of most, the only citizen of the world on the other side of the river Styx whom he had loved, whose body he had been inside, whose half sister he had married, was signaling from the land of the living. Before another sunset he could be in her breathing human presence. He quailed at the possibility. Maybe he had gambled to distract himself from thinking about what it would mean if Delaney were alive. Such thoughts could drive a person crazy.

He took out his phone again and snapped a few shots in each direction, the flash illuminating a vaulting sky cut off by a little land at the bottom. He could hear something, maybe a plane overhead, but not much. Out here the sky between the stars was as black as he had ever seen it. He could see the shape of the Milky Way end to end, like a clutch of fish eggs in dark water. He picked out Mars by its redness and the constellations he remembered from Boy Scouts. But there was no moon. The wind blew grit in his nostrils and teeth, and he heard coyotes not too far off. Movement close by caught his ear. Burrowing owls, snakes, prairie dogs? The desert was as full of complex life as any forest once you adjusted. There was no room in him to make that adjustment, though. He closed his eyes and the stars came through the sunglasses and the blood in his lids, like a sound behind a door. No escaping it, no second set of lids to close against the vision brought by the first. No escaping anything. He yelled, only knew it in the moment after, the wind whipping away his voice so fast he didn't hear.

Then something in him let go. He hollered something wild, an apology or a prayer, sound snatched by the wind. More like a surrender. *White flag! The vanquished request quarter, come what may, keep us all safe, do not give me what I deserve, and do not punish the innocent on my account. Whatever the blows that are coming, let them fall on me.*

"Are you okay? Hey there, fella?"

Keith's eyes flew open behind his shades and he sat up. He didn't know what time it was.

"Oh, thank God, I thought you might be dead. What the hell are you doing?"

Keith pushed the shades onto his forehead and looked up at the form of a man crouched on his hams and peering down at Keith like he was a struck deer.

Keith cleared his throat, full of sticky sand, and spat. "Didn't mean to fall asleep."

"You came to see Adobe Walls?" The man's voice was high and airy, like a whistle, pulled earthward by his thick Texas accent. "History buff, are you?"

"That's right." Keith felt grateful to the man for reminding him of the lineaments of his identity. "You ever hear of the Medicine Lodge Treaties? I'm researching Satank."

"Never heard of him." The man reached out a hand and pulled Keith to his feet. "Did he fight here?"

Keith felt lightheaded when he stood up. He bent his knees and planted his palms against his thighs, staring at the ground while he waited for the feeling to pass. "In the first battle."

"Hell, I didn't know there was more than one. Lived out here all my life and never thought much about this place. I guess I always meant to read up on it. You okay?"

"I didn't mean to fall asleep," he said again. Keith extended his hand. "Keith Frayne."

A huge hand gripped his, its calluses scraping his palm. "Tony Box."

"I'm on my way to New Mexico."

"Tonight?"

Keith felt for his phone. "What time is it?"

"Near eleven. I just come back from fixing an outage. Saw your car."

"You're—"

"Yeah, I work for the county electric." He ran a big hand through his thick, coarse-looking hair. Keith couldn't see his face well in the darkness. "My family used to have land out here, but it's all sold, so I work electric."

"Thanks for waking me up," Keith said. "I should get going."

"Hell, I was half scared to death to come up on you, tell you the truth. Wasn't sure what I was about to find. You're okay?"

"I didn't mean to scare you."

"You know, I recorded the Oklahoma City Thunder game Wednesday night, and I was just sitting down to watch it when I got the call about the outage I just fixed. You want to watch it with me, you're welcome. Start out in the morning?"

Keith hadn't thought much about the new NBA team, but he was one of the few people in the city, the state, the whole region, who hadn't. Like Tony intending to educate himself about Adobe Walls one day, Keith had intended to go to a game, check it out and see what all the fanfare was about. "Thank you," he said. "Who'd they play?"

"Timberwolves," Tony said, sounding surprised that Keith didn't know.

Walking to his car with his head down, Keith pulled his keys from his pocket. "Follow you?"

"I'm outside Stinnett," Tony said. "Just south of here."

Keith switched on his headlights and waited for the stout body of his new friend to swing up into his service truck. Under layers of dirt, areas of white paint glinted in the moonlight, and Keith could make out the Hutchinson County electric company logo under the mud.

His phone rang as soon as he turned the sound back on, and with the sound, the weird fugue state he'd enjoyed for the last several hours broke. Edie, worried about him. She'd probably been calling. And he had gambled. He saw his right pointer finger pressing the red button again and again on the Liberty 7s machine in the small, dark room at the gas station, its sticky carpet and the sickly sweet cherry smell of someone's vape smoke, the beeps and dings of the machines. It seemed like a long time ago or something that happened to someone else, a film he'd watched, one of those dreams you have in the morning right before you wake up. She might already know, if she had checked their account. He wrestled the phone from the pocket of his pants. "Hey."

"Are you okay?"

"People keep asking me that."

"What do you mean? Keith, where have you been? I've been calling."

He took a deep breath. "You won't believe this, but—well, I guess you will. You know Adobe Walls? Old battlefield where Satank and Quanah Parker fought? I found it, got out and read the marker—that's about all there is, just a marker. Then I fell asleep."

"At Adobe Walls?"

"Yes," he said, and the bright truth of it felt like a cold drink of water after a long hot walk in the sun. This was a truth he could tell. "I fell asleep at Adobe Walls." Now he would keep on telling the truth. He was on a roll. "This nice guy pulled up, thought I was dead. I guess he saw my car. I'm going to spend the night at his place."

There was a long pause at the end of the line. "Keith, are you okay?"

"You keep asking me that." He wanted to tell her everything, to get her smart, capable energy to work on the new problems he'd made, but that was another thing about gambling. It was lonely. "I'm doing fine."

"Who is this guy? And where are you? Adobe Walls, I have no idea."

"It's in Texas."

"That narrows it down."

"I'd hoped to get at least to Tucumcari tonight, but it didn't happen."

Another long pause. "You got distracted. By an old battlefield."

"Right, I—" How crazy was it to lose focus on finding Delaney? Edie must know him well enough to know only one thing could distract him that completely, and it wasn't western history. She might have checked the account. She might already know.

"Well, great." She was brisk now, like a doubt had been resolved. "What's this guy's name in case he kills you and buries you in his backyard?"

"Tony Box."

"Tony Box. All right."

"How's Ian?"

"He's wondering about ears."

"Ears?"

"Yeah, like if the fleshy part on the outside is their way to funnel sound down into the canal, why aren't they a lot bigger, like giant cones?"

"For looks?"

"I told him they'd get caught by the wind and make people fall over."

"Good answer, Edie."

"It didn't stop him, but it slowed him down for a minute."

They shared a sad laugh, joined in wonder at the ongoing experience of raising Ian.

"I'll call you tomorrow," he said.

The taillights of Tony Box's truck burned ahead of Keith, leading him south and east. He hadn't thought to ask Edie one thing about her day, but he was too weary to phone her back. Besides, nothing much would have happened today on the Landon Energy front. Theron Landon might not tell her a thing until he had already swung into action—that would be typical of him—and, strange as it seemed, it was still Sunday. She and Ian probably went to the park, maybe to the grocery store. They probably read and colored. They might have watched a movie. A normal day. And here he was in a dark Texas night following a complete stranger to his house in the ruins of a life he had destroyed, in the long pause before Edie and Ian felt the blast. Oh, to stop it from reaching them, to make the money back before Edie found out it was missing. He had already lied to Brad about the Landon announcement, a small victory now eclipsed by his gas station wipeout. He cranked up the heater in his car, his fingers so cold he could barely manipulate the controls.

Up ahead, Tony Box's right blinker started to flash, and he slowed down. Keith followed him onto a gravel road for about a quarter mile before he turned again, a left into a dirt driveway before a long, skinny brick house that looked a lot like a trailer that had been encased in a layer of masonry. Tony parked the truck next to the house and climbed out, giving a short wave into the glare of Keith's headlights. Keith pulled behind the truck. He felt cold the instant his car heater stopped. And he was starving. He tried to remember when he'd last eaten.

Inside, Tony switched on a floor lamp next to a couch and motioned for Keith to sit. The dog he had heard was smaller than the encompassing boom it made suggested, a yellow mutt with white feet that he planted against Tony's legs, imploring. "Let me feed this gal, I'll just be a minute."

Keith nodded. He settled into the couch's rust-colored cushions and found himself looking at a car headlight on a shelf behind the television, wires dangling from its back like veins from an eyeball. A movie poster for *Unforgiven* was tacked on the wall in the kitchen, Gene Hackman's determined face seeming to look across the room at the controls to an Xbox 360 controller on the coffee table. White lace curtains hung in the window and a bowl of potpourri sat on the end table next to his elbow, enveloping him in the scent of cinnamon and mulled cider. "Are you married?" Keith asked.

"Was," Tony called from the kitchen. "She moved to town. Amarillo. Said she was going crazy out here."

"I'm sorry," Keith said.

Tony came into the room from the kitchen with a bag of Doritos and a six-pack of beer that he set on the particleboard coffee table in front of the couch. The yellow dog climbed onto the couch and settled next to him. "I've still got Nellie," he said, patting the dog's flank. He switched on the TV. "You ready?"

Keith nodded. He felt stuck in that moment in a nightmare where you're about to die, so you wake up. But he wasn't waking up. He was in the bricked-in trailer of a total stranger who'd appeared out of the dark desert night. If he opened the front door, would he be in the Texas Panhandle or in some shaman's shadowland? He lunged for the Doritos on the coffee table. Maybe his blood sugar was crashing.

Tony pointed the remote control at the set and laid his heavy thumb on the volume button until the game announcer's voice drove back the empty night's silence to the walls of the house. He was lonely, that was clear. They talked more than they watched the game. Keith wondered how long it had been since Tony had a conversation with anyone else as he listened to the man unspool a series of bemused observations about the human condition between handfuls of Doritos. *Why don't people act right? What do you think about UFOs? You think I need a computer? Is it wrong to eat meat?* Given that Keith saw no books around the trailer except a coffee-table glossy on the history of Ford trucks, it was no wonder that Tony's metaphysical needs were so frustrated. The man had nowhere to go with his questions. Keith figured he was ripe for the picking by a local church with big-screen sermons and a bowling team. Until then, the NBA had a lot of needs to meet. On the screen, the bright modernity of the stadium, the positivism of the game, and the relentless commercials came at them like portents from another world. Out here on the Llano Estacado, where Tony's home sat, it still felt barely settled, and the battles at Adobe Walls felt closer in time at that moment than the Nike and iPhone commercials slamming at them from the television. Keith heard yips outside somewhere close. "Are those coyotes?" he asked.

Tony grinned and pushed aside the Doritos bag. "Want to see something?" He strained to his feet and grabbed an orange utility flashlight hanging on a hat rack by the front door. He hit a light switch and the floodlights outside the trailer went dark. The night poured in through the lace curtains on the windows. Smiling like a kid with a secret, he cocked his head toward the door. "Come here. Don't let Nellie out."

Keith followed Tony outside, squeezing through the door to prevent Nellie's escape.

Tony stood a few yards away facing north, his legs braced wide apart. In the dark, the land was only a dark presence Keith could feel rather than see, and the dome of the sky came down around them ablaze with patterns invisible in city skies. Behind them, Nellie barked inside the trailer. Around them, the coyotes howled. "Ready?" Tony asked.

Keith didn't know what he was assenting to, but he said yes, too defeated to ask questions or to object. Tony flipped on the flashlight and held it out in front of him. Slowly, he panned back and forth, shining the light into the sage and scrub that surrounded the trailer. "Oh my God," Keith said.

Tony giggled. "I know."

The beam of the flashlight showed white eyes reflected back at them, dozens of them shining inside the brush. Tony moved the light in a slow 180 degree arc a couple of feet above the ground, from east to west. Coyotes surrounded the trailer, rows of eyes casting the light of the flashlight back. In a hushed voice, Keith said, "They're watching us."

"Yep."

"Will they attack?"

"No," Tony said. "I like to think they're guarding me."

"I don't think Nellie agrees."

"She's just jealous."

Back in the trailer as the Thunder game went into its second quarter, Keith found himself telling Tony about Delaney. The whole story—the marriage proposal, the bombing, his marriage to Edie, the Facebook message. A long story, messy and personal, the kind of thing you only tell someone you'll never see again. He was on his third beer when he said, "So that's why I'm on the way to Abiquiu."

Sitting next to him, Tony never let his gaze leave the television, and he yelled and cheered at the screen, but finally he turned and looked at Keith. "The Murrah bombing," he said.

"Yes," Keith said. Was that all Tony had heard? Just as well.

"Everybody knows there was a second bomber. At least one other person involved, if not more. Everybody knows that."

"It's a popular theory."

"Ain't no theory! You know damned well there's people out there who know the whole story. Who helped McVeigh, and how and why."

"I expect that's true," Keith said.

"You want my opinion, that second bomber is somebody from Elohim City. You know about that place?"

Keith nodded. He had read about the white separatist compound near the Oklahoma/Arkansas line. The article he recalled said they believed white Americans were the true Christians while Jews and everybody else were of the devil. It said they were preparing for armed insurrection. "I'm sure the feds looked into it."

"I don't share your confidence."

"Knowing things doesn't change what happened, that's all I'm saying. When you've lost someone, the grief weighs you down. What that maniac was thinking and who he was involved with is of no interest to me. I'm not a vigilante."

"If I was you, I'd get to the bottom of it."

"That's what I'm doing," Keith said. "I don't need to know anything else but whether she's alive."

"Well, what do you think I'm telling you?"

Keith looked at Tony. "I don't know."

"I never heard anything like this story you told me. This girl—"

"Delaney."

"Delaney. Goes down to the Murrah Building on the morning of the bombing and you never see her again but she ain't among the dead? Don't you see?"

Keith waited. This wasn't going the way he had imagined.

"There was that sketch of another guy, you remember?"

"Terry Nichols?"

"No, at the scene. It was all over the news. Square jaw, ballcap? Then all of a sudden they're saying, whoops, you know what, turns out that was just a guy standing in line behind McVeigh at the Ryder truck rental place, that's all. Innocent bystander. Like, sure. Like, we believe you didn't think of that and check that business's records before you went to the bother of having a sketch artist come in and blasting that picture all over planet Earth. Sure, McVeigh acted all alone."

"That was weird. But they were looking for any kind of answers. Could've been a false lead, like they said."

"No, no, no." Tony shook his head. "You really think McVeigh would've planned all that out and not had a getaway car with a license plate? Course not! That car they caught him in was meant to be left at the scene—a signature. Had those crazy-ass brochures in the passenger seat, no plates, no tags. You kidding me? He didn't plan to drive that car away. His ride didn't show up—that's what I think."

"That theory, yeah. It does seem possible."

"His ride didn't show up. He had to drive the drop car."

"Could be."

"Now, I don't pretend to see the whole picture, but you sure do have my mind churning with this missing piece tonight."

"What missing piece?"

"Her."

"What about her?"

"Did you ever think she might have been the second bomber?" Tony was leaning forward in excitement, one butt-cheek off the couch. "You know, there was a story about a blond-haired woman driving a car behind the Ryder truck McVeigh was in. Lots of people saw her. Some people thought it was a wig, a blond wig. Could've been a man, but it could've been your Delaney. Was she blond? Could be she was down there to pick him up. Maybe she chickened out, I don't know. Then he got pulled over outside Perry and she had to go underground, see? Now think hard, do you remember a tall fellow with light-colored hair and a pointy chin around her place some? Eyes like a weasel. Maybe she told you he was just a friend?"

Keith planted his elbows on his thighs and laughed. He squinted at Tony. "Say that again? You think my ex-girlfriend—who probably died in the Murrah bombing, let's not forget, Occam's razor being what it is—you're saying this woman I've grieved for the last twenty years wasn't a victim of the bombing but was a domestic terrorist? She was in cahoots with Timothy McVeigh?"

Tony gave him a sheepish grin. "Shit, I don't know."

"Male, square jaw, ball cap?"

"Not her?"

"That was pretty good, though. You spun that out of nothing."

Tony pointed at the television. "It's already halftime!"

26

EDIE

2015

Edie unclasped her hands and told June, her assistant, to come in. She took out her earbuds and stopped the guided meditation she'd been listening to at her desk. A panic attack had struck earlier, and she had done what she could to stop it. Focused on her breathing, shut out external stimuli, even shut the blinds to her glass-walled office for as long as she could.

"You probably already know this, but tomorrow morning the Oklahoma Oil and Gas Association is going to put out a statement casting doubt on the Geological Survey's announcement." June stood in front of Edie's desk, her shiny hair curtaining her face as she looked down at her phone and read. "My friend over at OGA says they're going to say there *may* be a link but more research is needed. And that there's no way to prove that stopping wastewater disposal would stop the quakes."

"No way to prove?" Edie laughed. "Stopping would prove it. Let them stop and see if the quakes stop. If they don't, well then—"

June slouched into one hip. "Come on now. Stop making sense, boss."

"So that's it. I can predict how this will go. We're going to huddle behind OGA. No announcement. Do you know what that means, June?" Edie began closing the files on her computer.

"I give up."

"It means I'm leaving for the day."

"Really? It's only, like, noon."

"I have a—" She thought how to describe it. "A family emergency."

"You do?" June stepped back as Edie pulled her purse over her shoulder and came around the desk. "Oh, you really do."

"I really do." Edie ushered her out and turned off the light. "Keep me posted, all right?"

"Sure, of course. Does Mr. Landon know you're leaving?"

"Let him know, will you?"

"Me? I don't think he likes me."

June's look of consternation made Edie smile. "I think I can help with that." They left her office together. Light reflected from the floor-to-ceiling windows onto a black-and-white photograph of a pump jack under lowering clouds. Framed in gold, the photograph was the first thing you saw when the elevator opened, hung above a black leather sofa at the front of the suite.

The photograph's subject was a Landon Energy well site, one of many Landon had personally photographed in stark monochromes, working hard in the darkroom as in life to eliminate the vagaries of shadows. Landon managed somehow to capture in the black-and-white photographs his feeling for the nobility of his calling, the pump jacks looking determined and solitary, both at one with the environment and its centerpiece, like a cowboy on a horse, one of Landon's other favorite images. Edie, on the other hand, thought the pump jack resembled a carrion bird pulling out entrails.

"You see that photograph?" Edie said, pressing the elevator button. "Ask him about it. Then he'll like you."

When the elevator arrived, June waved goodbye and thanked her for the tip. "Flattery," she said. "I should have thought of that."

Edie stepped into the elevator and closed her eyes as the doors closed. She was exhausted. She should stay at work and craft a response acknowledging the likely truth of the OGS findings in case Theron pulled a 180 and she needed to produce a script for the occasion. She should talk to the geologists. She should provide a calm and confident presence, walk the halls and talk about the new opportunities in front of the whole Landon Energy team. At least they weren't a publicly traded company like most of the other O&Gs—they were less vulnerable to market reactions than most of their competition, if far more subject to the idiosyncratic management of their owner, whose fears and misperceptions, unchecked by investors, could drive the company singlehandedly into the ground.

She should stay, but she wouldn't. Since the bombing memorial the previous morning, her tolerance for empty gestures and uncertain outcomes was over. She'd had it. Standing in the cold drizzle at the Oklahoma City National

Memorial, looking around at the faces in the crowd and knowing that a fair amount of them were the family and loved ones of people who had died in the blast, she had felt like an outsider. The strain was intolerable. Twenty years of grief and uncertainty without even the minimal satisfaction of having the loss acknowledged. Enough. Living so long in the UK had allowed her to defer this crisis, but now it was here. She couldn't predict Theron's actions at work or Keith's actions at home, but she could answer, for her life, a much bigger question. Once and for all, no assumptions, no resignation when she hit a brick wall or the trail stopped. She was going to find out whether Delaney was alive or dead.

Edie thought of the route she had just downloaded. Distance from her home address on Northwest Seventeenth Street in Oklahoma City to Abiquiu, New Mexico: 548 miles. Eight hours and forty-five minutes there and back. She had to go. She'd be fine, and having Ian with her would keep her steady and focused. She called Keith as she walked to her car. "Who am I kidding?" she said, leaving a message. "Ian and I are headed your way. Call and let me know where you're staying tonight. See you there."

"How would you like to see a big rattlesnake?" Edie glanced back at Ian in the rearview mirror, squinting against the sun that poured through the back window. Her son was investigating the crack between the seats, sliding the flat of his hand into the space and pushing up treasures: a marble, the bright yellow arm of some dismembered action figure, half a dozen of the ubiquitous Goldfish that were his carb of choice and which stank up the car with the smell of processed cheese. What was the word for seeing smells and sounds? Synesthesia. She didn't usually have this gift, but the Goldfish smell was vividly orange. He was picking one up.

"Ian, don't eat that."

He glanced up, met her eyes in the mirror, then set the cracker down on the seat like a gunslinger lowering his weapon. "A real rattlesnake?"

"Big and real. In about four hours we'll be in Amarillo—that's halfway to where we're going. There's this place in Amarillo called the Big Texan. They've got billboards all up and down I-40, coast to coast—we'll see one soon. You get a free meal if you eat a steak that's about as big as you are."

"Do I have to do that?"

"No, no. The rattlesnake's in a big glass case in the gift shop."

"Does the rattlesnake ever get to go outside?"

"I don't think so, baby. It's not very nice, keeping her like that, is it?"

"They should let it go."

If Edie had to guess, she'd say that the rattlesnake frequently died and was replaced from the thriving population of diamondbacks to be found in the high desert region around Amarillo, but who could say? "You can tell them that."

They were still in Oklahoma City, headed due west on I-40 with the morning sun behind them. It would be a long day on the road. Ultimately, they'd stay wherever Keith was, but, knowing he probably wouldn't have, she made a reservation at a Rodeway Inn in nearby Española. All she could find in Abiquiu was a bed and breakfast with no vacancies, so she had made the online reservation, less because she was afraid there would be no hotel rooms to be had than to connect her in some real-world way to the journey she was about to make. With a bed and a shower to mark the journey's end, the road trip felt more real. She even remembered to pack all of their swimsuits. That night they'd be splashing around in the chlorinated water, their voices bouncing off the walls of the enclosed pool room, lights from cars passing by on the rural highway outside, maybe one of them carrying Delaney from her home to the nearest grocery store to pick up food for breakfast. The idea of her sister doing quotidian things hadn't entered Edie's mind before then—she had been too busy wondering whether Delaney could really be alive. But as she considered the impossible possibility, all the questions she'd never asked came flooding in. Did Delaney have a family? Kids? Was she married? What did she do for a living? She had wanted to be an artist, a painter. Was she? When Edie had told Kayli where she was going, her sponsor had surprised her by knowing the place. "It's up the road from Ghost Ranch."

"Ghost Ranch?" Edie said. She'd heard of it.

"I did a yoga retreat there a few years ago. It's way the hell out there, Edie—get your car checked before you go and call me, will ya?"

Edie had promised that she would. The dissonance between believing—no, knowing—Delaney was dead for twenty years and trying to imagine her living now opened a chasm in Edie's consciousness that she couldn't leap. Every few minutes she'd hit the possibility like a horseback rider at a gallop pulling hard on the reins just before tumbling down a canyon. Part of the problem was that she knew it was probably untrue. Delaney, alive. It was ludicrous. The very idea! Delaney would have let them know. She would never have left.

Edie breathed and tried to confine her thoughts to the present moment. That was the ideal, wasn't it? The heart of most spiritual practices, the ability to keep the mind from reaching to the future or past. She felt the slick leather of the steering wheel beneath her fingers, felt the air blowing from the dash, smelled the orange cardboard smell of Ian's Goldfish crackers, heard the swoosh and rumble of the road. This was how she had learned to ground herself. Anxiety is fear of the future, Edie. So stay in the present.

The day had started chilly and overcast, with a frost on the lawn that made her worry for her daffodils. Now, however, the sun flooded the plains like a glass of light spilled across a table as the morning rush-hour traffic clogged the city's major arteries and Edie made her way out of the mix to the city's westward edge. The absence of this big sky had never stopped bothering her or Keith during their years in a city where the sky was segmented space above your head between buildings. In this part of the world, the sky was better than fifty percent of your view, accustoming the eyes and the spirit to vast vertical reaches. To look at the sky was like looking into a clear sea through its depths and levels, the clouds that ran by fast, just above her, like minnows in shallow water, with cottony monoliths the size of mountains stretching beyond them, and the vast cloudless deep above where planes flew like deep-sea creatures, invisible but for the sun glinting off their wings.

She was in the fast lane, determined to clear the metro area and get out onto the long stretch between Oklahoma City and Amarillo. Keith had mentioned that he'd sent a message to whoever had friended him on Facebook under Delaney's name. She'd awoken that morning wondering if there had been a response. Before Ian was up, she had gone into Keith's study, flipping on the lights in the dark room—he never opened his blinds—and stepping around his boxes of unpacked books. She knew all his passwords—their wedding date or Ian's birthday, usually. In the year since his last, fingers crossed, gambling fiasco in the south of England, he sometimes used that date to mark the new leaf he had turned over. March 26th, 2014. She tried it first—32614LastBet. That wasn't it, but Ian's birthday worked. Once on Facebook, she went to Keith's home page, which featured a picture of the three of them grinning into the wind on the Millennium Bridge in London, then to his messages.

Sure enough. A new message to a new friend, sent Friday morning. *Who is this?* The user icon at the bottom of the message that appeared when the recipient had read a message wasn't there—no one had opened the message yet, although Edie knew that she could frequently read enough of a message to get its meaning without needing to open it when it flashed across her phone. A short message like this could've been read without the recipient ever needing to indicate having read it. Keith sent a follow-up message on Friday night, another in the middle of the day on Saturday, one Sunday morning.

Who is this?

This isn't funny.

Leave us alone. My sister-in-law is dead.

Edie warmed at the way he had referred to Delaney not as his ex-girlfriend but as his sister-in-law, routing their relationship through his marriage to Edie and not through their past connection. A semi in the slow lane had been running next to her for a few miles, keeping her locked in the fast lane with another truck behind her ready to run her off the road. When the semi on her right finally got over, she saw, up ahead maybe a quarter mile, the stark lines of a wooden cross, canted forward at 45 degrees, leaned against the green reflective surface of an exit sign. Below it, just a mass at first, the body of a man sitting cross-legged came into view and became more distinct the closer she got. Elbows on his knees, sandy hair. August? Oh, God. It was August. What was he doing? He should still have been in the hospital. "Oh, for shitssake. Hang on, Ian, we need to make a stop."

She made a fast lane change and pulled her SUV off the road a few dozen yards before where August sat. She engaged the parking brake and turned around in her seat. "Ian, you stay here, okay? Do not get out. Understand?"

Ian nodded.

"We may have to give somebody a ride."

She opened her door as little as possible and slid out, holding the door against the wind and the whoosh of traffic only feet from where she stood. Her eyes to the ground as she trudged up the road's shoulder, she kicked gravel painted yellow from the last paint touchup to the road lines. August didn't look up. "Hey, August?"

His bangs were hanging in his eyes. He swept them back with one hand and peered up at her. He didn't even seem curious. Profound resignation or maybe the exhaustion of illness showed on his face. But when he recognized her, he straightened his back and widened his eyes.

She said, "It's windy out here."

"Gracious, Edie. This is a surprise." He took off into a hacking fit that lasted nearly a minute.

"I thought you were at the hospital."

"I was, but I felt better this morning. I got to make my quota for the month."

"Quota?"

He gestured toward the cross behind him.

Since he hadn't stood, she crouched down to talk to him. Glancing back to the vehicle, she saw Ian's small head in the space between the seats. Traffic roared by them. "How does that work—monthly, weekly?"

"Monthly. If I don't set goals it's easy to put it off."

"Would you like a ride home? You should be resting. Those EMTs thought you might have pneumonia."

"I think they're right." August smiled sheepishly at her, admitting a secret.

"Well, for God's sake, August, then I'm going to insist. Come with me."

"What about my cross?"

She thought about it. "Tell you what, I'll call Kayli, ask if she knows anybody who can pick it up."

"The cross is better than ten feet—I don't know if—"

"August." Edie felt herself losing her temper as a semi barreled by and blasted grit into her eyes and mouth. She could see that Ian had climbed into the front seat of the Range Rover and was watching her, hands on the dash. He would be out soon. "Your cross will be fine. Lay it down in the grass—nobody will even know it's there. Come on, I'll help you."

He pushed himself up to stand. Each gust of wind from the traffic swayed him like a weed. He pulled up the collar of his big tan hunting jacket and sank his head into it like a turtle. He had wrapped its arms with reflective tape that stiffened the sleeves like armor. Edie made to help him lift the cross from off the sign and lay it down, but she stepped back when she saw she was in the way. He dropped the cross with a thud into the tall winter-dead grasses on the side of the road just starting to green up at their base. Only someone walking right over it would know it was there. August glanced back once at the cross and walked with Edie to her SUV.

27

EDIE

2015

When Keith finally called back, she was headed back into Oklahoma City to take August home. Keith's voice coming through the speakers had the strangled sound it got when he was freaking out about something, but all he would say was that he'd be in Abiquiu in a few hours. He could've been in Monte Carlo losing their house for all she knew. There was something he wasn't telling her, and whatever it was, he was terrified. "I'm in the middle of something," she said, glancing at August. He was studying his fingernails, using the long, sharp nails of one finger to scrape the dirt from under the nails of the other hand and wiping the dirt on his jeans. "Call me later."

"August, is this the fastest way?" She pointed at the Agnew exit. She had tried to talk August into letting her return him to the hospital or at least take him to the home of someone who could take care of him. It seemed dangerous for him to be alone. He didn't seem to understand how sick he was, kept mentioning cough drops. He seemed like the kind of person who could just drift away and not be found for a week. Yet the idea of going to his abode frightened Edie. She had texted Kayli—*August P.'s a good guy, right? Safe?* Kayli shot back—*He's a good one.* But what would the house of a good one look like? Could this man change sheets or wash dishes? Could he buy food or toilet paper or perform any of the tasks adults did to keep themselves together? She would not go inside, that was all. She wouldn't, Ian wouldn't. She'd drop August off and wish him well. Who was this guy, anyway? She knew almost nothing about him. He began to cough. "Are you okay?"

He waved a hand, body hunched in the paroxysms of coughing. "Left," he said, his voice raspy with phlegm. "Next left."

His house was on a street next to an overpass, the sort of place that, except for the concrete barrier wall that stretched along the opposite side of the street and the eight-lane highway on the other side of it, looked like the vestige of a preurban landscape, maybe even Land Run lots from the initial opening of the territory, with big spaces between the tiny shacks. She drove her Range Rover up the street past three other shacks, each with chicken wire for fencing, dogs, lots of dogs, a donkey, some chickens, old tires, car parts, and rusted-out cars, none of a more recent make than the mid-1980s, before she got to the one to which August directed her. Her Range Rover, sleek and huge and high-tech, cost more than his house, no question. Like a visitor from the future, she pulled into his driveway, more of a mud track where the grudgingly paved road petered out.

August's house was a shotgun shack in the true sense of the term, a narrow rectangle you could shoot a bullet through the front door of and it would come out the back. Its wood planks were unpainted and had been for so long she wasn't sure she could tell what color it had ever been. Someone had installed venetian blinds at some point, but these hung from the front windows crooked, their sides crushed in fan shapes that let the world in, probably by a big dog trying to get at something on the other side of the window. A slanted porch extended briefly with concrete steps leading up to it. In front of a stack of what looked like sodden wallpaper rolls, a white plastic lawn chair sat. There was a person in it. "Who's that?" Edie said.

The person stood up, a man, bearded chin thrust out, belligerent pose at the sight of the shiny silver SUV in the driveway. He wore filthy jeans and a black T-shirt with some sort of slasher lettering, a chainsaw, and an evil clown face, the logo for either a heavy metal band or a horror movie. Tattoos, dark and indistinct, crowded his arm, and greasy hair dangled above his shoulders. In one hand he held a shotgun.

August expelled a sound of disappointment.

Edie hit the lock button, and all four door locks slammed down with a uniform shunt. "August, who is that?"

"That's just Sam."

"Sam?" When August continued to stare straight ahead, she said, "Who is Sam?"

Dread rolled off August, and it was easy to see he did not want to get out. "Dammit!" She gestured at Ian sleeping in the backseat, as if his presence would galvanize August to clarity.

The man—Sam—descended the concrete steps of the porch with the shotgun hanging by his side. Ian was awake now, wanting to know what they were doing, who's that man, are we there yet.

"Just dropping August off at his house, baby."

"I met him at the midnight meeting," August said. "He needed a place to stay. When he's sober, he's right nice."

"I don't think he's sober," Edie said.

"No, ma'am, I don't believe he is."

"Drunk guy with a gun. Thanks a lot, August."

"That thing ain't loaded."

"How do you know?"

Sam had spotted August inside the vehicle. He was only about ten feet from the vehicle now, and Edie could see his face. Gin blossoms across mottled cheeks and head-banger hair. He was wasted, no question, struggling to make sense of August P. in a high-end SUV with an attractive woman, searching for a way to make this unexpected occurrence work for him. He squinted and stepped closer, running a hand along the front fender. "Hey, Forrest!" He tapped on August's window. "This sure is a big ol' box of chocolates, Forrest!"

"Forrest?" she hissed.

Ian made an indignant sound. "He said 'forest'! There aren't even any trees in here at all."

"That's his nickname for me," August said. "I think it's from a movie."

"Asshole. Sorry, Ian." She put the SUV in reverse and whipped it out of the driveway, spinning the steering wheel as she turned around at the top of the street. "If you want to get out, now's the time, August. I wouldn't want to leave that guy alone in my house—"

August looked at his hands. "He won't hurt nothing."

Through the rearview mirror she saw Sam standing at the end of the yard with the shotgun dangling from one hand, for all the world like a pioneer watching a spaceship fly off.

"Well, come on, then." The adrenaline from the encounter coursed through Edie's body as the threat receded. She fought a strong urge to stop the car and make August get out. Instead she turned onto a main road and they were back in modern generica. She saw a Starbucks at the end of the block and put on her blinker. The tremor of an earthquake came up from the wheels of the car. She had noticed that they weren't as detectable to passengers in a moving vehicle. August and Ian didn't seem to feel it, but she got it through her hands on the steering wheel. "So, listen. I'm headed out of state today and it's going to be a long drive. I really need to get going. Where can I drop you?"

"I'm sorry. I'm sorry, ma'am, I didn't mean to be a bother."

She relented a little. "I'm the one who made you come with me, remember?"

"I'm sorry."

"Could you call your sponsor? Where does he live?"

He shook his head. "He's on a cruise. Him and his wife."

"Do you have any family?"

August commenced a coughing fit that lasted while Edie pulled behind two other cars in the Starbucks drive-thru and promised Ian a chocolate milk. She watched August cough like a tubercular in some pre–World War I sanatorium and half expected blood spatter on her dash. She opened the console and found a packet of tissues that she handed to him.

Finally, he said, "Got a sister."

"Okay, then. Where does she live?"

"She's out in Erick."

"Where the hell is that?"

"Off the highway. Last town in Oklahoma."

"Which highway? Which direction?"

"West. I-40."

"That's where we're headed. You want room for cream in your coffee?"

"Just black. Thank you."

"I'm happy to give you a lift, but are you sure that's where you want to go? Way to the edge of the state? You sure you want to leave that guy in your house?"

"It seems right, me coming with you, and I appreciate the ride. Sam will clear off before long."

"Okay, then." She scooted up in her seat. Whatever else happened, at least she would be leaving August better than she found him.

28

ROBERT

2015

Is there a stronger drug than the feeling of being in on a secret? Robert squinted at his computer screen, pulled off his reading glasses, and wiped the frames against his uniform. His office chair squeaked when he moved. The noise startled the dog, who rose and bumped his head against the bottom of the desk. "You okay, buddy?" He heard his wife and daughter and granddaughters laughing in the kitchen. A lawn mower revved to life a couple of houses down in the suburban neighborhood he and his wife had moved into when they were first married, a starter home that, in another ten or twelve years, would be a retirement home. It had been all of a piece and so fast, his adult life.

He leaned across his desk to draw the blinds against the sun, having withdrawn into his cave in the lull after he got off work and before pot roast with the girls. "Women!" as they correct in one voice again and again, the timbre of their voices so alike he couldn't always tell them apart on the phone.

He checked the usual sites, looking for responses to his post about Monsanto, a new interest, but the only comment called him a nut, the usual fear response of people afraid to know the truth. He wasn't afraid. In fact, he craved that dissonance, those moments when the official story simply does not satisfy an inquiring mind.

Two years after the bombing of the Murrah Federal Building, he had gotten his first personal computer and subscribed to America Online. He'd turned it on and was astounded when the actor that played Q on *Star Trek Next Generation* appeared on the screen to take him through the computer's features. When Q's tutorial ended, he sat bemused before the computer's new glow for a long second, thinking about what to do. Back then, he thought of the computer as a big electronic encyclopedia—that was how the salesman at Best Buy had described it to him—so he thought about what he might like to know. He leaned forward and typed in "Oklahoma City bombing second bomber." And that was it, the keystrokes that set the course of his ensuing years' private moments as he went down the rabbit hole of chat rooms and research dedicated to the question of who the second bomber of the Murrah Federal Building was, how many people helped, how many people knew, and why it was all shut down as they built the case against McVeigh. McVeigh. That squirrelly shit the lone plotter, lone terrorist? The only other people convicted, Terry Nichols and Michael Fortier, were but the tip of the coconspirator iceberg.

Robert's thirst to know what really happened had been part of him long before the Alfred P. Murrah Federal Building blew up. The Kennedy assassination was one of his earliest memories, and he dated this inexorable tropism to then, to the day he dashed across the dead grass of a November lawn, the crunch of morning frost beneath his shoes, and into the world of death. His mother had been watching him from a picnic bench on their back porch, smiling as he ran toward her. Then, just as she was about to sweep him up in a hug, his mother shot off the bench and covered her face with her hands. The transistor radio next to her intoned the news, an ominous buzz that they stared at as if it were visible on the air above the yellow lawn.

Sometimes he'd be doing some ordinary thing—taking a left at an intersection, turning off the light before bed, brushing his teeth—and he'd think *the second bomber is somewhere right now brushing his teeth, too. The second bomber drives around and takes left turns. Somewhere, he lives in a house and turns the lights off at night. He knows who he is and what he did, and so do other people. Other people know.* Other people were involved in ways Robert still didn't guess at. This thought kept him clicking, searching, reading. He wanted to know the secret. *A* secret, anyway. There were many secrets, not one big one, and knowing even one of them would be satisfying.

His fingers hovered above the keyboard. There had been nothing new about the Oklahoma City bombing in a long time, and now that there was a memorial and a museum, the narrative of the event seemed set in stone. Few new posts. No new theories to argue with or sightings to dispute or get excited about. Nothing. He left the site, went to an auto parts website instead, and ordered a new drive shaft for the old truck in his driveway he would soon give to his eldest granddaughter.

His father had hated Kennedy—ostensibly because Kennedy was Catholic, but that wasn't the real reason. What was the real reason? Another secret motive, another unanswered question. People don't like people about half the time, so maybe it wasn't so much a mystery as a statistical likelihood. His parents were Argentine immigrants who'd overthrown their Catholicism along with Perón. His father's virulent anti-Catholicism had the fervor of the new convert, Robert saw that now. But at the time, it was a circumstance that kicked off a chain of thoughts that led Robert to where he was now, in the back room of his house behind piles of folders and books, facing a computer screen in the dark, wondering if this would be the day he would find the truth.

His father had come home drunk and jolly the night Kennedy was shot. His face was red, and he leaned against the kitchen counter like he was on roller skates. "I don't know who got that *cabrón*, but I'd like to buy him a drink. Hell, a bottle." From under the kitchen table, where Robert pushed a tiny blue Impala with metal wheels, he had watched his father. Watched his mother. Standing in front of the kitchen sink, rubbing her top lip and eyeing her husband with a look Robert would later recognize as disgust. Into the space between his parents' reactions to the Kennedy assassination went the boy's imagination behind the wheel of a finned 1960 Chevy Impala, looking for the truth. How could two people he loved have such diametrically opposed reactions to the same event? Was there one truth?

Not on the Internet. He wondered sometimes what it would have been like if the Oklahoma City bombing had happened in the age of blogs, chats, the dark web. It would have been a very different story, and one that the prosecution wouldn't have been able to abridge so successfully. If Robert ever started to doubt the existence of John Doe #2 and a fleet of other conspirators behind him, the doubts were banished by the mosquito-like surge of trolls who showed up when a new book or video appeared online laying out the by-now-pretty-well-documented case for the involvement of other members of the militia movement. Their full-throated disavowal, their mockery, their misdirection, all showed Robert one thing, and that was how badly they wanted to discredit the idea and their eagerness to keep eyes off the pursuit of that notion. Which was why he kept going. Going at what? He wasn't an investigator. He was a guy at his computer, a guy with an itch. By now much was known—over twenty-five eyewitnesses the morning of the bombing saw McVeigh with a few other people—but those people were still out there unidentified, and that was what kept Robert hooked.

The interior world of his search had veered into dangerous spaces, shown him menace, what he'd go so far as to call evil, more than once. He'd been felt out by people assessing his loyalties, wondering if his interest in the bombing meant an interest in bombing in general, as in, *would you like to?* Was he in the Christian Identity Movement, was he Aryan Nation, Patriot Movement, did he catch on to *Turner Diary* references, did he know the name of the prophet who killed the mixed-race couple in the Bible and what invoking his name cued? Winks, coded language, like fraternities, but so much darker. He was a member of none of those groups. He didn't want to join McVeigh's hidden friends, he wanted to find them. What would he do, he wondered, if he ever found one?

What about the theory that a handful of uninformed people had been stationed around the downtown area to give McVeigh the needed ride, all given different stories about who they were picking up and why? Wouldn't those folks have figured out what they were being used for? What if one of them lived next door, what if he saw them every day? He wasn't even sure how he'd tell anymore. Was anyone else still looking? After 9/11, the country moved on, fixated on terrorism from the Middle East, and forgot about these characters, who were holed up, scot-free, focused. Couldn't other people feel it building? The antigovernment sentiments, the abandonment of truth, the disappearing middle ground, the racism, the sexism, the hatred, the hatred, the hatred.

"Change clothes," his wife said. She was leaning in the doorway watching him. He looked down and realized he was still wearing his uniform. "And shower. Dinner in ten minutes. Rayla and the kids can't stay long."

He tilted his head and grinned at her around the edge of the computer. "Just when I almost had it." A running joke. *Someday,* he tells her, *I will find out something—something real—and on that day I will turn off my computer and come out of my office and I will watch a whole evening of cop shows with you and I will rub your back.*

Good thing my back doesn't hurt, she'd say. She had been so patient with him. How could he explain? He'd served in two wars, saved lives every day, yet somehow this had been his crucible. Accomplished in a chair, in a dark room, in silence, yes, but it had been real, the path he took and the ways it tested him. He had learned about himself over the years. That he was full of fear and anger. Irritated by illogic. He preferred flight to fight—closing his browser when a search got him noticed—but if he had to fight, he would. He took orders well but was not a follower. He was in some ways a good man, better than he once would have thought. He recoiled from violence and words of violence, he wasn't vain or tempted by glory, he wasn't lonely and tempted by acceptance and camaraderie, he wasn't a racist and comforted by assurances of superiority. When the Christian Identity Movement noticed him on the sites and opened a crack in the door of their organization, he melted away, *no thank you, man. Not for me.* The only thing that tempted him was the need to know the end of the story. People out there knew what he wanted to know, and that carrot dangled before his eyes kept him trudging forward down the path.

He heard small feet running down the hall, and his youngest granddaughter appeared in the doorway, hands on hips. "Papa, it's dinner time!"

"Ah, my goodness! Already? I'm coming," he said. He put his computer to sleep and stood up. "Oh, but Gina, you have to help me! I don't know the way!" He hobbled in mock-woundedness across the room, and she took his hand.

29

KEITH

2015

Here was Abiquiu, a town with more vowels than citizens, by the look of it. Gorgeous country. Sixty-three hundred and some feet above sea level according to the sign he had passed on Highway 84. The yellow mountains must have reached to ten thousand feet. Thank God his phone had lost its signal a few miles back—it stopped Brad Odel's calls and long messages that Keith hadn't had the guts to listen to yet, but it meant he was without GPS guidance. Still, he knew the small gas station on the right had to be his destination. It was one of the few structures in the tiny village. This was where one of the only other friends on the Delaney Travis Facebook page worked. Anna Hernandez, manager. He put on his blinker.

Keith had never been this far north in New Mexico. Gravel crunched under his tires as he pulled into the parking lot. Inside, he could see a Black man with a full, gray beard in a green flannel shirt moving around behind the counter. Keith reached into the backseat and grabbed his coat. It was cold up here in the mountains, the air thin and bright as metal.

The store was surprisingly busy for a Monday morning. Hiking supplies lined one wall, and two teenaged boys in Gore-Tex jackets looked over the ropes and carabiners. Three younger kids were peering into a glass case, ordering scones from the man behind the counter. He glanced up at Keith and smiled. When he had wrapped the scones and taken the kids' money, he turned to Keith. "Help you?"

"Is there an Anna Hernandez working here?"

"Uh, yeah. I'm Bill." He extended his hand over the counter. He wore silver Navajo-style rings on most of his fingers. "Her husband. What're you selling?"

"I'm looking for a woman named Delaney Travis. It's a long story, but—"

"Anna's more social than I am. She's got all kinds of friends I don't know."

"Will she be in? I'd sure like to talk to her."

"Normally I could just give her a call, tell her to come down and speak with you, but I'm sorry to say she's on a hike today. Up around the Continental Divide with our daughter and a couple of her friends."

"The luck!" Keith palmed the back of his neck and stood lost in thought. "I drove from Oklahoma City."

"To talk to Anna?" Bill chuckled. "You ever hear of the telephone? Not a cell phone, you know—not up here. But we've got a landline. Number's listed on the website. We have a website."

"I'm looking for Delaney Travis and the trail led me here. Anna's one of her only friends on Facebook."

"This lady run out on you or what?"

"No, she—yeah. Maybe so. But—well, you don't want to hear this."

Bill turned his back and was dumping a used coffee filter into the trash. Over his shoulder he said, "Who's the other one?"

"Other one?"

"You said she had one other friend on Facebook."

"Oh! Kennedy Stein. Her profile says she works at Ghost Ranch."

Bill poured water through the top of the coffeemaker and turned back to Keith. He drummed the countertop with his fingertips. "She does."

"You know her?"

"She comes here on her way to work most mornings. Stops for gas and coffee. Never can get her to buy anything to eat. I think she lives in Española."

"She works at Ghost Ranch?"

"Like I said."

"Did you happen to see her this morning?"

Bill nodded. "She comes early, right when we open."

"All right. I'll take a large coffee and a scone. How far to Ghost Ranch?"

Bill tipped his head to the west. "Twenty minutes?"

30

AUGUST P.

2015

"What's your story, August?"

We'd been on the road awhile, long gone from Oklahoma City, and the day was getting on. I'm not used to being around children, so I was having a high old time with Ian. That little fellow was funny as all get-out, and I was making him laugh without even meaning to. Edie was smiling, so I knew she meant the question in the way of just making conversation, not that she wanted to hear the nitty-gritty. I'm not the best judge, though, of what's nitty-gritty and what's polite and I only have one story so that's the one I told. I'd gotten to third grade in my story when she interrupted me. Maybe I shouldn't have started with when I was born. Maybe that's not what she was after. I was in the middle of a sentence when she said, "What do you have to feel so guilty about?"

"Now, why do you think I feel guilty?" She was like a mind reader or something.

She laughed. "Seriously? You lug a cross up and down the highways every day. Come on. What are you trying to make up for?"

I was surprised she would come right out and ask me like that, but I had a good vibe about her and an even better one about little Ian, so I told her about Elohim City, living there and meeting McVeigh. About the cicada shells and what his T-shirt said. I expected she'd freak out, but she got quiet and squinted her eyes and after a while she said, "It's not your fault your parents chose to live like that. Why do you feel guilty?"

"Because I am."

"You don't think you could've stopped him, do you?"

"Nothing like that," I said. It was something else. Something I never told anyone.

"Then what?"

"You can know in your heart that you've done wrong even if no one ever finds you out."

She nodded like she understood. "Maybe you thought he was cool?"

I nodded. "He was an older guy."

"Right, I bet you kind of looked up to him." She was telling my story to me.

"I was scared of him," I said. "But we talked about cars and the army."

"I see."

"But when the bombing happened in Oklahoma City and I saw it on TV? When I saw him—"

She laid a hand on my arm. "You must've been like, hey, I know that guy!" She tapped my arm with her fingernails. "That was it, right? You felt something close to pride because someone you knew was on TV for a second before you remembered *why* he was on TV. And then so ashamed. Oh, you must have felt so ashamed, and I bet that pride was nothing more than a fraction of a second."

I just looked at her. That was part of it, just how she said it. I felt something so heavy come off me it about made me gasp. I didn't tell her how after I saw him on TV, I stood up and went to my room. I got *The Turner Diaries* out of my sock drawer and I run it down to the dumpster and hurled it in. My feeling then was relief. All those innocent people dead, and there I was feeling relief because I could see ol' Tim wouldn't be coming around to quiz me about that book. I was free of that bad book. Now if that ain't selfishness. Edie's kindness made me want to tell her about it, and even to tell her the rest, but I can never tell that part. I looked out the window at the fields rolling by. Every so often a ridge rose up out of the grasses and showed the red dirt. I wondered how far down the red went.

"You poor guy," she said. "Let that shit go, you hear me?"

I grinned at her. She grinned back.

"Is that when your drinking started?" she asked.

I nodded. "Drinking, drugs. I didn't always used to be like this."

"Like what?"

"I always had troubles, but I was closer to regular. After I went into the army—they can drink to beat the band, those soldiers can. I got hold of some drugs. In Germany."

"I see," she said. "LSD?"

"I reckon."

"Did a number on you, huh? I'm lucky that never happened to me. It was mostly straight alcohol but once I was drunk, I'd take anything anyone put in front of me. My sister—the one I told you about? She hated that about me."

"The one you lost."

"That's the one."

"For me, the drugs scrambled things but they didn't get rid of the stuff I wanted gone."

"I can't see that you did anything wrong. You need to let yourself off the hook. It's like you're carrying around a resentment towards yourself."

I smiled at her and told her I'd try. I felt tapping on my shoulder. Tap, tap, tap. Turned around and saw little Ian peering up at me, burning with a question. His booster seat raised him a bit higher, high enough he could see out the window, but he was still so little. "Hey, August! What if your leg was an old hollow log?"

I cupped my chin. "Just one leg?"

He thought about that, said yeah.

"You know, I guess you could have foxes living in it. Or raccoons."

"Foxes!" he said. His entire little body wiggled and moved. He was seeing what I said, little foxes in an old hollow log that was your leg. Children! Nothing stopped him from the vision of what that would be like. Then his face fell. "Would you have to let them out sometimes?"

"I suppose you would. Maybe there's a hole in the log."

"But then you'd have a hole in your leg." He shook his head, grimaced. He could see it would never work. Just like that, he kicked my idea to the curb. "Or you'd have dead foxes in your leg because they would starve."

This was a tough problem to get around and I told him as much. His mom noticed we were in a hard spot. "Ian?" she said, interrupting him. "How about a snack? I could use a bathroom, too. How about you guys?"

"A snack?" Ian saw stars! He started naming off junk food he wanted to try and a drink with the word "Monster" in the title. He was hot to shop around, see what the place had to offer by way of refrigerator magnets with animals on them and stuffed animals, maybe toy cars and trucks. Did Edie think they'd have Legos? I was saved from having to come up with a way to get those foxes out of the leg that was a hollow log! Thank the Lord for small favors. I could see he thought the rules he usually lived by didn't apply today. I guess getting a kid out of school for an unplanned road trip will do that. One of those giant gas stations, half for truckers, half for everybody else, was up ahead. Edie put on her blinker.

31

EDIE

2015

"Come with me," Edie said. She placed her hands on his shoulders.

"I'm not a girl."

She felt Ian stiffen. He crossed his arms over his chest and stuck out his chin.

"I know that, Ian, but we have to go to the bathroom."

"I'm a boy."

They were standing in the travel center next to a rack of U-shaped neck pillows.

People milled through the store, only their heads visible above the rows of shelves and stands of products. Edie wouldn't have thought there were this many humans for fifty miles out here in the empty plains, but here they were, concentrated like bugs around a light. She had noticed this phenomenon before when she ran into people she'd seen fueling up in Oklahoma City hundreds of miles later, stopping at the same points along the highway she did. Two or three times she was practically old friends with these fellow travelers by the time their paths diverged a thousand miles from home.

"Sweetie, do you want to be out here by yourself?"

Ian began to cry. She could tell he was afraid to be left alone but wouldn't say so. It had been a while since she had taken him into the restroom with her, and clearly those days were over. He had lately started to be aware of things he had been too young for just weeks before, to tell her not to treat him like a baby. Usually Keith was with them and could handle the restroom visit, but he wasn't here and there was no way she could leave Ian unsupervised.

"How about I guard the stall so no girls see you? We can have a password. My sister used to say the password was always 'Swordfish.'"

She thought she had him—"Swordfish" intrigued him, she could see him mulling it. "It's always 'Swordfish'? Why?"

"It came from this Marx Brothers movie she liked."

"There can't be any other password ever?"

"It doesn't always have to be 'Swordfish,' I guess. You can have another password if you want. Whatever word you want."

He seemed about to capitulate, but only for a second. "I don't want to go in there!"

"Hang on," she said. She pulled him by the hand to the other side of the coolers at the back, past rows and rows of beers and sodas to the men's restroom door at the other side next to a sign with an arrow that pointed to "Men's Showers." Two other men exited the restroom before August, who pushed through the door wiping his hands on the sleeves of his coat, an abstracted expression on his face. He smiled down at Ian when he saw him. "I hate them sinks that won't let you turn them on and off, don't you? The electric kind? I must be a ghost because they never know I'm there. I wave and wave and they don't turn on till I done gave up and moved to another sink."

"Hey, August, I hate to ask you . . ." Edie pointed at the top of Ian's head.

"Why, sure. Come on, little dude."

"I'll be right out," she said. "He doesn't need help, just make sure he doesn't wander off." She spotted the coffee bar, a line of tall metal vats and plastic tubes full of cups and lids, against the far wall. "Meet by the coffee?"

"Let's go see a man about a horse, Ian."

Ian looked up at him with wonder and took his hand. "There are horses in the bathroom?"

"Figure of speech." August winked at him.

Aligned now in the company of men, Ian gave her a pitying look. "You're not allowed in here, Mom."

She laughed. "Well, in that case."

―――

Edie finished washing and drying her hands. Her phone was ringing. Sleater-Kinney's "Price Tag," her ringtone for Theron Landon's private line. "Hello?"

She tossed paper towels into the wastebasket and smoothed her eyebrows in the mirror.

"Edie, goddammit, where are you?"

"I'm sorry."

"A family emergency? That what your girl said?"

Her regret at lying to him about her whereabouts receded a bit when faced with his offhanded sexism. "She's not mine," she said. "I signed her emancipation papers a while ago."

"Now, it's a figure of speech. Don't be so damned sensitive."

Figure of speech. The second time in five minutes that she had heard that phrase. She wondered how Ian and August were doing. If she wasn't at their meeting spot soon, Ian would start looking for her. "I know it's not a great day for me to be out of the office—"

"See, that's what makes you so good at your job. You're the queen of understatement. Not a great day! I'll say!"

She found a comb in her purse and ran it through her hair. It left momentary lines like rows of corn from above, as she'd seen them from a crop duster with her dad at the controls.

"You told me we weren't going to react to the OGS statement, boss."

She could hear the quick exhalation of Landon's frustrated breathing. He wanted her to read his mind and anticipate his needs without him having to admit to them. Like Ian. "You know I like to talk stuff over with you."

"As of Friday there was nothing to talk over. Unless you've changed your mind. It doesn't matter, anyway. I couldn't be there today." She looked at the time on her phone. The offices had closed at 5:00, although Theron would probably be at work until late into the evening. In the morning, the Oklahoma Geological Survey, the state government, and even the governor would publicly acknowledge what Theron wanted people to ignore. How would he sleep?

"You're letting me down, Edie."

"You told me we weren't changing course. On the dam Friday, remember?"

"The situation is sensitive and I need you at your post."

"Like I said—"

"A family emergency."

"I'm sorry, Theron."

"That's just fine, then. Anybody can make a damned announcement. I can do your job and mine, too, if I have to."

"No! Theron?"

Theron: Private Cell flashed off her screen. She stared at it. Had he hung up or did the call drop? What was he about to say? At that moment she did not know his mind. Bad things happened when Theron made statements on the record, though. The unfortunate combination of his direct manner of speaking and the homilies he had inherited from generations of poor Southern ancestors tended to come across as either simple or offensive. Neither outcome was good. The last time he had spoken on the record, to a reporter for the *Wall Street Journal*, he had earned a comparison to Frankenstein's monster with his square head and his less-than-sparkling intellect. But of course, Theron was bright in his own inimitable way, and it was a mistake to underestimate him. At a moment like this, though, straight talk from the horse's mouth was not a good idea. She was needed at work.

She flattened her palms against the cool tile of the countertop and stared at her reflection upside down in the faucet's chrome. Maybe finding Delaney could wait. What if she went ahead and let Keith find the source of the Facebook invitation? Find Delaney? Or come back home without results and a story that she would always wonder about, leaving her with even less closure than before, even less certainty.

The need to know, that deep, familiar tug, part of her being now, fixed her in its undertow. She stood up, facing her reflection. No, it was work that could wait. Theron hadn't even asked after her family. *What's the family emergency? Is Ian okay? Keith? Your dad?* He hadn't even asked. And after twenty years, news of Delaney was happening now. She wasn't used to looking at herself while she made up her mind about something, but she could see that Keith was right—when she was revved up, her nostrils flared. *Like a bull, one of those cartoon bulls about to charge.* She took out her phone, typed *Screw you!* to Theron. Deleted it. Typed, *You selfish prick.* Deleted it. Then: *I'll be in touch.* She hit send.

Her phone call with Theron had kept her in the restroom longer than she had planned. She scanned the store, expecting to see August and Ian perusing the junk food. Ian would sometimes try to persuade sympathetic adults to buy him things he knew Edie and Keith would say no to. It was hilarious. The place was busy, and Edie had a hard time seeing around people and over the long rows of shelves. She didn't see them by the coffee as agreed, so she stood outside the men's restroom door. A long minute passed with no one going in or out. She paced, staring at the door and turning around, scanning the store. They should have been out by now. Reasoning that they had probably gone outside, she crossed to the glass doors and pushed her way into the windy afternoon. She walked up and down the sidewalk in front of the store, running her eyes over the rows of gas pumps, over to the edge of the asphalt where the pressure gauge and free air machine was, to a grassy embankment where a heavy woman in red capri pants stood while her small white dog lifted its leg. No Ian. No August. Where the hell were they? Her breathing got shallow, and even as she told herself to relax and not to worry, she began to panic. Rushing back into the store, she saw a sandy-haired man standing with his back to her. August. She grabbed his arm. "Oh, thank God. You had me worried for a second, August."

August turned around. His hairline was soaked with sweat, his expression rigid. "Is he with you?"

"What?" she said. She took a step back and stared at him. "What?"

"Is he with you?"

She looked down and around August, nonsensically, as if Ian were a small pet hiding behind his leg. "I left him with you. Where—?"

"I told him to wait on me. I told him. But when I come out of the stall he weren't there. He left the restroom. I been looking."

Edie grabbed August to steady herself. Her vision pinwheeled and her breathing narrowed to a whistle of choked air. "Where is he?"

August raised his hands, empty.

She spun away from him and began to run. *Ian.* She ran up and down each aisle, she sprinted the length of the coolers, moved to the side of the store where the Subway restaurant was, pushed her way through clusters of people, looking, looking. "Ian!" She was in front of the row of registers screaming, calling his name. "Ian! Ian!" She caught August's sheet-white face across the store, his body in a crouch like someone trying to catch a wild boar, scanning the people coming toward the front door, calling Ian.

The cashier, an acne-scarred kid with a pierced septum, drew himself up. "Ma'am, what's going on?"

"Have you seen a little boy?" She flattened her palm at her ribs to show Ian's height.

The cashier clasped his hands in front of him and looked around. "That's—hang on a minute." He yanked open a drawer under the register and pulled out a dog-eared employee handbook. "There's things we're supposed to do."

Edie ran outside, calling. She ran all the way around the building to the back, past the stockade fence surrounding the dumpsters and the piles of empty boxes. She ran down the stretch of wall that connected the gas station to the trucker facilities and saw a cheap motel in the shape of a staple set a little off the road and down a rise. She ran down the hill toward the hotel, her feet kicking high behind her as she gained momentum. "Ian!"

The air roared in her ears. "Ian!" She ran toward the hotel, imagining Ian inside one of the rooms with someone, with some adult. The she felt herself stopped, firm hands on her arm. She looked into the flushed face of a young woman.

"Ma'am." The woman had been running behind her, calling her name for a while, Edie hearing it like a buzz in her ear. The woman looked Edie full in the face now. Eye contact. "Ma'am. I was getting gas and I saw you run out of the store. My name's Carol. What's going on?"

"I'm looking for my son. He's seven years old." She broke into a sob. "Ian! Ian!"

"Are you sure he's not inside? Come on, let's look. How long's it been?" Carol held Edie by the elbow while she strained to look behind her at the hotel. Numbered gray doors next to windows with blackout curtains drawn, cars and trucks parked in front like horses tethered before a saloon.

"I don't know. A minute or—minutes. I don't know."

Carol pulled her along, back up the hill and across the blacktop toward the gas station. Edie stared at I-40 stretching to the horizon east and west, and a two-lane county road that ran north and south into God knows. Roads led away from her in every direction. The dome of the sky reached away above her, making everything small. Ian was out there and could be in any direction with anyone. He could be in someone's car. He could already be miles away. Her vision pinwheeled and her knees buckled. Despite the woman's firm grip, Edie hit the ground, her hands planting on the warm, rough asphalt, grit piercing her skin. *Oh my God, oh my God. Not this. Anything but this. Take anything else, take everything else, I don't care, but let Ian be okay. Oh my God, oh my God, oh my God. I will tell the truth to the world, I'll come so clean, I will do anything if you bring him back. Please God.*

Carol helped her to her feet. "Ma'am, let's get you inside. Let's call the police." They came around the front of the building, and she saw August, his head low and nodding, talking to a small group of people in the parking lot. Keep an eye on her son, that was all August had to do. That was too much for him! The things he had told her about Elohim City, about his shameful admiration of Timothy McVeigh, were suddenly portents. He was right—he was guilty. There was something wrong with him and he might have hurt her son. He might have done something. She broke and ran at August. "You! You!" She punched him as hard as she could in his soft gut. She wanted to reach into his body with her bare hands and pull out the truth. "You freak! Where is he? Where is Ian?"

August wept. "It's true. It's my fault. It's all my fault."

"Hey!" Carol clapped a hand on August's shoulder. "What do you mean?" She cast a fierce look at the people gathered. "What's he been saying?"

"Are you sure he's not inside?" a redheaded teenaged girl asked from the edge of the group.

"Can't get him to make much sense," a man in a yellow golf shirt said. "He says he's to blame. But, I mean, he's here and the child is—"

"It's all my fault." August's voice rose in a wail.

The guy in the yellow shirt grabbed August by one bicep and shook. "Do you know something about the whereabouts of this child?"

"I had him," August said. "I had him with me."

The crowd drew closer. Danger lit across the air. Edie felt it. She looked at Carol, who felt like an old friend. She said, "Had him where?"

"To see a man about a horse."

"A horse?"

In the midst of his weeping, August had a coughing fit. He doubled over, his hands on his thighs.

"He was traveling with us," Edie said. "I asked him to keep an eye on Ian in the restroom while I was in the women's."

August stood back up, wiping his nose with the back of his hand.

"So you know him," Carol said. "When was the last time you saw the boy?"

"He was at the sinks. I told him to wait right there."

"Right where?"

"Um." August passed a hand over his face. He stared in a panic. "The sinks?"

Yellow shirt braced his hands on his hips, seemed to understand something about August. "You didn't see him leave the restroom?"

Behind her, Edie heard her name called. She turned toward the travel center. The redheaded teenager was running and calling her name, stooped to one side to hold the hand of a running child. Her child. Ian. A blur of Ian and then Ian himself, hugging her legs. "Hi, Mama!"

She crouched and grabbed him by the shoulders, crushing him to her. She wept into his hair. "Ian, baby, are you okay? Did anyone hurt you? What happened?"

"Found him in the casino," the girl said.

"A casino." Edie echoed the word in a daze. "In the gas station?" Her own voice sounded strange to her. Wind blew through her words. In the span of two or three minutes she had spun through space and landed back in a self that felt permanently altered.

Ian was crying too. She ran her fingers over his cheeks. "Has someone hurt you?"

He shrugged, a big one that said *yes and no*. "Daddy left my dream catcher."

"What?"

"He left it. I made it for him, and he left it."

"Honey, your dad took your dream catcher with him, remember?" She looked down at Ian's clenched fist and saw blue suede strings extruding from between his fingers, Yoda and R2-D2 and a bunch of other tiny Star Wars figures dangling from them. He opened his palm.

She picked up the dream catcher Ian had spent the last week making. "Where did you find this?"

"In the Chuck E. Cheese room."

"The Chuck E. Cheese room?" The casino. She and Keith joked whenever they had to take Ian to a kid's birthday party at Chuck E. Cheese that it was basically a kiddy-casino, grooming kids for a gambling life. She didn't think

Ian had heard them, but obviously he had. "Where is it?" She straightened up and gestured at the building. "I looked all over that damned place!"

She followed him back into the gas station. The cashier with the pierced septum let out a whoop when he saw them. "Shit, man." He shook his head. "I was about to call the cops. Where was he?"

"I don't know," Edie said. "He's going to show me."

And she followed Ian down the hall past the men's restroom, past a turn in the hallway, past a room marked "Theater" to a room marked "Games." She hadn't known this area was here, had run forward into the gas station when she realized Ian was gone, without noticing that the hallway turned and continued past the restroom. August and the redhead and Carol followed. Ian led them into a small, dark casino, a ten-by-ten-foot room lined with slot machines with a group of four back-to-back in the center and an ATM, its bland white light stark against jewel-toned neon blinking and strobing from the slot machines. They were greeted first by the machine facing the door from the center grouping. It featured an American flag waving and a giant Liberty Bell that tolled on a video screen. It was called Liberty 7s. Ian placed his little hand on the machine's button panel.

Edie looked around. "This is where you were?"

"Am I in trouble?"

"No, no."

"I saw the games like at Chuck E. Cheese. Then I saw Darth Vader hanging off this." He tapped the top of the game. "Where is Daddy?"

"I'm not sure."

"I guess Daddy didn't want it but I made it for him. He said he liked it, Mama. I didn't mean to be gone too long. I didn't mean to scare you."

It was a huge travel center, and the only one for miles. Of course, Keith had stopped here, too. Of course, he was gambling. Edie looked at the red bet button on the game. She pulled Ian to her. "It's okay," she said. "It's okay."

3 2

KEITH

2015

The highway was lined with mountains that had famous names. He had seen them in watercolor, Georgia O'Keeffe's distinctive style seeming far less impressionistic now that he saw firsthand what she had been looking at while she painted. No, she was more of a realist than anyone knew who hadn't been out here. It really looked like this. But not just Georgia O'Keeffe—he had seen this geography in films, too, lots of them.

The turn off Highway 84 into Ghost Ranch was at a dip in the road and let onto a deep-rutted dirt lane. He passed a squat log cabin with three late-model cars parked askew off the road in front of it. Five people stood or paced the area with phones to their ears. He finished the scone and gingerly lifted the coffee from the cup holder. Taking a sip despite his nervous stomach, he was hit by the realization that he was close now—definitely close—to someone who might know something about whoever set up Delaney's Facebook page, might even know Delaney herself. As he continued into the valley, facing into a wall of red and yellow cliffs, the low adobe buildings of Ghost Ranch came into view dotted along a dirt road under gigantic cottonwood trees.

A low-slung administration building with a wide, covered porch at the top of a steep hill was the place to start, clearly enough. He parked and climbed the hill. Inside the building, a rack of brochures about the facility and the area stood to one side, while a room to the left showed a long counter with three women behind it in front of computers. One of them, a young Native American girl with headphones on, stood up and smiled at him when he walked in. She pulled the headphones from her ears and let them dangle over her shoulders. "Welcome to Ghost Ranch," she said.

"Hi." Keith looked down at the registration forms on the counter. Cups filled with pens dotted the countertop. "What do I do?"

The girl laughed. "What would you like to do? Are you here for an overnight visit or a tour or are you visiting one of the museums?"

"One thing I really need is a phone. I need to check in with my wife." He peered over the counter at a white multiline phone. Edie's message had said she and Ian were on their way and would meet him that night, but he didn't know where or when. "Do you have a landline you let people use?"

"You can go out to the City Slickers cabin."

"Sorry?"

"On the way in? You passed it—it's a cabin the film crew for that movie *City Slickers* built when they filmed here. You know it?"

"The movie?"

"The cabin. You noticed it when you drove past? For some reason there's cell reception on top of that hill. Maybe because it's far enough away from the mountains. My phone can get two bars."

Christ, he was in a state. Seeing but not seeing. "Of course. People were out there on their phones. I didn't even—" He shook his head. "I'll give it a try. And I have another question."

She nodded.

"I need to speak with Kennedy Stein? She works here?"

The girl gave him a blank look. "I don't know," she began.

One of the other women behind the counter leaned over. "We can't give out information about our employees."

"I understand. But she does work here?"

The woman shrugged.

"The paleontology museum is open for another hour," the young girl said, her voice consoling. "It's pretty cool."

Keith didn't imagine himself looking at dinosaur bones, but it was an apt metaphor in its way, for what was he doing but digging up the past? More and more he was convinced nothing good could come out of his trip. He had been gone twenty-four hours but it seemed like days. Another lifetime since Edie came back wet and sad and defeated from the Twenty-Year Remembrance Ceremony and peeled off her black jacket in the kitchen. His heart caught. How much destruction could one person wreak in twenty-four hours? He choked on all he had lost and lied about in the last day. And it wasn't over.

He left the registration room and walked down the hall, past a gift shop, and into a common room with round tables dotting the space. Two men with long hair under straw cowboy hats, both zipped into North Face windbreakers, sat at one table leaning over a map, walking sticks resting against their chairs. Above them, a wall-mounted television showed Santa Fe tourist spots, and below the TV was a coffee counter. It didn't look open, but he could see someone moving around. An open cabinet closed, revealing a tall woman with dark blond hair in braids to her waist. She tucked a handful of coffee filters into the front pocket of her plaid shirt and passed her eyes indifferently over Keith as she pushed open the back door of the building, dropping down to the desert ground and trotting off. Clods of dirt dotted the wood floor of the room where she had walked.

The day had passed getting to this remote spot from Tony Box's trailer in Texas, and now it was late in the afternoon. His job interview was less than twenty-four hours away now, and the drive home would take nine hours at the least. He ached to be home preparing for his interview, watching Ian, cooking dinner with Edie. He had no idea where they were, as if all three had been blasted into space and didn't get to know where they would land.

33

EDIE

2015

Thank God August's sister, Malory, had an Xbox, courtesy of a boyfriend she'd run off before he could pack his toys. Edie could hear Ian laughing in the living room. The television was mounted on the wall on the other side of the bathroom, and she could feel the game's sound effects vibrating the water. She stretched out in the warm bath and slid her arms up the side of the old claw-footed tub. She held her hands up and saw the white tips of her French manicure were trembling—a vibration she couldn't blame on either the game or an earthquake. It was all her. She closed her eyes and tried to meditate but gave up. She gripped the slick sides of the tub and pulled herself up. The bathroom was small, with daylight coming through the crack at the bottom of the window's blinds. She could have turned on a light but didn't. A set of old but clean blue towels sat on the bathroom sink where Malory had put them before assuring Edie she could take as much time as she needed.

Malory had taken in her uninvited guests with admirable grace despite her surprise at seeing August for the first time in twenty years. Edie had felt exposed, awkward, standing at the front door of a stranger's house. August had convinced her to spend the night at his sister's place, although she knew from watching the hesitant sibling reunion that he hadn't even known how Malory would receive him, much less a woman and child.

Edie's phone gleamed atop a small table next to the tub where it shared space with a pink scented candle and a tube of Neosporin. She thought of Keith when she looked at it, but the strong co-parenting impulse to call him and tell him about losing Ian in the travel center was replaced with the shock of the casino room and Ian's dream catcher dangling from his small hand like a crushed bird. She was still too relieved to have Ian safe to process her fury at

Keith. She wasn't sure she'd ever be able to look at her husband again. There was no continuing the trip to Abiquiu, that much was sure. She was too rattled and angry to join him. *What now* was the question, but before she could properly answer it, she had a debt to take care of. Unlike Keith, she was uncomfortable with debt. Unlike Keith, she tried to keep her promises. She toweled off, dressing in one of the clean tops she had brought and the sweatpants, wishing the washer and dryer were faster.

Ian and August were shouting at the television in Malory's cave of a den. They were both wrapped in blankets, like the trauma victims that they were. Malory came in through the sliding glass door by the kitchen with a handful of rosemary sprigs. She had August's lank blond hair and small build. She wore tight jeans and round-toed cowboy boots with a pink sweatshirt under a tan Carhartt work jacket.

"Smells good," Edie said, leaning against the kitchen counter. She saw a pile of mail next to the toaster and saw Malory's full name. "Terrell? August is August Price, right?"

"Different dads. My mom used to say 'the Price is right' when she married his dad. For a short time."

"Then the price was wrong?"

"So wrong."

"You need help with dinner?"

Malory shook her head. Edie pointed outside with her phone and stepped into what, for a house with less acreage, would have been called the backyard. But here the land stretched ahead to a distant tree-lined fence. Outbuildings lacking structural integrity dotted the space, their brokenness imperceptible but sure, the way you can tell an old dog from a good way off. She identified a chicken coop, a smokehouse, a little barn with a corral out front, and a newer-looking corrugated shed that was probably for storage. She meandered through the tall grasses until a voice came over the end of her phone. Then she stopped walking and stood looking out into the low April sun cutting across the greening fields. "Thanks for picking up, Fiona."

"You call for the latest on Zach? I hope not, because you're in for a disappointment. I dumped that shitkicker."

Edie tried to remember who Zach was. "Your latest cowboy?"

"He was as phony as my tits." Her friend was driving, her voice like it came from the bottom of a well. "What's up?"

She had promised. What was the term for those prayers thrown up to a long-ignored higher power in life-or-death moments? Foxhole prayers. She had prayed a foxhole prayer—*God, save Ian*—and the prayer had been answered. To walk away from the promise now that Ian was safe felt like tempting fate, and she knew how savage fate could be, even though she didn't believe in it. Maybe she was being superstitious, but she would take no chances with Ian. Now she had to deliver her end of the bargain, come what may. *I will tell the truth to the world. I'll come so clean.*

She began. "Landon Energy has been aware of the scientific concerns about fracking for a long time." She took a breath. "From the beginning."

"Edie!" She could hear Fiona pound her steering wheel. "Are you serious right now? Are you giving me this story?"

"I don't know how much of a story it is. Maybe if I'd done this a year ago."

"You let me be the judge of that."

"Do you need to record?"

"I—yes. Hang on. I love you, Edie! Love you more than cowboys! Shit. Okay, we're recording." Fiona prompted, "By Landon Energy do you mean Theron Landon?"

"I'm the spokesperson for the company, not the man. I mean Landon Energy."

"That's not as fun, but okay."

"I don't know how it is at the other O and Gs, you understand. I don't speak for them. But at Landon, there's a certain front—a certain way of dealing with the issue—that has been," she pushed at the cuticles of her left hand with her thumb, "less than honest. It's not true that he doubts the science. His geologists are telling him the truth all the time and he knows they're right. He just doesn't want to hear it."

"I can't believe this. Girl, we might make national news, you understand that? Are you going to get fired?"

"I expect so."

"What happened to change your mind?"

"It's a long story."

"I sure hope Keith's not gambling again—you may not be in a good place to absorb his losses."

"He is."

"Gambling?" Fiona observed an uncharacteristic moment of silence for the bad news. "Christ, Edie. You're making me feel guilty. Have you lost it? Should I recommend you take some time and think about this?"

"I'm fine. Really."

She pushed open the door to the chicken coop and stepped inside. Reaching out for the string hanging from a bare bulb in the low ceiling, she turned on the light. Edie's gratitude to Theron was still there in the background. She searched accordingly for the right words to soften the blow. "He's never wanted to hurt anyone. There's no active malice—you know? Just indifference. It's disconcerting. Disappointing."

"The results are the same."

"That's what I've noticed."

"Thank you, Edie."

"How about this? '*Landon Energy spokesperson Edith Ash stated that Landon Energy, despite its past failures to adequately grapple with the fracking issue and its causal relationship to the plague of earthquakes afflicting land near drill sites employing horizontal drilling and wastewater disposal technologies, would now begin a review of its practices with a willingness to implement change.*'"

"That's your official statement?"

"Official."

"Does Landon agree with this? You're really boxing him in. What's he going to do?"

"We'll see. If there's any fallout it won't be your fault."

"Edie, I can't thank you enough. This is going to help *All the Red Dirt*."

"You bet. I hope it gets you some sponsors."

"This goes up bright and early Tuesday—before the OGS and the governor's statements hit."

"I'll brace myself."

"Speaking as your friend now, what will you do if you lose that job?"

"Open a meth lab."

Fiona laughed. "Always so droll."

Edie hung up and looked around her. She was in the chicken coop, or what had once been a chicken coop. But now—this was a meth lab, right? She stepped across the bare ground, soft with sawdust and old feed, to a long table and picked up one of a dozen empty plastic gallon containers. She stuck her nose inside and winced.

She heard a cough behind her. Turning, she saw Malory standing at the door, her shadow long across the dirt and hay floor. "I tried to catch you before you went in."

Edie stammered, "It's a chicken coop." A statement, an official one, to be agreed upon.

Malory crossed her arms and walked over to the table. "Look like one to you? No, this is what you think it is. I ran off my old man couple of weeks ago because of this shit. I never come out here. He was doing it for months before I caught him."

"So—not in business anymore?"

"I'm not a criminal."

"I didn't think this fit what I—my idea of who you are. Granted we just met."

"I should've known. He acted so head over heels in love with me, but it was the land he had his eye on." She looked down and jammed her fists into the back pockets of her jeans. "You need a lot of space to cook meth. It's got a bad smell. That's how I finally found it."

"I'm sorry."

"I'm so hard on my momma for her taste in men, but I can't say that I'm much better. I don't think I'd have gone into a place like Elohim City the way my mother did. But I could've been put away for years if he'd got caught. Hell, I still could. Got to clean this shit up and he ain't helping. Maybe I can get August to stick around."

"I hope so. He's sick. He needs to rest."

Malory shook her head. "Don't get your hopes up. I expect he'll leave with you. I never thought I'd see him again, you know? Turns out he knew all this time where I was. That tells you something."

"Why do you suppose he didn't contact you?"

Malory rubbed her lips and looked off. "I think he was mad at me. I think he wanted me to come get him out of Elohim City, you know? But I was a kid myself, stationed overseas, and I had no idea what kind of place it was."

"He's not mad at you." Edie felt sure she was right, despite her limited acquaintance with August. "If that guy is mad at anyone, it's himself. No one but himself."

"I'd have seen him by now if I'd known where he was. What a family we are. He was asking me about our mom. Lord, she broke his heart. *How's Momma? Is Momma okay? Does she ask about me?* Shit if I know. I don't see that crazy bitch."

"Families are tough," Edie said.

With her blue eyes damp with tears and thin lips pulled down, Malory resembled August. It wasn't hard to guess what their mother looked like.

She eyed Edie. "You aren't going to tell on me are you?"

"Tell what? Oh, this?" Edie gestured to the room. If she'd found herself standing in a meth lab a week ago, she might have had some moral deliberations about what to do, but not anymore. Not with the evaporative mien of her marriage and her job, while her sister took on life and likelihood. "Your secret's safe with me. I've got bigger things going on right now."

"I can see that you do."

34

KEITH

2015

First, the gift shop. He would buy something for Edie, and for Ian the hugest stuffed animal they had, or the coolest toy. The woman at the front desk had mentioned a paleontology tour. Had they found dinosaur bones on this place? It was likely—he'd walked by a map on the wall that said Ghost Ranch was the size of the island of Manhattan. How could there not be dinosaurs on such a vast stretch of land, and if that were the case, how could this gift shop not have dinosaur toys? It had to.

The gift shop smelled of juniper incense and had T-shirts and hoodies in every color and size featuring the longhorn cow skull of the Ghost Ranch logo. Along one wall there were books about the area and about Georgia O'Keeffe. Along another were camping supplies, toothpaste and toothbrushes, small black combs, the sort of travel-sized toiletries that hotels gave out for free. There was bug spray and bottled water, sunscreen and lip balm. There were artisanal soaps, candles, and salsas. And along the back wall, there was art for sale.

A hand-printed sign in the middle identified the work as being donated by artists who had come to Ghost Ranch the previous summer to take classes or independently to paint. Unframed, with titles, painters, and prices typed neatly on cards affixed to the wall next to them, the paintings ranged in sizes and ability but not much in subject matter. Each painting grappled with the otherworldly landscape at Ghost Ranch, each one a single mind's effort to truly see and to duplicate that light, those stones, what the thin air did to the colors. Keith stood before the wall, deploying the meager art criticism skills Delaney had imparted to him, looking for something that rose above the rank and file. He found it near the bottom left of the wall, a smallish painting, maybe a foot square. It was one of the mountains he had driven by on Highway 84 outside of Ghost Ranch, a vast, flat-topped mesa with one of those profiles as distinctive as a face. The painting showed the sun at midday, light on the high points of the mountain's descending layers with the hollows shadowed in deep grays and browns. The signature in the bottom right corner was done in a purplish hue, its loop and lines clear against the yellow grasses. The big *D*, the long *y*, Delaney's signature was unmistakable.

He crouched to eye level with the painting. Gently he picked it up off the nail that held it, and framed the painting with both hands. Inside him, everything went still. He held it in front of him like a book, then stood to see it better. Maybe in a different light her signature would disappear or reveal itself to be another name entirely. He held it close to his face and read it letter by letter as much as he could. It still said what he thought it said. He turned it over, but the canvas was just white on the back, and he wondered, noticing his own disappointment, what more he had expected. This was proof. He was holding proof.

"I think that's the best one," the cashier called in a thin, reedy voice from behind the checkout stand.

The white card next to the painting said: "High Noon Over Pedernal. 12 × 12, $400. Delaney Travis Brown." There was her name in type, clear as day, with a new last name added on. Keith picked it up. He crossed the room and set the painting down on the counter before the cashier. "Do you know the painter?"

The man behind the counter looked like a retired professor, with small rimless glasses and longish white hair. He glanced at the name on the card and shook his head. "Doesn't ring any bells. I don't live on the ranch, so I don't see a lot of the people who come for classes. They come and go."

"Where do I find out about them? The classes."

"Front desk? That's a good place to start."

"Good as any." Keith smiled. Lightness coursed through him. He couldn't keep it out of his face. "Say, do you have any stuffed animals? Any dinosaurs?"

The man looked at him like he was crazy and gestured behind him. Above eye level atop shelves lined with Ghost Ranch stationary and postcards, half a dozen brightly colored stuffed dinosaurs leaned against each other.

Keith laughed. "That big one, the biggest."

The clerk reached up and pointed. "This one?"

"Perfect."

"That's our Coelophysis. He's a big deal around here. You can see him if you want. I doubt he was really purple with green stripes."

"You never know."

"Hey, that's the truth. I think I have some bubble wrap for the painting. Hang on a sec."

As the clerk disappeared into a back room, Keith took out his phone. He took a picture of "Sunset over Pedernal" and a second picture of the card with Delaney's name on it. As soon as he had a signal, he would send it to Edie.

35

DELANEY

1995

If I look at it one way, my larcenous tendencies saved my life. When I left the social security office after taking a number and tossing my jacket over a chair to save a seat, I was on the hunt for pencil and paper. I couldn't handle staring into space or flipping through dumb magazines. I didn't have any doodling paper, and I go a little nuts if I can't draw when I'm just sitting there. I thought about all the churches nearby and of those little squares of paper that they put in the pew boxes for new people to write their contact information on if they want some church people to come to their house unannounced and talk to them about their beliefs. There would be those little half pencils in their own little pencil holes in the side of the pew boxes. Pencil and paper, that was what I needed so I could draw. So, yeah, I was heading to a church to steal some art supplies.

Seen another way, and this is the way I've worked hard to view it in the ensuing years, my artistic tendencies saved me. Instead of emphasizing the part about going to steal pencils and paper, I focus on *why* I needed them: to draw. That was the prime motivation for me, and I'd have happily stopped at a store and paid for pencil and paper if there had been one in the Murrah Building, but there wasn't. The stealing part, as I've come to think of it, was just necessity. I don't think most people would even consider pencils and paper as theft-worthy, but to me they were essential tools.

I didn't make it to the church. When the bomb went off, I'd made it as far as the east side of the Journal Record building across the street, near the front steps. If I'd walked a little slower, I might not have been protected by the massive gray stone building from flying debris. I might have died or been wounded. I was not without a scratch—windows shattering at the Journal Record building showered glass shards on me, and I had hundreds of cuts in my scalp and on my face and arms that I didn't notice right away. There on the sidewalk, the blast turned me inside out, made me into a cell soup, suspended all of me in the air for a second and then let me drop, the orderly systems of my body converted to disorder like a new religion. The air was surging, the air was loud, the air was thick with flying matter. I may have passed out for a few seconds or minutes.

When I woke up, I watched the people around me and followed them. I sensed the Murrah Building before I could look at it, and when I did, something went through me that changed the course of my life. I should have been in there and I wasn't. I wasn't! I was out here, alive! Pure energy tore through me—Alive! I was alive!—joy followed just as quickly by the blackest low for what was before my eyes. And guilt, as if by being in the building where I was supposed to be, it would have made anything better for anyone. Being me was too complicated in that moment, unsustainable. I couldn't process everything, and the extremes of what I was feeling were pulling me apart. I stood there in a daze, feeling the sun beat down on me. People were in motion all around me. Coming out and going in, alone and linked together, carrying people, and carrying babies. People. Tiny children. Babies. Those are just words but they weren't just words. They were people. Little kids. Babies. The immensity of a human life! I could see it like a force field on the immanent air—these people were going and gone.

You go into shock, I think. I did. You don't feel anything and you're like an animal and your mind is all survival. I swung into motion then and started to help every way I could. I stayed down there through the morning and the afternoon and the evening. Through the sun and the rain, through the second bomb scare and the all-clear on that. The rain was what finally made me stop and think. I had been so caught up in helping people that I hadn't even thought about the people who would be worried about me. It hadn't occurred to me that Edie and Keith would think I might have died, but then I felt terrible. Keith's Bronco—he loved that thing!—was undriveable, and I'd lost the keys somewhere along the way, anyhow. It was late when I finally got home, imagining I'd seen my share of tragedy for the day, but no, the day wasn't over yet.

I guess that's when I got the idea. Not so much an idea, more of an event—the realization that I could get a break from myself if I would just be someone new for a while. There was much to escape. That terrible joy! That shame! Every horror I was seeing in that moment! The unacceptable absence of my mother, who was my home, gone in a stupid car wreck. Not to mention the crappy jobs, the sister I didn't know what to do with, who didn't know what to do with me, the marriage proposal I hadn't wanted, and the father who hadn't wanted me. All those things lived inside of me, so all I had to do to lose all that was lose myself. It was like when you realize that instead of trying another layer of detail on a painting that's not working, you're going to toss it and start with a fresh, white canvas. What I had been was bad. So I was going to be good. Bad, good, black, white. Just like that.

36

EDIE

2015

August had convinced Ian to come outside into Malory's big backyard and play a real game. The two of them were tossing a yellow Frisbee. Ian didn't have the hang of it yet, so Edie was doing a lot of instructing, bending down to show him how to hold it level, how to flick his wrist. Most of Ian's throws were wild and high, sending August running all over the yard to grab them. Malory stood next to Edie watching her brother run. "Thank you for bringing him to me," she said. "I'm so glad he's here."

Edie's phone sounded, Keith's text tone. "Excuse me," she said, and stepped away. About damned time. There was so much to say she hardly knew where to start. But she didn't start. She looked. He had sent her a text with a photograph. She opened it and saw a painting of a mountain. Why would he send her a painting? Just as the answer to her question began to dawn, another photo came in. A typed white card listing a title, price, and the name of the painter. And then she sat down in the grass and wept.

Then he called. She pulled herself to her feet and answered, glancing back at Ian as she strode toward the outbuildings. "Hi."

Reception was terrible. He asked her if she was okay. What could she say? Yes, she was fine. His voice was high and singsong, and she could tell he was probably pacing like she was, but his words were hard to discern. She heard, "City Slickers."

"That old movie?" Bits and scraps of dialogue coming over the phone like torn shreds of cloth.

She heard, "Summer classes—"

"What are you talking about? I want to know about Delaney! Dammit, Keith."

"Sorry!" The static quieted for a moment. "Okay, okay. I just stepped inside. Can you hear me now?"

"Yes."

"You use the cabin as a shield."

"For God's sake!"

"So—" There was a long pause that wasn't due to bad phone reception. She held silent too. They joined together in the hush of Delaney's living. She began to cry again.

"I don't even know where to—" He paused, started over. "It's—she's alive!"

"She really is, isn't she? Keith? I—"

"I know." He was crying, too. "But—"

"She left us." Edie paced up and down Malory's backyard, watching Ian and August toss the Frisbee. It was nearly dark and beginning to sprinkle. The rain at the bomb site the night of the bombing filled her nostrils. The new reality opened new questions. New fury. "I'm going to have some anger," she said, impressed with her own matter-of-fact tone. "I don't want to, but I'm thinking she didn't even care enough to tell us she was okay. Why would she run away from us?"

Keith exhaled. "Because of me? The proposal. That morning. It was the last conversation we had."

Edie laughed. She saw August and Malory look at her, and she waved.

"This is funny?"

Hysteria edged her mirth now, and she wasn't sure she could stop or that her laughter wouldn't turn into tears. "Oh, get over yourself. You didn't cause her to disappear. Stop that line of thinking."

The rain began to come down in earnest, sweeping in with a hard east wind. Ian ran inside through the sliding glass door at the back. August followed him, glancing back at her with concern. He stood in the door with his head cocked, trying to get her attention, but she turned to the side. She pulled up the hood of her jacket.

Keith's footfalls inside the cabin punctuated his voice. "But why? People don't just step through a hole in the world and vanish."

"Unless a hole opens up right in front of you," Edie said. "One you didn't expect. Then maybe you step through."

The rain began coming down harder, and she stepped back into the chicken coop–turned–meth lab. She stepped around a lot of broken glass and found a plastic bucket that she flipped over and sat on.

Keith said, "Looks like she's married. Delaney Travis Brown."

"Could she still be there?"

"At Ghost Ranch? No. But she came here to paint. Always talked about it, remember? Georgia O'Keefe and all that?"

"Then where is she?"

"Maybe her friend will know. The one who works here. I'll try to find her."

"I was sure the Facebook invitation was fake."

"It's hard to take in."

"We have a lot to talk about. Ian found your dream catcher."

"Found it? Where?" She heard his footsteps stop. He paused for a long moment. She could almost see what he was seeing, the dark travel center casino rising in his mind, the sticky slot machine surface where he'd set his good luck charm. She didn't try to help him. "Oh—fucking shit. The dream catcher, my God."

She picked up a stick and poked it into the sawdust ground. "I really just—I can't listen to you."

"Fuck, fuck, fuck."

"I don't want to talk about it right now." After a long pause in which she tried and failed to form words, she said, "I'll see you at home."

37

KEITH

2015

The place would soon be closing. Bill, the guy at the gas station, had said that Kennedy Stein worked at Ghost Ranch but lived in Española, which meant she would be leaving for the night soon if she wasn't already gone. "Where do employees park?" he asked at the front desk. Across the counter, the young woman who had been so cheerful earlier in the afternoon looked a little wilted.

She waved vaguely with her right hand. "Over there, most of them. Depends. Kitchen help parks by the kitchen. Maintenance has their own spot, too."

Keith nodded. "You have a good night."

He hurried out of the store, clomped down the visitor center steps, and stood in the gravel parking lot basking in the warmth of the lowering sun. He had at least an hour of light left. The vast face of a gold mesa behind the structures received the light like a battery charging. The white bark of aspens newly leafed out glowed as shadows crept into the valley. A pale dirt road led down into what looked like the main buildings of the ranch, but the girl had gestured the other way for employee parking, so he pointed himself to the right and walked. There wasn't much to see this way: public bathrooms, a warren of concrete dormitories that looked vacant, and the horseback riding stalls. Through the fence of the horse corral, he saw that the barn door was still open. He could hear music coming from the inside. As he drew closer, he made out something classical. Yes, it was Bach. He poked his head inside the fence and called out.

"Hello?"

A figure appeared in the doorway of the barn. Long braids swung as she walked. It was the tall woman he had seen helping herself to coffee earlier in the day. He repeated his greeting. She approached the fence smiling. "I'm sorry, you just missed us. We're open tomorrow, though. Are you staying on the ranch?"

"Actually, I'm about to head out."

"Thought you'd squeeze in a quick horse ride before you got in the car?"

"I'm looking for someone. An employee. Not having much luck."

"Well, there aren't that many of us. Who are you after?"

"Kennedy Stein?"

She pulled back. "That's me. I've paid everybody I owe, you understand? You can't come out here to where I work."

"I'm not a bill collector. You're friends with Delaney Travis. Brown."

Relief crossed her face. "Hey, I'm sorry! Shit, I thought you wanted money. I had a bunch of credit card debt before I came out here and left behind materialism, you know?"

She said "materialism" like it was a proper noun. He said, "That must feel great."

"Spoken with feeling."

He thought about Brad, about the fate of his bets and his marriage. "You have no idea."

"Why are you looking for Delaney?"

"You know her?"

She shrugged. "Sure. You want to come in?" She strolled through the dirt of the corral to a gate, which she swung open and stood holding for Keith. As he passed through, she said, "You want to get high?"

He laughed. "Tell me about Delaney."

"I will, but you seem way tense."

"You know what, yeah. I'll get high." He hardly ever drank or smoked anymore out of solidarity with Edie, but there was no reason he couldn't smoke a joint right now. He couldn't think of a better moment for one.

Walking ahead of him, she nodded and reached into the breast pocket of her flannel shirt. She held a small joint up with two fingers. "Come on in."

The inside of the barn was lit by a desk lamp on a small metal table in the front corner. The long barn recessed behind them with the moving and breathing sounds of horses in the stalls that lined each side. She dropped into a metal folding chair next to the desk and gestured to an empty one on the other side of the table. She lit the joint and took a long drag before she passed it to him.

"Delaney," he said, prompting her before he took a hit.

"She was here again this summer."

"Again?"

"She's come a few times."

"Do you have a picture?"

She nodded and reached for her phone on the table while she held in a hit. She raised a finger telling him to wait, then scrolled through the photographs on her phone, slowly letting out the smoke.

If the pot hadn't hit him then, slowing his mind way down, he might have lost it. Kennedy took her time, flicking by photo after photo until she stopped. "Here." She held up the phone to him. "Here she is."

The photograph was taken somewhere around there. Delaney was standing on a high promontory of yellow stone smiling at the camera. She wore sunglasses, so he couldn't see her eyes, and her dark hair was in braids like Kennedy's. She wore green shorts and hiking sandals and a white T-shirt.

"Do you have any more?" he asked. "Anything without shades?"

"Sure, that's just the first one. Here, why don't you have the phone."

He took the phone from her and scrolled through the photographs. There were shots of Kennedy, then a selfie of the two of them in front of a stream. And then one taken in the shade, Delaney resting against a tree looking at the camera wistfully. Seeing her eyes, he finally accepted that it was her. Those were her eyes—that spark of light was her own. The more he looked, the more familiar the face around the eyes became, not really much changed, but she wasn't wearing the pale makeup she had always worn. Her face was tan, the rough spots from acne scars barely visible. Her lips were bare, and her eyes looked smaller without the heavy black eyeliner he'd always seen her in. Her hair was clean and straight, the dreadlocks gone. She looked better, really.

Without looking up, he said, "Where does she live?"

"Chicago for a while. Not anymore, though. I'm not sure. I only see her like once a year when she comes out here to paint. She mentioned Austin once. She's married to a finance guy. She's talked about wanting to move to Denver."

It was all so normal and nice. The kind of catching up he had done a dozen times with people from his past when he moved back to Oklahoma City. Usually it was a happy thing, a good-for-you-man kind of feeling, but what was he hearing? How could he assimilate this new narrative—Delaney the painter, the wife. She had been dead for twenty years. "Does she have kids?"

"No. Hey, did you come looking for her because of that Facebook page she put up?"

"Yeah."

"That was funny. I don't why she put New Mexico as where she lives. Well, I mean she loves this place. But still."

"What's she like?"

"Delaney? Delaney's cool, you know? Sad, I mean, but who's not?"

"I thought she was dead."

"Dead?" Kennedy's eyes widened and she pointed at him. "Are you that dude? Are you the guy in Oklahoma that asked her to marry him?"

He pressed himself against the hard metal of the seat back. "That's me."

"Yeah, she was pretty fucked up about that whole thing. I get the idea it kind of ruined her life. It hurt her deep—her sister. That was tough. Do you know her?"

"She's my wife."

"Wow, that's right. She said something about that."

"Delaney told you that I married Edie?"

"She Googled you two. The Murrah bombing?" Kennedy made an exploding gesture with her hands. "Messed her up. Bad, bad shit."

What could he say? "Yeah, bad."

"She friended you on Facebook? That's a pretty big deal, right? I hope it makes her feel better."

Keith slapped the tabletop with the flat of his hand. He saw the rubble of the Murrah Building steaming and debris everywhere. There were those latex gloves, endless discarded medical gloves strewn high and low in the rubble of the building like an infestation of small, white creatures, a proliferating ghost white herd that bespoke urgency. There was Edie crashing against his back when he stopped walking and stood looking at his Ford Bronco. And that was just the beginning. The first night, followed by twenty years of hard grief and unanswered questions and trying to have a life in spite of it all.

Kennedy leaned back and made a pile of dirt with the heels of her boots. "She used to talk about this story, 'Yellow Woman.' Do you know it?"

He shook his head.

"There's a line from the story Delaney used to bring up like it explained something. Something like, *I didn't decide to leave, I just left.* I don't know if that means anything to you."

"Not really," Keith said. He was suddenly exhausted and not nearly high enough.

"Do you want me to tell her anything for you? I mean, I guess you can write her now, but—"

"No," he said. "I can't imagine what I'd say."

PART THREE

RECOVER

Human kind cannot bear very much reality.

T. S. Eliot "Little Gidding"

38

BRAD

2015

Brad Odel whistled softly when he pulled up to Keith and Edie's house. The two-story stucco building was lit up like a riverboat on the outside, showing off its teeming flowerbeds. "Not bad, old buddy. Not bad at all." It was one of those nice old places in Mesta Park. Not one of the mansions, but a boxy place with a screened-in porch and a look like the house version of a big-chested woman who wants to hug you and forgive you for knocking out her windows with your baseball. Some people were just lucky, and Keith had always been one of those people.

Brad parked in the driveway, pulling his emergency brake up as far as it would go against the steep upward slope. At the end of the concrete, tucked into the backyard, stood a separate garage that matched the main house. Box hedges lined the walkway up to the red front door, and the doorbell sounded like bells inside the house. Through the glass on the side of the door, he saw a lit foyer with stairs leading upward and a living area to one side. Beyond that he could make out a light in the kitchen, brass pots and pans hanging from the ceiling. He rang the bell again. No one came to the door, but Brad was sure they were home. It was ten o'clock on a Monday night—where else would they be? The motherfucker was not going to just avoid him. That was not going to happen.

He walked around the house and didn't see anything except an army of daffodils and hyacinths by the kitchen light. The backyard was long and neat with wind chimes tolling from the trees. That racket would drive him nuts. There were lights on in the windows to an apartment above the garage, and he could see from the porch light outside the door that the stairway attached to the side of the garage had a new wooden guard rail. He tried to think who could be living up there, but he didn't know enough about Keith's life anymore to guess. Not Keith's parents—he was pretty sure they still lived up in Quail Creek in the house he'd visited as a kid.

He took the stairs and banged hard on the door. No one answered, but he could hear some kind of commotion inside—a rhythmic banging close to the door, the steady whish of something mechanical. Blinds were open at a window about three feet to the left of the door, but it was too far over for him to see into. He tried stepping down the stairs until he was directly under it. From that position the window was above him, just out of reach. Jumping, he grabbed the ledge but couldn't get a good enough grip to raise himself up. He jumped a few times then stopped, panting on the staircase. This wasn't cool—it was beneath his dignity.

He had to remind himself about the matter of dignity often. It was a second, and sometimes a third, thought. His knee-jerk sense of self still settled low, to the pitiable figure he had cut most of his life, and it took running through his lineage to bring his self-esteem up to the point where he was inhibited from peeping in the window of his old friend's garage. He was the great-grandson of the Zabel clan of Comanche County, after all. His granddad had been the biggest gambler, gangster, and racketeer in the state for three decades, and the FBI had spent millions in the '60s and '70s trying to convict him. His mom had been her father's top bookie, and his uncle Stanton was a scary dude to this day, with fingers in every pie he could think of, whose low opinion of Brad had supposed to be improved by a big win on Landon Energy's fracking announcement. But would it?

Keith had sounded cagey on the phone, and the more Brad thought about it, the more he was convinced Keith was about to screw him over. He'd come to his house for assurances, and the fact that nobody was home was a bad sign. If Keith gave him bad info, he would appear to be more of a dipshit than ever, laying everybody's money—including his uncle Stanton's—on a guaranteed announcement in the morning that might *not* transpire. It had better transpire. It had just better.

He heard a voice. There was no mistaking it, a voice was coming from inside the apartment. No words—it was more like a moan. Who the hell was it? Brad ripped open the beef jerky stick he kept in his shirt pocket and gnawed on it. He was on a high-protein diet and had to be careful not to let his blood sugar drop or he'd be face-first in the first tub of ice cream he could find. Basically, it was none of his business what was going on behind that door and who it was. He chewed. He took a few steps down the stairs and looked over the back windows of the house. Fucking Keith! While addictions made people predictable, and Keith surely had a gambling problem, he wasn't sure enough about Keith's possible actions to feel safe. Keith had always been hard to get ahead of.

He had been kind to Brad's mother, though. Brad would never forget coming home one day during their senior year and finding Keith reading aloud to his mom, who was down with shingles. Keith didn't know who she really was—the Zabel bookie. He thought she was some kind of low-end clerk, some sad-sack divorcée that he felt sorry for. He'd come by every afternoon for a couple of weeks and read her the whole biography of Quanah Parker. Brad would hover around and listen, wishing he'd thought to read to her. Not that he would ever want to, but he would've liked his mom to look at him with the sort of admiring gratitude she directed at Keith. And it had been damned nice, that was an unfortunate goddamned fact. What if that was Keith's mom behind that door moaning right now? Oh, it wasn't. Eleanor Frayne would never end up on the floor. But what if it was?

Hell. Brad bit off the last bite of jerky and let the wrapper drift to the bed of daffodils beneath the stairs. He slammed the door hard with his shoulder. A cheap particleboard door, hollow, it gave right away, and he found himself looking down at an old man on the beige linoleum of a small kitchen. His arm and leg on one side were thumping the cabinets. His lips were blue, eyelids fluttering. A few feet away lay a backpack with tubing that Brad reached down and picked up. Breathing tubes that fit into the nostrils were at the end, the source of the whooshing sound. He stuck them up the old guy's nose. That was the right thing to do, but it wasn't enough. He dialed 911. Then he dropped onto his butt and leaned against the cabinets next to the old guy while they waited. When the ambulance got there, he rode in the back to the hospital with the guy, whose wallet solved the mystery of who the hell he was—Edie's dad. At least he and Keith were even now when it came to parents.

39

AUGUST P.

1995

The phone was ringing when I let myself into my dad's apartment in Tulsa after school. I crossed the short distance to the kitchen, rounded the motorcycle my dad had disassembled on the linoleum where you'd expect to see a table and chairs, and slung my backpack on the kitchen counter. Why did I answer? I hardly ever answered my dad and Angie's phone. The call was never for me, and it was usually nobody they wanted to talk to either—a bill collector or a boss asking can Angie work a double or one of the long line of people calling to say they'd kick my dad's ass next time they saw him. I never knew why, but he provoked that response in people quite a bit. Still, I picked it up, and there was my stepdad, who made my real dad look like a pretty good guy in comparison.

"August? This's Gary. How you doing, son?"

I allowed that I was doing okay and told him that, no, spring break wasn't coming up, it already happened. I hadn't seen him or my mom in a couple months since I left Elohim City in February.

"Your mom sure misses you."

"I miss her, too. Where are you?" There was only one phone on the compound, and I couldn't picture him calling me from there. "Can I talk to her?"

"She's not around. I'm at a pay phone in town. I'll tell her you said hello." He kept saying how much my mom missed me and I should come back to the compound. Said it was just a visit and I could leave whenever I wanted. She sure missed me.

"Spring break is over," I said. I wanted to ask were Phil and Roger still around, but I didn't dare. His begging me to come for a visit, it was weird. Gary never could stand having me around.

"Why'n't you come, anyway?"

"I got a job."

"Working, are you? Come anyway."

"I don't have a car." I told him how I took a bus to the barbecue place where I was a dishwasher. No busses out there in the sticks where he was.

He kept on. Funny I should mention a car! He had a great idea, one he knew I was going to like. Could I catch the bus to OKC? Wrong direction, true, but there'd be a car for me at the Oklahoma City bus station and all I had to do was pick it up and drive back to Elohim City. The whole thing—Tulsa to Oklahoma City and then to Elohim—might only take six, seven hours if I could find a bus for the first leg that wasn't going to stop in every little town.

I pulled the yellow phone cord with me to the fridge, where I stood and looked at a mostly empty case of Natural Light, a bunch of condiments, and a to-go box that was my dinner. I grabbed the white Styrofoam box of barbecue I'd brought home from work the night before and set it on the counter. "You want me to take a bus from here in Tulsa down to Oklahoma City, then pick up a car and drive out there to y'all?"

"For a visit," he said.

I was quiet, trying to wrap my head around the route he had just described. From where I was, there in Tulsa, south and east to Elohim City was only about ninety minutes. Why would I drive way out of the way south and west to Oklahoma City first? He could hear me thinking, seemed like. He'd usually be calling me a dimwit by then, but he kept his temper and stayed sweeter and more reasonable than I'd ever heard him. He explained how the car I picked up in Oklahoma City could be MY CAR if I did them this favor! My own car! And could I pick up Tim McVeigh—you remember ol' Tim? He might need a ride from downtown. He's dropping off a truck and may need a friendly lift. I'd need to be right on time. Tim's a stickler for promptness. All I had to do was stand outside the car so he could see me. If he didn't show up, why, I could just leave.

When I heard I'd have to spend time alone in a car with Tim McVeigh, I wanted no part of it. One big long quiz about *The Turner Diaries* was what I saw the trip being, and what would happen if I failed? But I could tell this wasn't really Gary asking so much as telling me what to do. "When?" I said. He told me next Wednesday.

"Day after tomorrow?" I said. That was awful fast.

"No, next Wednesday," he said. That sweetness was draining out of his voice fast. "The nineteenth. April nineteenth. Got it?"

It was a school day. Did he not know? He didn't care. I knew that. "Yes, sir," I said. "Got it. Why am I getting a car?"

"You don't want it?"

"Course I do!"

"Tell your dad you're getting a car he ain't going to have to pay for and he won't mind."

That part was true.

Tuesday night rolled around and I took a late-night Greyhound from Tulsa that took four times longer than a car ride would have and got me into downtown Oklahoma City a little before 7 AM. I found the car like he said, in the parking lot of a New York Hotdog restaurant with a parking lot that backed up to the bus stop. It wasn't much—a red Datsun 710 with a faded Rock 100 the KATT bumper sticker in the back window. The grinning feline face of the state's big rock station gave me a hearty welcome, like, now you're cool, August. Now you're rock and roll. It was a decent old car, but the idea that it was mine made it glow. I stepped around it, taking it all in. I couldn't believe it! I cupped my hands over my eyes and peered inside. The tan interior was pretty beat up, with some rips in the upholstery and a split in the front dashboard, but I was already thinking about how I could repair those things, how I'd buy Armor All and Windex and paper towels and make it shine. It even had a CD player—something somebody had put in not that long ago. I kicked the tires. They hurt my toes. That seemed right. I found the key in a black magnetic box under the back fender and opened it up, sat inside and listened to the radio for a few minutes of a song about are you gonna go my way that I heard a lot at the barbecue restaurant. I found a penny in the passenger seat. 1968. I put it in my pocket for luck.

Then I went back into the bus station and had some breakfast at the café inside. It had wagon wheels for decorations and orange vinyl seats. I sat in a booth by the window and drank a Coke, eating sticky eggs and thinking about Tim McVeigh strolling across the bus station parking lot and waving, ready for his ride, about the drive back to Elohim all alone with McVeigh in the car.

I'd been trying not to fix on that part of the deal, but now it was the next part of getting my car. The man made me nervous, and he had squished one of my cicada shells. I didn't know what I'd have to say to him, but I knew he'd have plenty to say to me.

I had tried so hard to read that danged *Turner Diaries*. I'd used a ruler, I'd gone slow. I figured I could answer some of his questions, but I didn't know if it would be enough. I would've bet anything that he wouldn't like me listening to the radio. I tried to come up with some questions for him—Where are you from? What's your favorite food?—but I knew those weren't good questions and I had no others.

I finished eating and went to the restroom where this scrawny fellow with blue scaly feet and yellow toenails and red-white-and-blue flip flops asked me if I wanted to get high.

"Sure," I said. I'd smoked a few joints in Tulsa and knew it could make me worry less about picking up McVeigh. It might even make me funny. We stood by the casement windows and looked out at the parking lot while we smoked. I could see my car, but I didn't feel right about calling it my car. He wanted all kinds of things from me in exchange for the joint, but I just said, I gotta pick up a guy. I gotta go. No, sir, I gotta go.

Over the loudspeaker a man's voice announced an arrival and a departure at 8:30 and 8:45—arriving from San Antonio, departing for Albuquerque. The names of those cities sounded soft and nice, and the stray thought of sneaking onto a bus for Albuquerque crossed my mind before I remembered I had a new car and commitments to fulfill. I trotted down the urine-smelling stairs and walked across the waiting area on the way out. Rows of seats, shiny plastic with a fake wood pattern and metal armrests, were full of people. Some looked fresh, some looked dog tired. An old man in plaid pants was reading the paper and had made a big mess all around him, pages everywhere. One part was sprawled open across the bench, and I saw a headline, just a word, "Waco." I kept walking out to the car.

The word "Waco" took hold, and my discomfort found a focus. April 19th? I wouldn't have thought of it without seeing that headline, but now it clicked, and I knew it was the second anniversary of the siege at Waco that killed all them people. Gary about lost his mind when he talked about it, all of them at Elohim did, they held it up as proof positive that the government was as evil as they said. That real life was like *The Turner Diaries*. That *this* was a war.

What was *this*? I never quite knew. Life itself? It should have occurred to me right then, walking across the parking lot to that beat-up car with somebody else's KATT sticker on it, that I, myself, needed to choose sides. But it didn't, not quite yet. I was really high now and sleepy from not much rest on the Greyhound, and I was trying to stay out of sight of the bad man with the blue feet, so I crawled into the backseat and closed my eyes. I didn't mean to fall asleep, but I must have because I was woken up by a sound that shook the car like a toy. My innards trembled. I scrambled up and out of the car and stood there looking around. People standing around the loading docks at the bus station were all freaking out, pointing, yelling. What was going on? I stepped over to where a woman was pointing and saw massive smoke gushing over the buildings, rolling like water out of a broken dam. The air around us turned dark and thick.

I turned to the woman and could barely find her right in front of me. She smelled soapy clean and had curlers in her hair. Her hands were thick and dark and clasped out in front of her like she was praying. "Ma'am, what time is it?"

She pulled her watch up close to her face. "About 9:02."

"I'm late!"

She looked me up and down like I was crazy. "These buses got a schedule. You just wait, that's all you can do."

"I'm picking a guy up. I was supposed to be standing outside the car at nine o'clock." I cast around, tried seeing through the flying dust, looking in case McVeigh was standing around the parking lot looking for me.

"Well, something blew up. Maybe tell him that's why you late."

The air looked like one of those pictures from the Dust Bowl. I ran to the car and stood there. I even waved a few times, just in case McVeigh was looking for me, hoping he was okay. With mayhem all around me, I waited a few more minutes before I decided it was safe to leave. That was what my stepdad said to do—if he doesn't show up, just leave—but I thought I'd drive up toward whatever was happening and make sure he wasn't coming along late. I started up my new car and swung a left out of the bus station, then another left on

Robinson, and what had happened was right up there, just right up the road. People were running. I could hear sirens. I pulled over. I got out. I was so scared. I stood next to the car and flattened my palms on the hood, which was still cold, and I looked around and I couldn't understand what had happened. My mind was moving through molasses. A woman in a business suit ran by screaming, holding one shoe. She was calling to someone behind me. She screamed, "The federal building!"

Then I did understand. Waco. It was April 19th. Earl Turner blows up a federal building in *The Turner Diaries*. Uses a moving truck to carry the bomb and gets away in another car. *Another car*. Whatever this was, it was ol' Tim. Then I knew what *I* had almost done. I was supposed to be his getaway car.

I drove to Elohim. I pulled over and got sick a few times. My eyes were dry like I had a fever. I shivered and couldn't stop. I didn't know what else to do but drive, and I wanted to see my mom. I needed to know if she knew what Gary had got me into. I could never tell what she was thinking after we moved to Elohim, and I didn't know if she offered me to them, thinking it was an honor for me to be the getaway driver, or if she let them use me knowing it was trouble, or if she didn't know what Gary was using me for. I wanted to believe she didn't know. Where had McVeigh gone? I drove and listened to the radio. They didn't know who did it. The voices on the radio said lots of things, but nobody had any idea about Tim McVeigh. I hoped I was wrong about him, but I knew I was right. I never had such a strong gut feeling—didn't doubt it for a minute once I figured it out. When I was about a quarter mile away from Elohim City on the dirt road that leads into the compound, my mom came at me out of the scrub on the side of the road, jumping out and waving her arms. Her face was like an animal's. Tears streaked through the dirt on her face. "Turn around," she said when I rolled down the window. "Turn around and never come back."

"Momma?"

"I love you."

I cried then. She said it. She loved me—that was what I drove out there to find out. "I love you, too."

"Ditch that car. Stay with your dad. Don't ever tell. Don't come back here." She handed me a bunch of money, loose and dirty. My mind was spinning, trying to understand, hoping I was wrong about McVeigh, hoping none of it meant what I thought it did. I drove back to Tulsa fast as I could. My dad and his girlfriend had the TV on when I walked in, and they nodded like they weren't surprised to see me home. I sat down and watched the coverage.

McVeigh got caught so fast. I think he planted that old yellow Mercury he was driving with antigovernment brochures on the seat right near the scene for a signature, no license plates cause it weren't supposed to be for the getaway—I was. I believe he must've drove off in the Mercury out of necessity when he couldn't find me, driving a car bound to be pulled over the minute a cop saw it. Over the years, there have been times when I liked to tell myself it was me that got him caught. If I'd been standing outside the car looking for him like they told me, he wouldn't have had to resort to that Mercury with no plates. He'd have gotten away with me driving him in a red Datsun 710 to wherever it was he'd have told me to drive. But other times I think, what if I had told Gary to keep his danged car, I didn't want it? What if I'd gone to school that day instead? Would Tim have called the whole thing off?

People wonder a bunch about all this, and lots of folks realized his getaway ride must not have shown up. I've also heard that there could have been a few of us waiting around to give McVeigh a ride, all in different spots on the streets around the Murrah Building, told to give a guy a ride and not knowing why or what it meant, not involved in his plans. I wonder if that's true. Somehow it would be helpful to me to know I wasn't the only one. But if they're out there, then whoever got them involved probably said something to them like my momma said to me. *Don't ever tell. Don't you ever tell.* And so we all kept on silent, carrying that heavy weight.

40

EDIE

2015

August had discovered a tube of hand lotion in a side pocket of the passenger door and had asked her if he could use it. Edie had said yes, never guessing that August would spend the next two hours rubbing the entire tube over his chapped hands and dry arms, even his neck and the red and flaking tops of his ears. Now the interior of the Range Rover smelled like Honeysuckle Heaven. She looked over at him. He was burnishing his elbows, attending to these private ablutions in an absorbed way, as if he were alone, stopping every few minutes to cough, a deep, wet sound that wracked his whole body.

It was nearly midnight, and they were on I-40 just coming into the western edge of the Oklahoma City metro area, passing hotels and all-night breakfast chains. Ian had been asleep the whole way. She was barely able to keep her eyes open. Not since the day of the bombing had she been through so much. She wanted to be home, to tuck Ian into his clean Teenage Mutant Ninja Turtles sheets and to climb into her own bed and turn off the light. When she woke up Tuesday morning, she would be in a new world. She would open her eyes on a world in which Delaney was alive, and she would begin to understand the story as it had changed Delaney from victim to—what? Nobody had ever hurt Edie more, that was for sure. Her father swooping low above the Spanish mine in the Wichita Mountains: *People don't abandon valuable things.* That was what Delaney had done, abandoned her in a way that made the way her dad took off seem humane. And her unauthorized Landon Energy announcement would be out there. She would be facing those consequences soon enough, and Keith would be facing consequences, too.

But first she would have to do something about August. On the drive back from his sister's house in Erick, while Ian slept in the backseat, August had let her talk about Delaney and process the idea that her sister was alive and well, with all it meant for her and Keith. "Now that big hole in you can close up," he said. "No matter why she did what she did." August was a good guy, and she was glad he had been with her all day, but she didn't know where to take him now and he wasn't being reasonable. He wouldn't let her take him home. He didn't care what Sam had done to the place, had no curiosity about it whatsoever. Massaging lotion into his knuckles like a middle-school girl after her first trip to Bath & Body Works, he insisted that she drop him off right where she had found him, on the side of I-40 where he'd left his cross in the grass. Crazy! It was nearly midnight. Rain could come blowing through at any time, and anyway, it wasn't safe.

"Dammit!" she said under her breath. "You're a very trying person, you know that?" He glanced up in mild surprise. "You need to stop carrying that cross." She gave him a firm nod. "Nobody wants to say it to you, or maybe nobody cares, but August, I care, and I'm telling you, you need to cut it out."

He didn't seem offended or even surprised. He rubbed his lotion-soaked palms together and looked out the window. "Why?"

"Why? That's the question I would like to ask you. Why do you do it? All that grief and sadness you've been carrying, you think you've been carrying it for other people. You haven't. It's yours. That's *your* grief and sadness. You can let it go, my friend. Let it go. Just because you met Timothy McVeigh doesn't make you responsible for the bombing, okay? No matter what you thought about him. And you're not a Christ figure. You're not making your feelings more important with this masochistic display, and you're not having any effect on anybody else's feelings except to piss me off."

The crow's feet around his eyes deepened as he smiled and rocked back in his seat. He seemed genuinely touched. "I sure do appreciate you saying so, Edie."

"So, are you going to stop?"

"I've got the need to do it right now. I won't do it forever. But it means so much that you would talk to me about it. I guess it looks pretty weird."

"Why don't you work? You're in the prime of your working life—why don't you work?"

Here, for the first time, she saw he was hurt. "I'm sorry," she said. "I'm sorry. It's just—are you on disability? That's none of my business, is it? I'm not thinking straight. I need to sleep."

He gazed at her in surprise.

"Just up here is where you can let me off."

"August, I care. That's all I meant to say. I'm sorry."

"It's okay, Edie. I appreciate you and I'm going to give it some thought. But right now I want to pick up my cross and walk it home. It's what I want to do."

"Tonight?"

"Don't you know a little something about being compelled?" He waved at the road stretching out behind them, giving her such a direct gaze, it took her aback.

She laughed. "You got me there." He settled back and looked out the window, and she knew he thought they'd settled the matter in his favor. She kept driving, though, until she reached the exit for his house. Compulsion, yes. Right now she felt compelled to get him home safely.

When he realized where she was going, he asked her to turn around. Once she'd taken the exit, he gave up, as though asking her to drive back to where he'd left his cross was more inconvenience than August was willing to cause. He looked back at Ian, whose closed eyes and wide-open arms made him resemble someone midleap.

"I guess I could use a good night's sleep," August conceded.

The night was fair and bright. No lights shone from his house, which seemed a good indication that Sam had moved on. "I'm going to wait until you get in," she said.

"Edie, I'm sure sorry—"

"Stop it." She flexed her hands on the steering wheel. "Stop your apologizing, August. Things happen. We had an adventure together, didn't we? Some of us," she pointed at herself, "have things we need to apologize for. There's real harm to be owned, no doubt, but not by you. Okay?"

"All right, then." He pushed a newly softened hand through his hair and grinned at her. "You're wrong about that, but all right. See you at the meeting."

"See you there," she said.

Before pushing the door open, he reached back and patted Ian on the leg. "Tell him I said watch out for foxes."

She watched through the front windshield as August climbed the concrete steps onto his front porch and turned the doorknob. She couldn't see inside the house, but she watched him step into the dark and close the door. In a moment, a light appeared in the front windows. She drove on.

41

KEITH

2015

Keith bought a few to-go coffees in the hospital cafeteria. He didn't know how Brad took his coffee, so he loaded up his pockets with creams and sugars. He was surprised to see the Tuesday morning paper already there, next to the cash register. He bought one and sat down at an empty table to read the morning headlines. The announcement from the Oklahoma Geological Survey came as scheduled and said what everyone had known it must. The report explained the distinction between fracking itself and the injection and disposal of wastewater associated with the process, which was a hair-splitting that did not in the least soften the conclusion that the 700 percent increase in seismic activity was not credibly attributable to natural causes. There were some responses, most notably from the Oklahoma Oil and Gas Association. As predicted, nothing from Landon Energy, which meant Brad's bet was lost. He stacked the coffee cups under his chin and walked to the elevators, pressing the up button with his elbow. He had known Brad was going to be a problem when the bet didn't go his way, but he hadn't expected to be in his presence when the news hit.

Keith had heard from Edie sometime after midnight that her dad had been brought to the ER by some "angel of mercy" and Keith should drive straight to the hospital when he got to town. He got in before dawn, grateful to be summoned. It meant he was still part of the family.

"He's level four," Edie said. She had been standing at the side of her father's bed and had reached down unnecessarily to smooth the stiff bristles of his hair back. She had lifted the sheet around his shoulders, tucking him in the way she did Ian. The old man was asleep.

"How many levels are there?" It was not the question he had wanted to ask. Next to her, Brad Odel was stretched out companionably, reading, his phone propped up on his chest, his legs outstretched. No one seemed inclined to explain.

"Four is the worst," she said. "The final stage."

"But he'll survive today—"

"It's time for hospice."

"Oh, Edie. I'm so sorry." He had moved to hug her but stopped when he saw her stiffen. He dropped his hands to his sides and asked for details while Brad looked on.

She had been smooth as glass, not talking except to respond to his questions, and Brad's inexplicable presence wasn't helping him read her. She had gotten the call from the emergency room soon after getting home, and when she and Ian showed up at the hospital, Brad was there, full of his rescue story. He could have left but for some reason seemed to feel his presence was vital. With Ian asleep on the couch next to his mother, Edie and Brad had sat together for some hours before Keith showed up. Soon after, Keith's parents had come by to pick up Ian, and they had both given Brad the hail-fellow-well-met greeting, hugging him and slapping his back, reminiscing about times when Brad and Keith were kids. Eleanor surprised everyone with a story about helping Brad get a spider out of his sleeping bag during a sleepover. "You were so afraid I'd tell Keith," she said, "but Keith was as afraid of spiders as you were. I thought you were pretty brave." The son of a bitch was a bit of a hero at the moment.

Keith's parents seemed to know he had been out of town, but nobody asked. The gambling, he could see, was still in the precious pause between commission and full revelation, when he could still walk among his loved ones as one of them. Edie knew, but she had more than enough to deal with at the moment, and his parents and Ian were clueless.

He figured he was still safe from Brad, too. The business day had just begun, and it would be a while before Brad could be sure that Keith had screwed him over and that the Landon Energy announcement wasn't coming, although the fact that Edie was in a hospital room with them instead of at work might tip him off.

When Keith got back to Calvin's room, he handed coffees to Edie and Brad. He emptied his pockets of the cream and sugar packets on the stainless-steel table next to the bed. He watched as his middle-school compadre doctored his coffee with a lot of artificial sweeteners. Then he said, "Brad, could I talk to you for a second?"

Brad stood up and pressed his palms into his lower back, rotated his head across his shoulders. Brad followed him out of the room, then leaned against the wall in the hallway. "What a night, huh? Damn!"

"Yes. Thank you. You saved his life."

Brad shrugged. He felt magnificent, you could see it all over his face. "I owed you one. You were nice to my mom. You read to her."

Keith nodded "You know, reading that book might've been the start of my profession?" Again with Brad's mother. You never knew when you were doing something that would define you for another person forever. At least Brad had him locked into a defining story that was positive. Keith wondered, if Edie's memories were boiled down right now, what quintessential actions would define him for her. "I didn't know anything about the West before then. Your mom picked that book."

"I told Edie you didn't want to bet on her."

"What?"

"I could tell she was happy to hear it."

"Brad." Keith grabbed him by the shoulders. "You told her about our bet?"

"Yeah? She acted like she already knew, but then I realized she kind of tricked me into telling her. She's a smart one."

"God help me."

"Bro, the important thing is I told her how bad you didn't want to be part of the bet. I could tell that meant a lot to her. Seriously. Like, she cried." Brad looked as rough as Keith felt, almost twenty-four hours out from his last shave and shower. "But you fucked me on the bet, man. You knew Landon Energy wasn't going to announce anything today. If it had gone the way you thought it was going to, I'd be in deep shit with my family."

"The Zabels."

"Right."

If he had heard the name in high school, he hadn't known to worry. Now he did. In lying to Brad, had he just cost Stanton Zabel a lot of money? "What do you mean, *If it had gone* the way you thought?"

Brad rubbed his hands together. "No thanks to you, you sonofabitch."

Keith stared at his friend. "What are you talking about?"

"I'm talking about Edie. She's so much better than you deserve."

"No question. But, what—"

"She saved you. Saved all of us just trying to be honest."

A nurse accompanying a man in a hospital gown and pushing an IV drip on wheels walked slowly by. Brad smiled and nodded at them. "Folks," he said.

"Morning," Keith said. He thought he might go crazy waiting for the nurse and patient to pass.

When they did, he leaned in. "Brad, what the actual fuck?"

"She's not talking to you right now, huh?"

"I guess she's talking to you?"

Brad waved a hand in the air. "We talked all night. I really like her, you know? I thought she'd be this stuck-up bitch, but she's good people. Told me what happened to Ian. Dude!" He shook his head. "Most people forget the promises they make when they're in a crisis, but not her. She up and made things right."

"I'm about to strangle you."

Brad looked down at his phone and grinned. "Here. Read. My uncle's going to have to pay attention to me now."

Keith grabbed the phone. *Landon Energy spokesperson Edith Ash stated* . . . It was *All the Red Dirt,* a blog Edie's friend Fiona wrote. He read Edie's announcement.

Blinking, he handed the phone back to Brad. "My God. She'll lose her job."

"We won our bet."

Keith pinched the bridge of his nose and closed his eyes. When had she made that statement? He had never known Edie to be willing to risk her job. For months now, she had held steady, convinced that Theron Landon would stop his company's fracking. When? Any day now, any day now. But this statement meant she had given up on Landon. She had taken matters into her own hands. He was proud of her, but—"Hell."

"Dude, we won! Listen, I'm heading home. Saving lives—" Brad thumped his chest. "Wears a body out."

"Thanks for helping Calvin."

"No problem, man, for real. It actually makes me feel good. Weird, but true."

"I'm glad the bet worked out." Visions from gangster movies flashed through his mind—broken kneecaps, sleeps-with-the-fishes. Yes, he was damned relieved he'd landed on the good side of the Zabel family. "That's it for me, though, okay? No more gambling from this guy."

Brad laughed. He took a beef jerky stick from his pocket and ripped it open with his teeth. "Sure. We'll talk sometime. I'll be seeing you, bro."

Keith watched his friend walk off down the white hallway. Was he losing weight?

Back in the hospital room, Calvin's pearly shins stuck up from the bed, the bones of a shipwreck at the bottom of the sea. Still asleep, but stirring, he had kicked off his covers. Edie was standing at the window wrapping up a phone call. Keith could hear Theron Landon's big voice booming from the phone. When she hung up, her expression was set in a rictus he couldn't interpret.. She sat down on the edge of her chair, perched with her fingers steepled atop her knees.

"What's a—what's happening?" He sat down next to her, in Brad's vacant chair.

She wouldn't look at him while she told him about the events that led to her making an unauthorized statement on behalf of Landon Energy. She spoke in a low, breathy voice he knew meant she was trying to keep it together. He had to slow her down a couple of times—that nut that carries the cross? Ian! Foxhole prayer? Yes, I know what it is. A meth lab? He got the gist. "So, after I gave Fiona my statement, I fully expected to be fired today," she said. "I accepted that I'd lose my career. Even knowing about your gambling relapse, I was ready to be unemployed. I felt so clean for a minute, before you called about Delaney. Fiona put my quote up on her blog this morning, called it an official statement from Landon Energy spokesperson Edith Ash. And she posted it before the Oklahoma Geological Survey statement this morning. It didn't make the early paper, but it's everywhere now."

"And now you're out of a job?" Ian's dream catcher was on the window ledge behind them. He picked it up and pressed it to his chest, feeling how Ian had tapped him on the leg to give it to him, looking up at him through the hole in the center. Keith dragged his forearm across his eyes. Watching him, Edie turned away.

"Who wouldn't want to hire you, Edie? You'll get another job. I'm proud of you. Besides, I've got that job interview this afternoon—" His stomach cratered at the thought. He hadn't slept. He hadn't prepared. He was terrified that he would bomb it, and another tenure-track spot in his subject area, in the city where he lived, might not come along for years.

"That call just now?" Edie pulled her hair across one shoulder, a weird gallows-grin flashing across her face for a second. "Theron was full of good cheer. Told me how indispensable I was, how brilliantly I had read his true meaning. Thanked me."

"His true meaning!"

"Yep." Edie widened her eyes and pressed her fingertips to her lips.

Keith laughed for the first time in days. "Oh, that's perfect. Of course. It was Lego Head's idea all along! You saved company face but you didn't, because it was all his doing, really."

"Right. I was just an instrument of his will. A very finely tuned one, though, one that reads minds."

"Wow." For a second, he and Edie were in accord, and he ached to remain inside that pocket of goodwill with her.

"I'll give him my resignation tomorrow," she said.

"But you don't have to. Hell, you could ask for a raise."

Even as he spoke, he could see she meant it. She invited no discussion. Her entire working life since college had been at Landon Energy. Being their principal breadwinner had seemed like a key to her identity. All of that was going? Something big had changed for her.

He looked down at his hands. If her career was out with the trash, what else might she be done with? The room stank of Calvin's sickness, and behind him, the heat of the new day was warming up the window at his back. "You're really quitting?"

"Quitting, yes. A concept you should try."

He couldn't look at her. There was no need to ask what she knew or to tell her what he'd done. It was all there between them. "You told me we were through if I did it again."

"I assume that's why you did it."

"What?"

"To force me to leave you."

"What?" He stared at her, struggling to absorb her meaning. "You don't believe that. Come on."

"That's the only way it makes sense."

"It doesn't make sense. Addictions are crazy. You know that."

"I do," she said. She softened as she spoke, and he knew she was remembering what it was like before she quit drinking. "I do know that. But Keith—"

"I know." He reached for her, but she moved back. He had nothing to offer her. That-was-the-last-time declarations had lost all believability, I'll-go-to-meetings promises rang false even to him. He knew as he had never known before that his gambling was hopeless. He couldn't predict it, couldn't stop it, couldn't reason with it. About the only hope he had to hold onto was the memory of how Edie's sobriety happened. He had seen her like he was today, at the bottom. He'd broken up with her, convinced she'd never stop drinking and it would only get worse. She had promised him over and over again to stop, and it never meant anything. Until one day it did. One day was the first day of her sobriety.

"I'm sorry," he said.

She waved away his apology. She slid down in her chair and studied him, her eyes roving his face as if she was seeing him for the first time. Her dark hair fanned out around her face, her long legs stretched out before her. "Remember when I hit my bottom?"

Sitting in an AA meeting in the basement of a church near the Highgate Cemetery in London, his hand on her thigh as she shook through the meeting. He had felt like he was holding her to the earth, wholly believing that she would die soon. He remembered.

"Maybe this is your day."

He pressed his palms to his eye sockets. Somehow her empathy made him feel worse.

"Understand you'll have to do it on your own. With your people—your kind of addicts. You'll need to practically live in those meetings for awhile, you understand? I'm going home to sleep. We'll talk later."

She walked out and he moved closer to Calvin, watching the old bastard's labored breathing and envying his unconsciousness.

42

AUGUST P.

2015

The grit in my mouth is part of the road. Pain slows time and fills all the space inside me. That hot creosote smell is like home, and the sounds of cars and brakes and sirens is not so different from the everyday sounds when I walk with the cross, only today the sirens are right here, real loud and close. I reckon they're for me. Faces look down at me. They're all strangers until my friend, Robert, leans in, his dark eyes on me hard.

"August!" he says. "You're supposed to be in the hospital!"

He's in high gear, asking me questions, putting something over my face that helps me breathe, wrapping my chest. He's stern and busy, and Blanca is, too. They're talking to each other about my vitals and my chest and my legs, then she's behind my head and he's down at my feet and they lift me onto a stretcher and into the back of the ambulance while people watch. When they lift me, I see, behind the people standing close, my cross leaned against the legs of a billboard sign, but I can't tend to it. They say live by the sword, die by the sword, and I guess that's right, only with me it's the road. So it is, a sort of justice, and no surprise. That instinct for justice is deep. People need the pattern to finish. Lightning? Let's hear that thunder. Better see the ripples after the splash. People hate it when things don't make sense, and they'll find a pattern no matter what. We're all little gods, wanting order in our kingdoms. To put things back where they belong. That's why I carried the cross. Not to be a holy man myself, but to satisfy a debt. Looking at the inside of the ambulance and Robert's solemn face, I understand as I never did about letting go. It breaks the cycle. It's so hard for people to do. Damn, you want somebody to pay. This here, it's just an accident, some old boy driving an eighteen-wheeler, probably on his phone, whisked me right off my danged feet. What good will it do me to worry about that fellow getting into trouble on my account? I have bigger matters at hand. I reach up and touch Robert's shoulder and say I need to tell him a story.

"Another time, my friend," he says, busy.

But what does that mean? Another time? There's only this time.

"No," I say, and I start to tell it. I must be hard to hear under the oxygen mask and he pays me no mind, working on me, until I say ol' Tim McVeigh's name, then Robert, why, he sits up straight and looks me full in the face. He moves up closer to me and he leans down and listens to the story about *The Turner Diaries* and my stepdad calling from Elohim City and that Datsun 710 at the Oklahoma City bus station, McVeigh and Waco in the paper, and how I fell asleep. I can see that he understands what I'm saying and the full importance of it.

An expression comes over his face that I can't describe. He pushes both hands through his hair and stares at me like I'm a different guy, but not like I'm a bad guy. I'm losing my sight, but I see him crying, and I hear him say—the last thing I hear and he's saying, "Oh, my friend! Right under my nose. You're the puzzle piece. All this time! All this time?"

43

EDIE

2015

Edie and Delaney messaged back and forth for days. Edie wrote long messages full of history and explanation—her sobriety, Keith, Ian, London, Landon Energy, their dad's emphysema. She sat on the couch where she'd been when she saw the Facebook invitation, continually relieved by the relative stillness of the ground, a dramatic seismographic calming that had happened since the Oklahoma Geological Society's announcement. The fracking hadn't stopped entirely, and the earthquakes didn't either, but they were going and, she hoped, soon to be gone. Now that the earthquakes had slowed to a pace that seemed, by comparison, almost leisurely, she was grudgingly willing to internalize what Keith had always said. If they had been her earthquakes, then she could feel that these new spaces between the quakes that remained were hers, too.

Fiona thought so, at least. Breaking the Landon Energy statement had put *All the Red Dirt* over the magic subscriber number she had been shooting for, and now she had sponsors, a change she credited to Edie.

Edie wrote and wrote. Delaney offered up vignettes, sometimes detailed but always without a larger context. She described a long camping trip in a Botswana nature preserve, a night at a Chicago bar where she was working when she broke up a fight between two old men in love with the same woman, a showing of her work in St. Augustine, Florida, and meeting her husband at an art festival in Wyoming. It was the way you talk to a stranger on a plane, Edie realized. You tell entertaining stories. They tiptoed around how they had parted, avoided mentioning the bombing, and swapped stories as though they had merely grown apart.

Edie would grow frustrated at Delaney's indirection and want to force a confrontation, but fear that her sister would fade away again restrained her for the most part. One day, she did ask point-blank if they could talk on the phone and didn't get a response. She didn't know if she would ever hear from Delaney again, so she broke the silence a couple of days later with something innocuous—news of a band they had liked getting back together. Then the correspondence resumed, but Edie had learned her lesson about pushing for answers. Now that she knew Delaney was alive, she had Googled her sister and filled in some of the gaps in Delaney's impressionistic narrative. She had even seen Delaney's work online at a few gallery websites and read a write-up in a Chicago art magazine about a group showing in which Delaney's work was described as "dense and unyielding" but "full of power and portent."

On the day that Delaney finally opened up, Edie was busy at the house with movers and hospice workers, rushing them to finish so she could attend August's funeral that afternoon. She was standing in the kitchen with Ian, watching out the back windows as two men shouldered her father's dresser down the steps from his apartment, soon to be Keith's. Ian sat down on the floor and tied his shoes, full of purpose. "I'm going to help."

"Stay here, sweetie. They've got it under control."

Ian scrambled to his feet and splayed himself against the door like a starfish on the glass of an aquarium. "I want to hold the door open."

"Okay," she said. "Hold the door open but stay out of the way. Watch your fingers." The idea was to move her father into Keith's downstairs study where he would spend his remaining days. Keith had never unpacked his boxes in the first place, so they were hauled out along with his computer to create space for a rented hospital bed and a comfortable lounge chair for Edie and the hospice workers, who would be taking shifts. Now that Edie wasn't working, she planned to devote as much of her father's remaining time to him as she could.

A few days before, he had woken up at the hospital and seemed to know he didn't have much time. He touched the oxygen tubes going up his nostrils and gave her a wry smile. In his raspy voice, he asked if she liked the flowers he'd picked for her. She hugged him and told him about Delaney. The news seemed too much for him—he closed his eyes and did not open them again for hours. When he woke up, they kept talking and she told him she'd quit her job. He locked eyes with her. "I knew you would." The approval knocked her back, though objections flooded her mind. His deathbed expression of support was surely what the phrase "too little, too late" was meant for. Like Theron

Landon, he would get on the Edie train after it had left the station and act like the conductor. Why he was the way he was would remain a mystery, but for the first time in her life, it didn't bother her.

She had resolved to do her best for his last days. That morning she'd cleaned out his closet and drawers and wept at the sight of his heavily starched jeans and pearl-button western shirts that he would never wear again. His favorite belt hung over the bedstand, brass horseshoe belt buckle dangling. She wrapped the belt around her arm and took it with her, along with a cardboard box packed with some of his personal effects. The curtains, the carpet, the walls—everything in the apartment smelled like cigarette smoke.

The movers lugged Keith's belongings outside and up the stairs to the garage apartment. He had already packed his clothes and shoes to be moved into Calvin's old bedroom. He'd been in his parents' guest room since the night he returned from New Mexico and was eager to get out of there. He would live in Calvin's apartment, kicked out of the house but on the property for Ian, and for hope, until he hit some milestone that convinced Edie and himself that he was on the road to recovery, or he relapsed, and they divorced.

It was up to him. In the last few days, her friends had let her know they were rooting for a divorce. *What did she see in him? What was between them?* Not even his new job impressed them much. Even his mother. Eleanor loved him hopelessly but thought her son was hopeless. Who didn't join this choir was anyone in recovery. The changed believe in change, though they were also flintier about the low odds.

What no one knew but Keith and Edie was what passed between them seventeen years ago in the last days of her drinking. How he forgave her. She had been given a second chance—so many, really, in so many areas of her life. Because of that, she felt honor bound to extend second chances to anyone when she could, but especially to Keith, the person whose forgiveness had started it all. He would have to kick the gambling, that was the truth, but stranger things had happened. For example, her formerly dead sister was texting her. Edie heard the ding on her phone and picked it up off the kitchen counter.

It's good talking to you, chica, but I guess I'm wondering if you're ever going to apologize. I'd like to get past it all, and I know I have a big part in all this—I didn't have to stay gone, I guess. But I can't start. It starts with you.

Edie stared at the phone. The fury she'd suppressed since finding Delaney tore through her. Her hands shook with the adrenaline surge as she typed. *Hey! I'm so glad you're bringing this up finally. Have to say I can't see how I owe you an apology.*

Which sounded too harsh. Aiming to soften what she'd said, she deleted and typed, retyped, and settled on *Keith and I grieved you, you know? For years. I've got PTSD from that shit. Still in therapy. You let us think you were dead.*

Edie's breathing was shallow and her heart was pounding. She walked through the house watching the ellipsis dance on her phone. "Ian," she said. "Let's watch a movie." She reached for the remote and turned on *How to Train Your Dragon 2*. Ian came running.

"Right now? In the daytime?" He was grinning like Christmas morning.

"Right now!"

She paced behind the couch until Delaney's message came in. She didn't know what she expected, but something more than she got.

Are you fucking kidding me?

She stopped walking and typed back, *I deserve more than this from you, Delaney. You had to know we'd think you died in the bombing.*

Why would I think that? I didn't die in the bombing. I talked to you that night. What????????

Delaney sent back a laughing emoji. Then, *Not that it's funny. Are you gonna act like you don't remember running me off?*

Edie looked up and took in the room. She breathed deeply, 1-2-3-4, like she'd been taught. She stayed in the moment. She wrote, *????????*

Sure. That night. April 19, 1995. I should've come home sooner, but I got caught up in the rescue downtown. When I got home you were so fucking furious! You threw a beer at me. You and Keith had been looking for me. His Bronco was ruined. Obviously, you were drunk, I saw that, but I mean you were looking right at me and speaking English. Are you saying you don't remember? You told me I was bad for Keith, that you loved him, that you never wanted a sister. The unvarnished truth. Ringing bells?

Edie tossed the phone onto the couch. She got up and made Ian popcorn on the stove. She took the popcorn to Ian, then grabbed a couple of bottles of water from the refrigerator and ran them up to the movers up in the apartment, who were unloading Keith's boxes of books. She laid out her black dress for the funeral. She called the skilled nursing facility where her father had been staying while his room was set up and told them they could begin his discharge. She tried to think but couldn't. She texted Kayli but then deleted it. Finally, she sat down on the couch.

It was her turn to be terse. *I don't understand what you're saying.*

You really don't remember?

Remember WHAT?

You're saying you were in a blackout?

I'm not saying anything.

I swear I couldn't tell, Edie. You ask Keith or anybody who ever saw you in a blackout. I knew you were drunk but I had no idea you wouldn't remember it at all.

If you were there, why didn't you take any of your stuff? Why didn't you just tell me to fuck off and go to bed? Where did you go?

You were just so cruel, Edie. After that day? Seriously, you wanted me gone so I went. And I did take some stuff—I was there for like an hour. I packed a bag. I told you to tell our fucking dad I was okay and to look me up. I went to stay with this girl I knew in Chicago to give you time to cool off. I gave you the phone number and I waited. I've been waiting for years. I made sure I always had a phone number listed in the white pages wherever I lived in case you called. You never did.

Edie leaned back and closed her eyes. Ian was on the floor in front of the television holding his action figure of the dragon from the movie, swooping it through the air. Was this all her fault? *Can't we talk? Skype?*

No.

Okay. I know I was a blackout drinker, and I know I was in a blackout that night. It was the worst night of my life, hands down. But I can't believe you were there. You didn't even leave a note.

Why would I leave a note, you fucking pinhead? You were right there talking to me. Yelling at me.

No, no, no.

Edie, you were going on about Vera Wrede, lumping me in with her somehow, writing these letters.

Then a picture appeared below the last text. A light blue airmail envelope with handwriting on the back. Edie saw her own drunken scrawl, unreadable but for the giant block letters with which she'd written HILLBILLY HOLOCAUST.

She remembered finding most of the airmail envelopes she'd bought to address overseas graduate programs ruined when she came to on April 20th. Sick and brainless, reverberating with shock, she had taken a look at the empty beer cans and ruined blue envelopes scattered across the living room, and she'd done what she always did after a blackout. Swept the debris into the trash, made resolutions, swore she would never drink again, showered, cried, and looked for constructive action to take. That morning she'd tried to give blood for the rescue effort before a woman in the line called her out for smelling like alcohol. After seventeen years sober, it was hard sometimes to remember the true debasement of that life, but staring at the envelope brought it up like vomit in her throat.

She held her thumbs above the screen for a long minute before she responded. *You didn't have to stay gone.*

I know. That's why I sent you the Facebook invitations. I'm trying.

You used the bombing. You used it to cover your exit.

THAT is BULLSHIT. You're the one who ran me off. Get it through your head, Edie. I had no idea you thought I died in the blast.

It's a pretty big adjustment.

Used the bombing? How fucking dare you?

It's hard to assimilate.

What—that it's your fault? Edie, if we had fought like that on a normal day—a day when our fight was the worst thing about it—I know we would have made up. We'd have been okay. But I went through the bombing that day. I spent twelve hours down there. To come home to that assault—

Assault?

Damn near. Listen, I just fractured. Split in both senses of the word. Broke into pieces and took off. I split. You were totaled, too. I see that.

Pink mist.

What?

Pink mist. That's what a forensics guy told us could explain why we didn't find your remains. That you were so close to the bomb you were vaporized.

A long pause followed. Edie watched the ellipsis dance then disappear on her screen. She could feel Delaney taking in for the first time what she and Keith had been through. That it had not been necessary or intentional felt like an affront. And also the best possible news. *You really came home,* she wrote. A statement. A question. A whole new reality, and an admission of fault.

I really did.

I need a little time.

Me too.

Edie got up and walked into the kitchen, staring at the picture of the airmail envelopes on her phone.

She saw Delaney as she had been the first time they met, teenagers with curly perms and mall bangs in a slick plastic booth in a truck stop with their dad, who was acting like they were silly girls for making such a big deal of having sisters he'd forgotten to mention. Moving in together in their early twenties like that was sneaking a victory on the old man, giving themselves the family they never had. She saw the muck of feelings when they lived together, the way Keith had divided the air like a magnet, and she saw Delaney in the past tense, the bright-eyed deceased sister in the picture they never took down but could not look at straight on, who had lived in Edie's heart all these years.

She wrapped her arms around her waist and doubled over. Somehow the long, straight highway of memories circled around now, an ouroboros that came back to Delaney alive again, pissed off at her, imploring and confusing and telling her how she was the one to blame. And she was, too. It was a different story altogether. It was guilt as she'd never known. And it was too wonderful. She heard Keith's voice in the backyard. She watched him greet the movers as he pulled a carpet cleaner across the lawn.

"You're here," she said, walking over to him.

He set the carpet cleaner at his feet and waved. "The cigarette smell in there is going to take some work," he said. He was in the paint-ruined sweats and T-shirt he had worn painting Ian's bedroom robin's-egg blue when they were getting ready for his birth. "I was reading about this stuff you can paint the walls with that seals in the smoke smell. Do you mind if I paint?"

"Go ahead, sure." She was amazed he couldn't see the new world in her face, but he just smiled, mild and distracted. "How are you doing?" she asked.

"Lots of meetings, lots of therapy. Lots of new employee training. I'm okay."

"Are you still coming with me to the funeral? The sitter will be here in an hour."

She'd tried to make him understand why she was grieving so hard for the loss of this strange friend she'd known so briefly, how August had connected with Ian and how devastated he had been—like them—by his own thoughts about the Murrah bombing, his own damaged way of dealing. She could tell Keith was puzzled, but he was putting up no resistance these days.

"I dug out my suit," he said. "Even ironed a shirt."

She held up the phone with her and Delaney's text conversation on the screen. "Could we talk?"

They sat down in a pair of Adirondack chairs on the back porch and watched the movers go back and forth. Things were uncertain between them, but they were getting along. Facing into the weirdness of Delaney's contact, agreeing together that Edie should be the one to talk with Delaney for now had given them common purpose. She scrolled to the top of the conversation and handed him the phone. "You're not going to feel like the only guilty party after you read this."

He took the phone and shot her a puzzled look. He held it at a distance and squinted. She didn't think she could stand to watch him read, badly wanted to hustle off and check on Ian, the movers, her dad's imminent arrival, a message from the headhunter about a job interview, but instead she sat next to Keith and focused on her breathing like the meditation app had taught her. The wind was picking up and the sky was green. She looked at the daffodils, dying with the month of April, and thought about summer plants. She could put in bluestem grasses, zinnias, roses, and a desert willow to shade the porch. She'd string lights and set the table for whoever was still there. Her father could last the season. Her sister might come, and they could make dinner and turn on the bug zapper and spend the evening under the sky if the heat wasn't too bad and there weren't any tornado warnings. Ian could search for cicada shells, which he'd encountered at the house of a friend who had a shoe box full. Now he couldn't wait to collect them. They look like aliens, he said. And they crunch, and they're see-through, and also, Mama, they stick to things.

44

EDIE

2015

August's funeral was held downtown, in one of the churches that had all its stained glass blown out in the bombing. The sanctuary was tall, the stained-glass panels looking as if they had been there for a hundred years, not replaced twenty years ago. Sound echoed off the walls. While Keith sat at the end of a pew holding their seat, Edie circumnavigated the lobby with Kayli, telling her about what Delaney had said. She was crying hard, and people politely averted their eyes. It was a funeral, after all. "So, you see," she said, "we've been apart all these years because of me. It was all my fault."

Edie could tell Kayli was more shocked than she was allowing herself to show. She twisted her turquoise rings without looking at Edie. "Look," she said. "It's a big surprise, no question. But you didn't remember. I know what that's like—I woke up in Cleveland one time. Came out of it and I was standing in a group of people at a pool party. No idea. You can't change what happened. What you've done since then, though? You stopped. You've been sober all these years, you've made amends, and you try hard. That's all you can do."

"I've caused a lot of suffering."

"No way around it."

"What if it means I don't deserve all this? My life?"

"You're about to start feeling sorry for yourself. Cut that shit out. This doesn't feel good, but that's just how it feels."

Edie nodded. "Right. You're right."

"And, Edie? Your sister told you her version. The one where she's blameless and it's all your fault. But you and I both know that's not quite it, either. She held the grudge, she could've contacted you, and, girl, I bet she knew it was at least possible you were in a blackout, no matter what she said."

Edie looked at her feet as she walked. Her black heels and black tights absorbed the sunlight cast across the floor in kaleidoscopic jewel tones from the windows. "Nobody's innocent."

"Or everybody's innocent, one of the two. Look around." Kayli gestured at the motley group of mourners signing the guest book and filtering into the sanctuary, people for whom any black was funeral black, and so they appeared arrayed in leather jackets, rock T-shirts, steampunk blazers, and emo skirts with safety pin edges, the pews full of people from the many meetings August had attended. Edie saw the woman who had called her The Fracking Lady, some old timers in western-style leisure suits and Stetson hats, Sam, the drunk guy with the shotgun at August's house, looking sober, his hair slicked back from his forehead and a gray dress shirt buttoned at the wrists and tucked into khakis.

The paramedic who had gotten August to the hospital for pneumonia was standing in front of a photograph of August mounted on an easel by the guest book. Robert. Their eyes met across the room, and he gave her a long look like he wanted to tell her something but appeared to change his mind. He stood next to a bespectacled, carefully dressed woman whose shoulders he kept rubbing.

The photograph of August was old, an official army photograph taken when he was still a teen. It must have been right after he enlisted, a couple of years after he left Elohim City, a couple of years after the bombing. There he was, his blond hair in a GI crew cut, his blue eyes clear, his complexion unravaged. He looked mild as milk. He had already been damaged then, she knew. You couldn't see it on him. You couldn't tell what he thought about himself or what he thought he'd done. So it was with everyone, though. Most of the time, you couldn't tell anything but what they thought you'd like to see. She was the queen of such concealment, herself.

She pulled her dark hair over one shoulder and twisted the earring in her left ear and looked around for August's sister. Who else could have provided the photograph? She had nearly decided Malory wasn't in attendance when Edie saw her step out of a private room designated for the family. Malory held the arm of a small, stooped woman with faded blond hair pulled into a tight bun. Her skin was mapped with capillaries, her forehead etched with lines. The woman peered around at the crowd of people in mute discomfort. Here was the source of August's and Malory's similarities, the source of August and Malory, period. Malory raised a hand in greeting when she saw Edie. They stopped in front of a water fountain and waited for Edie to join them.

"Malory, I'm so sorry."

Malory wore black slacks and a short-sleeved turtleneck, her light hair curled around her shoulders. "You know, I'm so damned glad you brought him to see me. What would I have done if he passed and I hadn't seen him again?" She looked down at the woman on her arm and winced.

Had August's mother ever talked to him after he left Elohim City? Did she still live there? Edie had no idea.

"Always thought I'd see him again," the woman said. "Thought he'd turn up."

"Edie, this is our mother, Loreen. Loreen—" She seemed to be reaching for a last name she didn't have. "Momma, what are you calling yourself these days?"

Loreen squeezed her hands into tight little fists that flew to the sides of her face. She started to cry. "You don't know my name."

"I'm sorry. Shit. I'm sorry, Momma."

"Nice to meet you, Loreen," Edie said. If she had ever thought about August's mother, it was to wonder at her missteps and all the harm she had done, but it was another matter to have the woman before her in an ill-fitting dress that looked like it came from a donation box and August's tear-rimmed blue eyes staring out of her older female face, a person who stood in relation to August as she stood to Ian. What a thought! Edie hugged her. The woman felt like dry sticks. "Your son was quite a person," she said. "He was a good one."

Loreen cracked a smile, her yellowed teeth showing for a moment. "So they keep telling me. Dang if I know how. He sure didn't get it from me."

Mother and daughter moved slowly up the hallway to the sanctuary, and Edie found her seat in a pew a few rows from the front with Keith, who squeezed her hand.

"Looks like a lot of people knew him," Keith said.

Edie leaned back in her seat and rubbed her eye sockets, mascara be damned. "You couldn't help wanting to watch out for him. A lot of people must have felt that way."

"Did you ever find out why he carried that cross?"

"Guilty conscience," she said. "And speaking of—"

"Yeah. Wow, Edie. Delaney's version—it's a hell of a thing."

"I might be a terrible person, Keith."

He patted her hand. "Maybe, but that's not good news for the rest of us. You cut yourself less slack than anyone I know." The organ music came in loud then, the service started, and they rose with the rest of the mourners.

On their way home, they passed by the bombing memorial. The bronze walls from the Gates of Time gleamed in the sunlight on either end. Edie could see people strolling by the eternity pool, hands in pockets. The lawn was green and flowers lined the sidewalks, daffodils fading out and tulips starting to bloom. The survivor tree was budding. She imagined that for people who didn't remember the bombing, it would be an attractive park, a place with a certain gravitas and narrative about it. Someday, it would be like Adobe Walls, like the Alamo, or like Nelson's column commemorating the Battle of Trafalgar in the center of London. The bite of the pain would fade. The struggles that brought the event into the world would be remembered through the safe lens of history. Such a time was still a long way off, though. Today, it felt closer than ever. "Do you still think about it?" she asked.

"Every day," Keith said.

"Me too." At some point each day came the thought, *it could happen again,* and every day that it didn't she thought, *good,* and then she thought, *but it could happen tomorrow.*